HAVING THE DECORATORS IN

HAVING THE DECORATORS IN

REAY TANNAHILL

headline
review

First published in Great Britian in 2007
by HEADLINE REVIEW
An imprint of HEADLINE PUBLISHING GROUP

10 9 8 7 6 5 4 3 2 1

Cataloguing in Publication Data is available from the British Library

ISBN 978 0 7553 3307 3 (Hardback)
ISBN 978 0 7553 3308 0 (Trade paperback)

Typeset in Sabon by
Palimpsest Book Production Limited,
Grangemouth, Stirlingshire

Printed and bound in Great Britain by
Mackays of Chatham plc, Chatham, Kent

Headline's policy is to use papers that are natural, renewable and recyclable
products and made from wood grown in sustainable forests. The logging
and manufacturing processes are expected to conform to the
environmental regulations of the country of origin.

HEADLINE PUBLISHING GROUP
An Hachette Livre UK Company
338 Euston Road
London NW1 3BH

www.headline.co.uk

This book is dedicated to
Richard Rees, architect
who designed Vine Regis
with more hindrance than help from the author

Chapter 1

'DECISIONS, decisions!'

With any other woman, it might have come out as a wail, but wailing was not Dame Constance's style. Her tone was perfectly conversational, though there was the merest hint of exasperation in it as, placing her elbows on the table and resting her chin on her elegant fists, she fixed her husband with a hopeful gaze and waited.

And waited.

After a while, he became aware that something was expected of him and raised his head, eyes gleaming with amusement, from the legal papers and parchments that surrounded him. 'Decisions? You can't possibly want my opinion on whether the walls should be painted red or green!'

She laughed. 'I don't. I was just trying to find out whether you'd been listening or not!'

'Off and on.'

'Purely as a matter of interest, *do* you have an opinion?'

'Yes, of course I do. But it is not – praise be to God – *my* Great Chamber we are talking about. It is your son's.'

'And you think Gervase might have some ideas of his own?'

'Well, he might, if you asked him. *Have* you asked him?'

'Not yet,' she admitted.

Sir Guy's smile broadened. 'Scared, are we, now that he has got out of the habit of saying, "Whatever you think best, mother"?'

She grimaced at him. 'Oh, very droll!'

Gervase was the elder son of Dame Constance's first marriage and had inherited both title and lands when his father, Lord Nicholas, had been killed in the Scottish wars. The boy had been twelve at the time and for most of the fifteen years since then had left to his mother everything to do with the management of the estates. 'Whatever you think best, mother,' had become a litany, and a very tedious litany Dame Constance had found it. He had even said, 'Whatever you think best, mother,' when almost three years ago she had proposed adding a large and costly extension to the rather grim old castle of Vine Regis to provide him, as Lord, with an up-to-date Great Chamber that would serve him as bedroom, office, reception room and dining room when he was at home, besides making the whole castle more convenient and livable-in for everyone else.

Soon afterwards he had been appointed equerry to the new boy king and royal service had done much to give him the confidence to develop opinions of his own. He had always had opinions on subjects that interested him – such as wars and weaponry – but Dame Constance was still not accustomed to his taking the initiative in matters that had always fallen within her province. She had told him, often enough, that he should concern himself more with the management of his extensive lands and estates but, now that he was showing signs of doing so, she was not at all sure that she liked it. Especially since he had acquired the royal habit of tossing off ideas and leaving others to sort out the difficulties he had no desire or ability to foresee.

It had been sheer bad luck that he had arrived home on a flying visit just when Dame Constance had been blissfully contemplating the departure of the builders who had made the construction of the castle extension such a nightmare.

'Before they go,' he had suggested airily, 'why don't we get them to put up a bailey?' Observing her expression, he had added, 'What's the matter? Don't you think it's a good idea?'

It was, in fact, an excellent idea. The castle had been built a hundred years earlier by an ancestor steeped in the traditions of war. It was more fortress than castle, tall and square and rather forbidding, solidly grounded on its own little moated island and containing within its thick stone walls all the necessities of life for its inhabitants – including a food supply on the hoof.

By 'bailey' Gervase meant a separate ring of low buildings round the periphery of the island, and Dame Constance would not have hesitated had she not seen enough of builders to last her a lifetime.

She widened her eyes at him.

'Come, now, mother!' he said authoritatively. 'The inhabitants of *royal* castles don't have to live cheek by jowl with bakers and brewers and cellarers, with hens and pigs and cows, and I don't see why *we* should have to. They could all be rehoused in a bailey, with the noises and smells kept at a decent distance from the living quarters. It was certainly necessary in time of war for besieged castles to be able to provision themselves from within their walls with meat and eggs, bread and ale, but that no longer applies. Yes, a nice little bailey is what we need.'

So saying, he had vanished back to court, leaving Dame Constance to put his suggestion into practice.

It had all been very trying, with a mason who had not really wanted the extra work and weather that had been consistently atrocious from start to finsh. After the crisis-ridden experience of building the extension, Dame Constance had felt it necessary to keep a close personal eye on the work herself instead of delegating the task to the castle steward. It had proved so time-consuming that she had been forced to shelve a number of other matters requiring her attention.

She sighed heavily. 'If it hadn't been for the bailey, I would have had the Great Chamber finished, decorated and habitable by now. Oh, I am so weary of the whole business.'

Sir Guy said, 'But you must have made *some* progress or you wouldn't be asking me about wall colours?'

'I am not sure that finding Signor Alberti qualifies as "progress", and I won't be sure until he actually turns up and starts work.'

She had gone to the greatest trouble – via cousins, acquaintances, friends, and friends of friends – to find an artist-decorator who specialised in wall painting and had finally discovered Signor Alberti, who was reputed to be *au fait* with everything that was currently in vogue in Florence. He had been working in London on a project for one of the royal dukes, but had deigned to pay a visit to Vine Regis to decide whether it was the kind of place worthy of his genius.

'But I wish you had been there,' she told her husband with an unexpected chuckle, 'when I showed the Great Chamber to him.'

'*Si, magnifico!*' had said Signor Alberti, glancing round the main apartment in the new drum tower. He was a small, swarthy man, very full of himself and, even allowing for the language difficulty – Dame Constance's Italian being even

4

sketchier than Signor Alberti's English – she could already foresee that dealing with him was not going to be easy. However,
she had no trouble in interpreting his '*Decorazione dramatica!*'
to mean that lordly splendour was what should be aimed at,
while Gervase, who would have understood even less than Dame
Constance did, would have looked down his long, aristocratic
nose at the artist and said, 'Hmmm. Yes, a bit of splendour is
what's needed.'

Fortunately or unfortunately – time would tell! – the potential for lordly splendour had sufficed to persuade Signor Alberti
to agree to a contract. He would come, he had said, when his
present work permitted. Now, in mock heroic tones, Dame
Constance repeated, '*Decorazione dramatica!*' making a grand
gesture with her slender white hand as her husband showed
signs of retreating into his legal papers again. 'So, Guy, what
is your view? Ruby red, or forest green?'

'White,' he said firmly, just as they heard the sound of the
lookout's horn from above the Great Gate, blowing the series
of calls that signified friends approaching.

'Friends. Well, that's a relief,' said Dame Constance. 'I am
not in the mood for strangers.'

From where they were seated in the Great Hall on the first
floor of the castle, they could not see whose was the little
procession approaching through the grey November afternoon.
The castle walls were twelve feet thick and the windows small,
the Abominable Ancestor having held to the belief that small
windows allowed defenders inside the castle to shoot freely at
attackers *outside* while making it as difficult as possible for
attackers outside to shoot *in*. Dame Constance sometimes
thought that if the said ancestor had deliberately set about
designing one of the most inconvenient dwellings imaginable
he could not have made a better job of it.

Now, as she wondered, '*Which* friends?' her question was

answered, as so often, by Hamish MacLeod, the big, wiry, sandy-haired Highlander who had been at Vine Regis for twenty years and was her most valued and trusted servant.

Appearing at her side, unannounced, he said, 'It's the Lady Susanna, and I think she's got young William Burnell with her. If it's him, he's grown a lot since he was last here. And there's a lassie I dinnae recognise. Looks a bit like our Jinty up on Mull, tall and thin and plain, like a big long drink of water.'

Dame Constance, after twenty years, was accustomed to having hitherto unheard-of members of Hamish's vast and widespread family introduced into the conversation. 'Jinty?' she enquired. 'Have we had her before?'

'Maybe not. She's my third cousin, twice removed.'

'I'm never quite sure. I think my memory is beginning to fail. Advancing age, I suppose.'

Hamish, his pale eyes twinkling at her from under their almost invisible sandy lashes, said only, 'Oh, aye?' but Sir Guy raised a quizzical brow. 'Fishing for compliments, my love?'

It was no secret that she was forty-one years old, but her looks, despite a few fine lines round the startlingly blue eyes, had not even begun to fade. Her features were as flawless as they had ever been, her complexion as clear, her mouth as shapely, and her nose as fine-boned. Her lips might be firmer and her nose more autocratic than in her youth, but that was only to be expected. Before she had married Sir Guy she had usually worn a widow's barbe, a white nun-like headdress that made no concessions to flattery, hiding hair and ears and leaving the face starkly framed. Even thus she had been handsome. Now, the silky black hair with its distinctively white streak coiled over her ears and covered with either a sheer veil or, more formally, a golden net, she was strikingly beautiful.

'Compliments?' she responded blandly. 'Certainly not. I was merely teasing Hamish about the number and variety of his brothers and sisters and cousins. I have long suspected that he invents new members of his family as the occasion seems to require. In all the time he has been at Vine Regis, this is his first mention – ever – of "Jinty". *Do* you have a cousin Jinty on Mull, Hamish?'

A picture of injured innocence, Hamish replied, 'Aye, of course I do.'

'Who is tall . . .'

'Aye.'

'And thin . . .'

'Aye.'

'And plain?'

'Aye, the poor lassie. Mind you, I havenae seen her since she was ten years old – and that was a good fifteen years back – so she's maybe improved since then.'

2

They were still laughing when they heard the visitors clatter across the bridge over the moat, a bridge which had been demoted from its original role of drawbridge when the late and impatient Lord Nicholas had declared himself tired of waiting for the ponderous thing to be fully lowered every time he arrived home unexpectedly or wanted to ride out in a hurry. He had decreed that the castle had protection enough in the form of its huge wooden gates and iron portcullis, and a partly opened gate and partially raised portcullis were quicker and easier for one or two horsemen to negotiate than that misbegotten slab of timbers.

Sir Guy, murmuring, 'I have work to do,' scooped up his papers and vanished with a parting injunction to Dame Constance to give his love to his daughter-in-law, Susanna. He was just in time. Within a very few moments, sounds on the curving stone staircase betokened the closer approach of the visitors, ceremoniously escorted by the castle steward, Sir Walter Woolston, stately and white-haired, who liked to do things properly. Not for him the informality of Hamish MacLeod. He wondered sometimes why Dame Constance let the fellow get away with it.

'The Lady Susanna Whiteford. Mistress Flora Chandos. Master William Burnell,' he announced.

Susanna was seventeen years old, small, blonde, shapely, and fetchingly attired in a gown of deep rose pink under a surcoat of dark green. She had once been betrothed to Gervase but – fortunately, in Dame Constance's view, since she had been a tiresome chit – had fallen passionately in love with Piers Whiteford, the son of Sir Guy's first marriage. The pair of them now lived with their year-old twin sons at Lanson, a fortified manor house nearby, and marriage and maternity had improved Susanna almost beyond recognition, so much so that she and Dame Constance were now on better terms than ever before.

Welcoming her, enquiring after the health of Piers and the twins, Dame Constance observed that Susanna was not her usual sparkling self. It was a chill, wintry day and her nose was still pink with the cold even though she had cast off her outer wraps, but Dame Constance, turning to greet the young woman who accompanied her, realised that there was more to account for Susanna's subdued air than a mere shivery wind. Her companion was a girl who seemed to have no dress sense whatsoever and no interest at all in her appearance, which alone would have sufficed to cast a damper on Susanna's spirits without the further depressant of a face that said as clearly as words that Mistress Flora Chandos was a very serious-minded young woman indeed.

She was undoubtedly tall and thin, as Hamish had said. But plain? Dame Constance was not so sure. The current fashion was for neat-featured dainty blondes like Susanna, and the girl was certainly not that. She had an oval face with arched brows over hazel eyes that looked as if they might be a little short-sighted; a nose too aquiline for beauty; and a wide mouth with lips that were unnervingly tight at the corners. Her chestnut hair, which was heavy and very straight, fell almost to her waist over an outfit that looked as if she had given no thought to it at all but had dressed that morning in whatever had happened to come to hand. Her high-necked gown was in a dull shade of mud, with neither embroidery nor jewellery to lighten it, while her equally drab surcoat was of a loosely woven wool, trimmed round the armholes with tired-looking rabbit fur. No wonder Susanna was depressed.

The serious-minded young woman, glancing round the white-washed Great Hall with its huge tapestries depicting the deeds of ancient heroes, addressed herself to Dame Constance. 'How kind of you, Lady, to welcome a complete stranger to Vine Regis. I have heard so much about the castle and its hospitality that I have been most anxious to visit it. Even at this time of year, with the trees leafless, the castle's situation on its own private island is impressive, to say the least, and . . .'

Dame Constance, devotee of courtesy though she was, was perfectly able to recognise the beginnings of what promised to be a long and uninteresting speech. She put a gentle stop to it, therefore, with a gracious inclination of her head to Mistress Chandos, and turned her attention to William Burnell, who was beaming at her as if they were the oldest of old friends.

'And how is the West Country these days?' she asked with a smile. He must be sixteen by now, she supposed. He had grown several inches in the last two years and was no longer spotty, but otherwise he seemed not to have changed. His fair hair was still lank, and his air still that of a boy who was full of bright ideas and considered himself cleverer than anyone else – though, even as the son of Susanna's former guardian, he had not been clever enough to persuade Susanna to marry him. What a match that would have been, with the pair of them snapping at each other like brother and sister! Dame Constance smiled again at the memory of it.

'Fine, Lady,' he replied promptly. 'Winters are mild in Cornwall, as I think you know, but it's a bit cold and blowy there now, so I decided I should come and pay Susanna and Piers a visit and see how the family was doing and how Piers was getting on with his horse breeding . . .'

Everyone except Mistress Chandos could tell that he was well launched, but he had learned some sense in the last two years and a warning cough from Hamish was enough to bring his speech to a precipitate close – though, being William, he finished his sentence first. '. . . and whether there were any new barbary foals.'

Crisply, Susanna told him, 'And now you know, so you can go home again.' To Dame Constance she added, 'He's been here for weeks. We just can't get rid of him!'

William made a face at her, before turning back to Dame Constance to say, 'Vine Regis looks amazingly different with its new bailey. Are you pleased with it?'

'In general, yes.'

Now that the site had been cleared and even the thatched lath-and-plaster masons' lodge demolished so that it no longer offended everyone's eye, Vine Regis had begun to look civilised again, even if, as William said, strangely unfamiliar with the new buildings ringing the moat. It would, of course, take a while for the softening grass to grow again in what was now the outer courtyard, but time would rectify that.

'It will fulfil its function when everything is finished,' she went on. 'The wall plaster inside the new buildings is not yet thoroughly dry, and will have to be lime-washed before the baker, the brewer, the wine cellarer, and the livestock are able to enter into their new premises, but the castle itself will feel more comfortable and spacious once all of them are moved out. I seem to remember that, when you came here with Susanna in '78, you found yourself having to sleep above the horses in the stables, but we are planning guest chambers in the bailey which should eliminate such makeshift arrangements in the future.'

William's eyes lit up hopefully, but, 'Don't encourage him!' Susanna exclaimed.

Without giving William time to respond, Dame Constance said, 'Susanna, my dear, you haven't seen the Great Chamber since we've removed the timbers protecting the new plaster. It is going to be very handsome. Come, and I'll show you.'

It was only a few steps from the Great Hall to the Great Chamber – three steps up and a short passage widening substantially towards its end to form a small open room. This was obviously designed to be an antechamber but was at present furnished with shelves and easels, and a low table with porphyry slabs on it and pestles and mortars and empty containers neatly laid out.

'The painter,' Dame Constance explained. 'He is proposing to use this as his studio when he starts work. Whenever that may be! He has another commission to finish first, but anticipates returning here in due course, by which time I hope we will have decided what we want in the way of decoration.'

'Aaah!' It was William, who had an insatiable thirst for knowledge and new experiences. 'Can I come and watch him at work?'

Susanna said repressively, '*If* you are still staying with us at Lanson, and *if* Dame Constance permits. You will just be in the way, you know.'

11

William's look of yearning was almost too much for Dame Constance's gravity, but she said only, 'We shall see. Now, here we are. What do you think?'

The smell of new wood in the great circular Chamber was powerful in the extreme, and the floor clattered echoingly as the visitors trod on it, unlike the stone floor in the Great Hall. But it was certainly going to be a splendid apartment when completed.

Mistress Flora said politely, 'How very unusual.'

'Big, isn't it!' exclaimed the irrepressible William, beginning to pace it out along the diagonal. 'Hmmm. Twelve paces, about twenty-four ells. You're going to have problems with the decoration, Lady, aren't you? I mean, what about furniture? And you can't mount big flat hangings against these curving walls, can you? You'd have to nail them along the top if the blacksmith could make nails long and strong enough to penetrate the stone. And it would damage the tapestries and the weave would be bound to crease, wouldn't it? Or I suppose the blacksmith could make some kind of curved rail for them to hang from . . .'

Dame Constance looked at him silently for a moment. She had been so pleased with her lovely new round tower that it had taken weeks – months – for her to acknowledge that the shape brought problems with it. And here was young William Burnell recognising them at a glance. The furniture presented no real difficulties, but the walls were another matter.

Signor Alberti, as far as Dame Constance could discover from what he had said during his second visit, proposed resolving the problem of hangings by simply doing without them. He would paint the main part of the walls either ruby red or forest green – *very* fashionable in Florence, he had repeatedly assured her – and break up the overpowering expanses of colour with panels painted after the *style* of tapestries. She could not feel that this was quite what the Great Chamber required, but had so far failed to think of any satisfactory alternative.

She gathered herself together. 'We have an excellent joiner, who will build benches and possibly shelves round the lower walls. As far as hangings are concerned, there are several options amongst which we have yet to decide.'

William, who was no fool, wasn't sure that he believed her. But he said helpfully, 'Why not just have some nice panelling, with neat little heraldic devices painted on it – the grapes from the Vine Regis coat of arms, maybe?'

'We shall see.'

'That's quite enough, William,' interposed Susanna tartly. 'The Lady does not need your advice.'

The Lady caught Susanna's eye, a very slight frown in her own. Susanna's nagging at the boy was not only bad-mannered but very wearisome to listen to, though it didn't seem to trouble William at all.

3

Back in the Great Hall, Dame Constance and her guests seated themselves round her favourite table in the window alcove, and Susanna launched straight into the reason for their visit. 'Mistress Flora is a neighbour of ours and I have brought her to see you because she needs advice that I do not feel myself competent to give. William, go away, please, and find something to do somewhere else.'

'Women's gossip? Ho, hum. All right, I'll go and look for Lord Gervase. I want to ask him something.'

With impeccable timing, Gervase himself came striding into the Hall at that moment, a tall lean young man with haggard good looks, high forehead and cheekbones, strongly-marked eyebrows, and little resemblance to his exquisite mother. Heads were apt to turn when he entered a room, since the current masculine fashion for strong colours and fitted garments suited his tall, lean figure remarkably well. Today he was clad in a dark green doublet buttoned from neck to thigh, with a knightly girdle on his hips, and parti-coloured hose below – one leg mid-green and the other white. Buttoned over one shoulder was a short mid-green mantle lined in red and with a dagged border cut into scallop shapes.

'Susanna!' he said, bowing slightly. 'Welcome! I didn't know you were here until Hamish told me. Haven't seen you for a while.'

'No, indeed,' said Susanna. 'How are . . .'

William put a tactless end to this unpromising exchange of courtesies. 'Hah! Just the man we need!'

Gervase turned, hard grey eyes looking down on the boy from his superior height. 'Young – er – Burnell, isn't it? You have grown.'

William had never been impressed by Gervase, who seemed to him to be not very bright. 'Most people do at my age,' he muttered, earning a look of reproof from Susanna and shrugging it off. 'Yes, well, I thought that, spending so much of your time at court, you must know all about the new Poll Tax and I'd like to have it explained to me. Why do we have to pay tax at all? What's it for? In '77 it was only one groat a head. Now it's to be three. It's a lot.'

In no mood for being interrogated by a boy whose exploits on his previous visit to Vine Regis had been memorably disruptive, Gervase replied curtly, 'Governing the country costs money, and we all have to pay for it. The tax has gone up this year because we need one hundred and sixty thousand pounds to meet the royal debts and fund the war against

14

France. Every adult in the country is required to contribute. It's perfectly simple and perfectly fair.'

'Why can't the king pay his own debts?'

Dame Constance gave in to temptation. 'I hear that the crown jewels have already been pawned,' she murmured.

From anyone else, this provocative remark would have earned a blistering rebuke, but Gervase knew better than to do battle with his mother. He merely frowned at her.

Unexpectedly, Mistress Flora joined in. She had a perfectly pleasant if rather expressionless voice, with a very slight foreign accent. She said flatly, 'Well, I think it is a shocking imposition. Three groats from every man and woman in the country – why, that is more than most servants earn in several weeks! And I should think the peasants must be even worse off.'

Gervase stared at her, clearly wondering where she had sprung from, but she raised her chin and stared right back at him challengingly. Susanna, trying hard not to giggle, performed a belated introduction.

She knew that Gervase was still looking for a second wife to mother the two little daughters of his first and remembered how unimpressed he had been when she herself had been introduced to him as his bride-to-be, seeing her as a frivolous little thing with amazing eyelashes and no conversation. Which had been true enough, she supposed. It had been horrid at the time – she had been dreaming of romance – but what a relief in the end! If he had loved her, or even liked her, he would never have relinquished her to Piers, the husband she adored.

Vaguely, she felt she owed it to Gervase to find him another wife, but Flora seemed unlikely to qualify. She was not the kind of lady to appeal to him, being plain-looking, despising fashion, and having political opinions as well. A truly shocking combination!

Susanna could not have guessed that Gervase was confused.

Once, like most young men of the knightly classes, he had known of only two types of woman, ladies and whores, but his years in the royal household had taught him otherwise. Some ladies *were* whores, of course (even if paid otherwise than in cash), but although respectable females at court might hold opinions on poetry, fashion and music to which gentlemen dutifully listened, they knew better than to say what they thought – assuming that they *did* think, which Gervase doubted – about matters of state. Only the late King Edward's inamorata, Alice Perrers, had exercised political influence, but that had been in the king's last years and before Gervase's time.

Now, surveying this unusual young woman and always mindful of what his mother had taught him – that women were not by definition inferior to men and should therefore be treated with invariable politeness and respect – he inclined his head towards Mistress Chandos and said with slightly steely courtesy, 'Good day to you, ma'am.'

That he had no intention of entering into discussion on matters of royal policy was all too clear. Dame Constance, observing his expression, reflected that he was becoming more like his autocratic father, the late Lord Nicholas, every day. But in some ways life at court had improved him. From being a disappointingly dull young man with limited interests, he had expanded his horizons and improved his judgement – though not in relation to building and builders! – even if he still lacked the vital spark of his younger brother, John, who entered the Great Hall just then, looking as usual as if he had been dragged through a hedge backwards. She saw Susanna's eyes flicker and knew that she was withstanding the temptation to tidy him up, to tuck his shirt in, smooth down his hair, and pull up his socks. Dame Constance herself, after twenty-two years of her younger son's existence, knew better than to try.

Fortunately, hot on his heels came Gervase's two little girls,

16

Blanche a nine-year-old bursting with personality, and Eleanor, a quiet, placid seven.

'We haven't seen you for ages and ages, Susanna! And horrible William, too!'

Dame Constance said, 'Blanche! Manners! We have a guest.'

Both children greeted Mistress Flora with a curtsey and a prim, 'God give you good day,' but with Blanche it stopped there.

'When can we come over for Piers to give us some more riding lessons?' she demanded of Susanna, who said decisively, 'Not until the weather is warmer.'

The child tossed her head pettishly, but for once didn't argue and devoted herself instead to squabbling noisily with William, leaving Susanna and Gervase to try and carry on a remarkably unexciting conversation, with interpolations from John, about horses, the weather, and the difficulty of storing winter feed for the cattle.

Dame Constance, casting her eyes ceilingward, wondered without very much interest why the seemingly assured Mistress Flora should be seeking advice from an outsider. And why Susanna, never hesitant about expressing an opinion, should not feel competent to give it.

She was just about to tell the children to quieten down when silence fell of its own accord. Bringing her abstracted gaze back from the ceiling, she discovered that Mistress Flora, from some secret recess in her surcoat, had produced a pair of spectacles, whose lenses she was holding perched on the bridge of her nose, allowing the ribbon ear-loops to dangle at the sides. Through the lenses she was inspecting the girls who were staring back at her open-mouthed. Only once before had Dame Constance ever seen spectacles, and the children never.

Knowledgeably, Gervase said, 'Venetian, are they? There's one of the barons at court who has some, and he tells me only the Venetians can produce glass of fine enough quality.'

'Yes. He is quite right.'

'What are they for?' demanded Blanche.

'To help me see better.'

'Oooh, can I try them?'

'I'm sorry, but no.'

William said, 'I wouldn't mind having a peek through them myself. Those heavy black frames make you look awfully clever.'

Blanche bounced up and down. 'I want to try them! I want to try them!'

Dame Constance, Susanna, and the girls' attendant, Alice, all frowned at her, and Mistress Flora shook her head as she tucked the lenses away again. 'It's better not. They are valuable and would be very difficult and expensive to replace. I prefer not to take chances.'

Dame Constance reflected that it would be wiser to let the children try them now, under supervision, rather than run the risk of illicit borrowing – which Blanche would certainly attempt if ever the opportunity arose.

In the moments of renewed silence that followed, she said, 'Susanna, I think perhaps you and Mistress Flora should come up to my chamber to talk. It will be quieter there and we will not be interrupted.'

4

Upstairs in Dame Constance's austerely elegant chamber, with its pale wood panelling gleaming softly in the firelight, Susanna saw that the top of the painted clothes chest bore its familiar burden of parchments and accounts rolls. The room was faintly and pleasantly scented by the applewood logs on the fire.

All too well, Susanna remembered the occasions when she

had been summoned here to explain her failings to her future mother-in-law. But Dame Constance's manner now was relaxed and smiling as she waved Susanna and Mistress Flora to cushioned stools.

'Now, how can I help?'

Flora said, 'I think I had better begin at the beginning.'

'What an excellent idea,' agreed Dame Constance cordially.

She saw that Mistress Flora, serious herself and probably accustomed to being taken seriously by others, regarded her own lightness of tone as approaching dangerously near to frivolity. Certainly, the girl looked at her doubtfully for a moment before she recognised that she had committed herself, gave a faint sigh, and began her story.

'I badly need advice,' she said. 'My father is English, an expert on astrology, but spent much of his life in Venice before accepting an invitation from King Charles of France to be Court Astrologer at Paris. That was ten years ago.'

Tactfully but truthfully, Dame Constance murmured, 'I am impressed. Astrology is the most advanced science of our day.'

'Yes. It was a great honour. So we all moved from Venice to Paris. Unhappily, when King Charles was seen as being close to death, factions developed at court and it became clear that my father might become a victim of them. I am sure you can guess that when the *comte de Ceci* and the *marquis de Cela* are both striving for the same prize, anyone who happens to get in the way has to be very fleet of foot to survive. My father *is* – fleet of foot, I mean – but he decided to send me and my brothers back to England to be sure of our safety. This, of course, was before France and England went to war again.'

'Of course. And your father stayed behind?'

Mistress Flora raised a hand to toss back the curtain of her hair and took a moment to answer. 'Yes. I have no idea where he is or what has happened to him.'

'Oh dear. And what about your mother?'

'She died in Paris eight years ago, giving birth to my younger brother.'

Susanna, who had heard Mistress Flora's story before, murmured dutifully, '*So* sad!' Her own twins had been delivered with such obliging ease that she found it difficult to think of childbirth as a potentially lethal experience, although she knew that it often proved to be so.

Mistress Flora seemed to have lapsed into an indecisive silence, so Dame Constance said encouragingly, 'Your family, therefore, consists of . . . ?'

Mistress Flora gave another of her gusty little sighs. 'I am twenty-one years old and the eldest. I was born in Venice, as was my brother Stephen, who is a year younger than I. And lastly there is Frederick, who was born in Paris. We are at present living at the manor of Coteley Valence, of which my father has a tenancy, as his father had before him. Do you know it? It lies about a league to the east of Lanson.'

Coteley Valence was not on Vine Regis land and it was four or five years since Dame Constance had ridden over in that direction. She remembered it vaguely as a manor house much in need of refurbishment, and had wondered why the abbey of Stanwelle, on whose vast estates it lay, did not insist on the tenant carrying out improvements. Easier said than done, she now reflected, when the tenant happened to live in France. She said, 'I think I know it.'

Mistress Flora nodded her head slightly, then raised a hand and again tossed back her hair.

What, Dame Constance wondered as the silence lengthened, could this young woman need advice about? Not, presumably, about tracking down papa. Dame Constance was beginning to feel as depressed as Susanna had looked on the two girls' arrival. Flora's voice was sufficiently lacking in expression to send even the most kindly-intentioned hearer into a doze – and did she *never* smile?

Dame Constance shook herself back to wakefulness and said perseveringly, 'So?'

The girl had been sitting gazing down at the hands folded in her lap, but looked up. 'We have an elderly aunt who lives with us, but I am mistress of the household. My difficulty is that I do not know how long this situation will last. When we parted, my father told Stephen he must marry and beget sons as soon as possible. Otherwise, he said, everything would be bequeathed to our younger brother Frederick without more ado.'

Dame Constance, rarely at a loss for words, found herself murmuring, 'Unusual!'

'My father,' retorted Mistress Flora, 'is a very unusual man.'

'I'm sure he is.'

'And though Frederick is a tiresome boy, he is also a clever boy, much cleverer than Stephen. In any case, I wasn't much concerned at first because Stephen is far too lazy to go looking for an eligible bride. The trouble is that one has now fallen into his lap, so to speak.' Her tone changed, and she asked anxiously, 'I hope I am not embarrassing you by telling you all this?'

'No, no. Not at all,' Dame Constance assured her. *She* might not be embarrassed but she would have expected Mistress Flora to be. It was not customary for anyone to talk about intimate family affairs quite so openly to strangers.

'Thank you,' said that young woman, sounding as if all the cares of the world were resting on her shoulders. 'Well, then. We have an Italian steward at Coteley Valence and during the summer his niece, Benedetta, came to pay him a visit. She is a big, goodlooking girl with a mass of dark hair and I saw little of her at first because of course she stayed mostly in the

21

servants' quarters. She did strike me as being remarkably indolent, but I was wrong about that. She turned out after a few weeks to have been very busy indeed – persuading Stephen that he should marry her. And now . . . and now . . .'

She swallowed hard. 'He has always resented my being in charge of things. The fact of my being a year older, he says, in no way cancels out my natural inferiority as a mere female. I am very much afraid that he will encourage Benedetta to undermine my position as mistress of Coteley by running things as *he* tells her to, without reference to me.' Her narrow shoulders drooped. 'She doesn't speak even a word of English. Between them, they will do everything wrong, and my life will be made a misery. I don't know what to do.'

Dame Constance threw a glance at Susanna, understanding why she had not felt competent to give Mistress Flora the advice she was seeking. She said, 'But surely your father must have made some provision for you, personally, in the eventuality of Stephen's marriage?'

The girl sighed again. 'He told me he had set up a financial arrangement for me based on an estate of my mother's but he gave me no details and Stephen swears he knows nothing about it.'

Susanna volunteered, 'Didn't your father employ a man of law, who would know?'

'I don't think so, but we left Paris rather hurriedly and there may not have been time.'

Dame Constance and Susanna surveyed the girl in meditative silence. After a while, Dame Constance said, 'Yes, I understand your problem,' then, with a mental shrug, went on, 'but you must be aware that this is the way of the world. Whether or not Stephen marries the dislikeable – er – Benedetta, it would be very strange if he did not marry someone, some day. And then, like any other young woman in your position, you will have to resign yourself to handing the reins over to the new bride, or else find yourself a husband and set up a household of your own.'

5

'I don't want to find myself a husband,' Flora said sharply. 'I have *no* opinion of men!'

This was nothing short of heresy.

Susanna's eyes widened in shock and Dame Constance could see her thinking that men would have no opinion of Flora unless she made an effort to improve herself. At twenty-one, she should have been married long since, and it seemed to Dame Constance that, in a world where appearances counted for so much, the girl would lead a more satisfactory life if only she would face up to reality. She might not be a beauty, but she could at least look stylish. If she were to feel herself admired or even just appreciated by the opposite sex, she would very soon – human nature being what it was – modify her views about men.

Just then came a knock on the door and Hamish appeared bearing a tray with three silver cups on it. 'Here we are, Lady,' he said. 'I thought ye might be needing a restorative.'

Dame Constance looked at him suspiciously but, since she was accustomed to him reading her mind and anticipating her wants, said only, 'Thank you, Hamish.'

Mistress Flora was wearing a mystified expression as she watched the door close after the big man in the grey Vine Regis livery. 'He's not English, is he?'

'No. Scottish. The late Lord Nicholas, my first husband, captured him as a boy in the Border wars and brought him back here. And here he has remained ever since. I trust him absolutely.

23

'Now, you may think you don't want a husband,' she went on, 'but, if you will forgive me for saying so, it seems to me that your father would have done better to arrange a suitable marriage for you, rather than this undefined inheritance. It is, after all, a parent's duty to make such arrangements for his or her daughters. Failing matrimony, failing estates or money of her own, there is nothing a respectable unmarried girl can do in today's world but enter a convent or depend on the good-will of some relative prepared to take her in – and she all too often ends up as an unpaid servant or nursemaid, and is expected to be grateful for it.'

'I don't have a grateful disposition,' Mistress Flora replied rather sulkily. 'And in the case of marriage, *if* I wanted a husband I would prefer to choose one for myself. Though how I would find one here in the English countryside, which seems to me very strange and empty after the bustle and excitement of Venice and Paris, I don't know. Especially a husband I could bear to regard as superior to me in all things!'

Dame Constance laughed. 'You only have to behave *publicly* as if you regard him as superior to you. Privately, a clever woman can always get her own way.'

This did not go down well with Mistress Flora, who made it clear that she herself was a woman of principle. 'But why should she have to? Why should she have to resort to trickery, to being "clever", as you put it?' Mistress Flora glanced across at the businesslike piles of papers and parchments on the chest and, after a hesitant moment, went on, 'I know that you are in undisputed charge here. It's impertinent of me to ask, but how did you achieve that?'

Dame Constance, slightly nettled, might have replied differently if she had not been anxious to bring this uninteresting and singularly fruitless discussion to an early close. Her brows drawing together, she said, 'I was married at fourteen, and my children were still infants when my first husband was killed in the Scottish wars. I therefore had to assume control, and since Lord Gervase has grown up to be less interested in estate management than in war, I have continued, despite my recent second marriage, to manage Vine Regis on his behalf.'

'In effect,' Mistress Flora responded, hitting the nail smartly on the head, 'although you devote all your energies to it, Vine Regis isn't legally *yours*!'

'No, of course not.'

'But it should be. You have a right to it. That's what I mean. I think it's scandalous that women should be at men's mercy in everything, with no rights of their own. Legally, they are the property of their fathers until they wed, and of their husbands thereafter, and then their sons when they are widowed. I don't want to be my husband's *possession*. I believe women should have a say in their own destiny. I believe . . .'

Dame Constance, who had better things to do than debate the obvious, interrupted her. 'Yes, I appreciate that the men of your family lack charm . . .'

'I don't want them to be charming. I just want them to be considerate.'

'. . . but some men are perfectly reasonable beings. My advice would be that you try to put up with the present situation until your father reappears. If that is not possible, then you must make an effort to find out more about your mother's estate and the arrangement your father spoke of.'

It seemed to her to be a statement of the obvious which this possibly intelligent but undeniably dreary girl must already know.

'But . . .' the girl said helplessly, 'But how? How *can* I find out?'

'Have you asked the aunt who lives with you? She might have an idea.'

'I hadn't thought of that.'

Susanna, gazing out of the window at a darkening sky, said, 'It looks like snow. I must get back to my babies. Is there anything more you want to ask Dame Constance, Flora, or can we go now?'

'No, I . . . Thank you for your indulgence, Lady. I will do what I can to follow your advice.'

When they had gone, Dame Constance sat back with a sigh of relief. It was a perennial source of amazement to her that so many people – royalty included – were completely lacking in financial judgement. The great landowners, including the Church, compensated for their inefficiency by simply raising their tenants' rents or introducing new charges or taxes, but lesser mortals such as Mistress Flora's papa had no such recourse and as a result did nothing but land themselves and their families in an inextricable tangle.

She wondered again, without much interest, why such an apparently self-contained young woman should ask an outsider for advice – and, indeed, why she should be so explicit about her family's private affairs. Perhaps she was less sure of herself than she had at first appeared.

6

After that, save for when it occasionally occurred to Dame Constance that it might be useful in the future to have someone who spoke Italian to help her contend with Signor Alberti (when he condescended to reappear), she gave little more thought to Mistress Flora.

It was quite otherwise with Mistress Flora, who had been desperately impressed, first by Vine Regis itself and then by Dame Constance. She had lived and to some extent travelled in both Italy and France and thought she had seen everything in the way of grand buildings that the civilised world had to offer, whether in city or countryside. But Vine Regis had a personality all of its own – its high stone squareness redeemed from menace by the banners fluttering gaily from the corner towers and the at once sturdy and frivolous machicolations of the spectacular round tower attached to its east side. The ring of small stone buildings lining the inner margin of the moat had a further softening effect, and the moat was as bright and sparkling as the river that fed it. The vineyard and orchard on the rising ground behind the castle looked beautifully tended even as late in the year as this, and there were healthy-looking sheep in the meadows to the south, and a well cared for village nearby with a good stone church presiding over it. The whole landscape, Flora thought, would be wonderfully lush and green when spring came.

She had anticipated being interested in the castle itself, but she had gone there already in awe of Dame Constance, of whom she had heard so much from Susanna.

That she managed Vine Regis very well indeed had been obvious to Flora as she rode with Susanna towards the castle. It had encouraged her to hope, just a little, that the Lady's wisdom would offer her some respite from her worries. But she had left feeling even more discouraged than before. She had been haunted for months by nightmares of the future, had been racking her brains hoping to come up with some acceptable solution, and had reached a stage of depression where she had thought that even a stranger's confirmation of her own gloomy conclusions would come as a relief. It hadn't, of course. Dame Constance had simply told her what she already knew.

What disturbed her more than anything was the knowledge that she had displayed herself to the redoubtable Dame Constance in the worst possible light. Even to herself she had sounded uninteresting, unconvincing, and not very bright. She considered herself to be clever, but knew that she must have appeared rather stupid as well as plain and badly dressed.

She might not choose to make any effort where her own appearance was concerned, but that did not mean she was unable to appreciate Susanna's eye for style and colour, or the refined elegance of Dame Constance's slender, sapphire-blue gown, its simplicity emphasised rather than diminished by the exquisite gold-clasped, pearl-embroidered girdle that was the only jewellery she wore other than her rings.

Flora was vain of her cleverness, if not of her looks. She knew herself to be no beauty. She was almost as tall as a man, her nose was too pronounced, her mouth too wide, and her hair was not blond but brown and refused to curl unless with the laborious application of the curling iron or the nightly discomfort of curl rags. She knew that, if her father had been a different kind of father, he would have made sure she was married off long ago, but, without his impetus and in a world where appearances counted for so much, she had neither the looks nor – as far as she knew – the dowry to attract a husband. She could understand the importance of a dowry, but would have had no respect at all for a husband who chose his wife on the basis of her looks.

The more she thought about it, the less was she prepared to make any concessions. She had no intention of trying – and failing – to make herself look pretty.

Arriving back at Coteley Valence, a very ordinary manor house surrounded by fields, she left her palfrey in the care of her groom and hurried indoors, where she found her brother Stephen lounging before the fire in the hall.

'Where have you been?' he asked as she warmed herself gratefully at the blaze.

'Out. Where's Frederick?'

'I don't know. You're supposed to be in charge of him. Out where?'

She was too tired and depressed to embark on a tale in which he would not be even remotely interested. Briefly, she wondered whether she had been unfair to him when talking to Dame Constance and Susanna, emphasising his bad qualities at the expense of his good – such as they were. But he *was* spiteful and lazy and self-centred, which was what was making her life so difficult.

All she wanted to do was go to bed and hope that she would wake on the morrow feeling more cheerful, and more competent to put vague, silly Aunt Edith through a catechism about the inheritance from mama, who had been Edith's sister. She had no real hope of a sensible answer, certainly none specific enough for her to follow up. Why, oh why had papa not told her more about the 'financial arrangement' he had made for her – an arrangement with whom? How? Where?

She came close to tears every time she thought about it. But if Aunt Edith knew nothing, she would have to wait until papa reappeared, if he ever did, or hope that some steward who had been left in charge of mama's reputed estate would condescend to turn up at Coteley Valence one day to make a report on the condition of the land, the buildings, the rents and other matters of that sort.

To Stephen, she said, 'I rode over to Lanson to visit the Lady Susanna. That's all.'

'Oh. Is it snowing?'

'Not yet.'

He yawned. 'I hope Benedetta has not gone outdoors.'

Flora laughed for what felt like the first time for weeks. The thought of the languorous Benedetta venturing even as far as the front doorstep unless the sun was blazing down out of a clear blue sky was too improbable to contemplate.

If only she would! If only she would catch her death of cold! If only she would take an irrevocable dislike to England and go back to Italy, where she belonged. But she wouldn't. Not while she had her claws in Stephen.

Chapter 2

1

UNTIL Signor Alberti turned up again at Vine Regis with his journeymen and apprentices, his canvases, his pots of pigment and his fashionable ideas, there was nothing Dame Constance could do in the decorating line other than snatch a word with Gervase before he vanished back to court, about the style he favoured for his Great Chamber.

'Lordly splendour, hmmm,' he repeated. 'As long as the fellow's not thinking of plastering gold leaf all over the place. Very vulgar. It's not lordly splendour but lordly *grandeur* we need.'

She had carefully refrained from mentioning either ruby red or forest green, in case he said yes to either of them, although she later claimed that her omission was designed to leave the question completely open for Gervase himself to decide.

Unequivocally, he rejected William's idea of small, formal, heraldic motifs. 'No. It's a big chamber. It needs *big* pictures

31

even if they have to be painted – which I don't much fancy, I may say – rather than hung.'

He was quite right, as it happened, so she said, 'Pictures of what? I feel we have a superfluity of ancient heroes in the Great Hall.'

'Why not some Classical gods? They'd make a change. We can talk about it next time I'm home.'

'And perhaps a goddess or two?' she asked politely.

'Yes, why not?'

And off he went.

With a shrug, she returned to studying her plan to introduce the warrening of rabbits into some of Vine Regis's less product-ive acres – a cheap but profitable enterprise, since there appeared to be a growing market for rabbit meat and fur in London. She had not mentioned the idea to Sir Guy, who had only a limited interest in estate management. Horse breeding was his passion when he was not engaged on the legal affairs that absorbed so much of his time.

One afternoon early in the new year, wearing an expression of acute annoyance, he tossed a parchment roll down on the table in the Great Hall. Dame Constance, immersed in calcu-lations of likely profit and loss on the coney project and un-accustomed to seeing her husband in any mood other than urbane and humorous, raised an enquiring eyebrow.

'Yes,' he said. 'You may well ask.'

She raised the other brow.

'This benighted Poll Tax!' he complained. 'The money is not coming in, and the royal council has ordered the collectors to redouble their efforts. But *they* claim there is systematic tax evasion. It seems that almost half a million people who were registered for the first Poll Tax in '77 have disappeared from the rolls.'

'Goodness! That must be almost a quarter of the population!'

'Not quite, but near enough.'

'They can't *all* have died, can they?'

'It seems unlikely. The council suspects collusion between the collectors themselves and the people they should have assessed for tax. They say that collectors across the country are all local people and must therefore know when the existence of unmarried females and widows, for example, is being concealed. The council intends to investigate, and this communication requires me, in my role as Justice of the Peace, to hold myself in readiness to be appointed as a local commissioner to chase the arrears.'

'Oh, dear.'

'As you say, oh dear! Think of Weaver John in the village. You can see me – can't you? – pounding on his door and demanding to know why he has failed to declare the existence of the six (is it?) daughters who live at home with him.'

'Only three of them are of taxable age,' Dame Constance pointed out helpfully. 'The others are too young.'

'Indeed? And you think that should make it easier?'

'Well, you can't be expected to *know* that the man has three girls over fifteen. You might think them all to be younger.'

The corners of his lips twitched. 'Am I wrong, or are you suggesting I should connive at tax evasion?'

'Would I do that?'

He grinned. 'Yes.'

'Really!' After an artificially offended moment, she went on, 'I haven't seen the girls for quite a while. They may have gone off to stay with Weaver John's sister in the north. In that case, they would not be your concern, would they?'

She must, she thought, drop a word of warning in Alice's ear – Alice, the second of the weaver's seven daughters, who lived at Vine Regis and acted as chamberer to Blanche and Eleanor. Alice was a sensible girl who could be relied on to recognise and act on a hint when it was given her. Though perhaps, Dame Constance reflected, it would be best not to become directly involved. Better to pass the hint on to the girl through Hamish, who for the last two years had been hovering on the brink of asking Alice to marry him. It was high time he made up his mind.

Sir Guy shook his head at her in mock reproof. 'My dear, Weaver John is only one of many. And I suspect that a goodly number of them will object strongly to being chased for arrears.'

'Strongly? You mean you might have to take a bodyguard when you go investigating?'

'Probably. Indeed, certainly.'

Dame Constance had always prided herself on the good relations the castle had with its tenants and retainers. That this relationship should be jeopardised by the officiousness of the royal council was quite unacceptable. It also worried her that much of the inevitable resentment would redound on Sir Guy, who had always been generally popular. It was quite unjust.

2

Just then, the castle's stately steward came sailing along the Great Hall towards them, followed at a few paces by the unmistakable and even more stately figure of Abbot Ralph of the nearby abbey of Stanwelle.

The abbot was a large man of middle age, well over six feet in height from his gleaming tonsure to the soles of his soft leather buskins and with a girth to match. The thick white woollen robe and the rope tied round his middle made him look, if that were possible, even larger. His air was in general imperturbable, although he tended to twitch slightly when confronted by Dame Constance, who stirred in him responses unsuitable in a man vowed to chastity. Seeing her and reacting to her, now, he bethought himself of the penance he would have to impose on himself – fifty days on bread and water – and sighed. He was a man who liked his food.

He had hoped to find Sir Guy alone, or as alone as anyone could ever be in a castle and, after the requisite exchange of courtesies, it emerged that he wished to consult Sir Guy about certain matters of legality.

'In civil law, I hope?' Sir Guy enquired. 'I am no expert on canon law.'

'I am aware of that,' Abbot Ralph replied. 'What I need is the opinion of a trained mind, uncluttered by – ah – Church orthodoxy.'

'In that case, you don't need me,' said Dame Constance with her blandest smile. But before she left, she was overcome, as so often, by the temptation to tease him by her continuing presence. It amused her, as it amused all the members of her family – except Gervase, who was impervious to such things – that Abbot Ralph should believe that his secret *was* a secret. So she enquired politely after the progress of the new chapel he was building at Stanwelle.

He inclined his head. 'It progresses, but slowly. I insist on quality, and the statuary and other carvings take time.'

'How well I know it. Even our own work here, minor though it has been by comparison, has consumed an amazing amount of time. And we are not finished yet. Now I am occupied with the decoration of Gervase's Great Chamber.'

'Indeed? But when that is done, you will be finished. A matter of weeks or months. Our new chapel will take years yet.'

Dame Constance, suitably chastened, lowered her eyes to hide the laughter in them, then went off quite unnecessarily to ensure that someone in the buttery had been instructed to send up wine and spices for the two men. Not that she had any doubt about it. Sir Walter was nothing if not efficient.

'So, what is it that concerns you?' asked Sir Guy. 'Please sit. How can I help you?'

Abbot Ralph surveyed the cushioned stool just vacated by Dame Constance but chose, for reasons best known to himself, to settle his large posterior on a hard wooden bench. 'I would appreciate your considered view of the schism in the papacy.'

It was totally unexpected. Sir Guy, who had no view on the papacy as long as it stayed away and minded its own business, murmured, 'Indeed?'

The struggle for power between Church and state in continental Europe, with kings, cardinals and the common people all taking a hand, had finally erupted just over two years before, with the result that now there were *two* legitimately elected popes, one in Rome and one in Avignon, both claiming supremacy, both trading in benefices, selling indulgences, appointing cardinals and bishops, and issuing excommunications with a fine, free hand. Neither of them had succeeded in establishing an absolute right to the papal throne, and the various rulers of Europe had chosen to acknowledge the authority of one or other of them largely for political and diplomatic reasons. France, Aragon, Savoy and Scotland were among those acknowledging the pope in Avignon; England, Denmark, Flanders and the Holy Roman Empire favoured the pope in Rome. Chaos looked like being the inevitable result.

After a moment of wondering what Abbot Ralph's interest was, Sir Guy made certain deductions. He said calmly, 'England has declared in favour of Urban in Rome. Do I deduce that you, personally, have reservations about him?'

Casting a majestic glance around, presumably to reassure himself that there were no dangerous eavesdroppers within hearing, Abbot Ralph replied, 'Reservations is an appropriate word.

Urban is known to be crazed and cruel, hardly the kind of man to inhabit the Holy See of the Christian Church. Whereas Clement in Avignon . . .'

'Is scarcely more Christian, surely? Only two or three years ago he was responsible for the massacre of five thousand innocents at Cesena, and is hated throughout Italy as a result.'

'A single episode for which no doubt he had his reasons,' said Abbot Ralph dismissively. 'Save for that, he is known to be eloquent, cultivated, well read in several languages, and artful in the management of men.'

Unimpressed, Sir Guy leaned back, hands behind his head. 'Possibly, but whatever your personal opinion, you are surely bound by the decision of those higher than you? If England has declared for Urban, you can scarcely take an independent decision as to which pope you and your abbey should follow.' Dryly, he added, 'If you did, you might find Urban appointing one of *his* adherents to take Stanwelle over from you. And then where would you be? Two popes may be all very well, but two abbots of Stanwelle?'

It was a danger Abbot Ralph had clearly failed to foresee. Had he not been so large a man, he might have leapt to his feet to stride around the Great Hall. Instead, 'That is all you can say, is it?' he enquired.

Sir Guy mastered the temptation to say a good deal more. What was it about Ralph, he wondered, that so often stirred mischief in him? Now, aware that Abbot Ralph's sense of humour was a frail thing at best, he refrained from suggesting that the abbot could always emigrate to Scotland, which (enemy to England and friend to France) had declared in favour of the Avignon pope.

'Yes, I'm afraid that *is* all I can say,' he replied.

'I suppose you are right,' the abbot conceded. 'I had hoped for something more.'

Sir Guy, anxious to return to his work, was inwardly congratulating himself on having dealt with the abbot's concerns so expeditiously when a servant appeared bearing wine and spiced wafers. So he had to listen to Ralph's views on another matter – John Wyclif's vernacular translation of the Bible, of which the abbot could not, on principle, approve, since it gave people ideas above their station by allowing them direct access to holy writ instead of having to depend on what their priests told them about the word of God.

And after that it was the unpopularity of the clergy. 'I hear complaints about our building vastly expensive chapels to house holy relics instead of using the money to feed the poor. Which sounds all very fine,' the abbot went on, an almost plaintive note in his soft voice, 'but, as you know, building our new chapel at Stanwelle was a condition of our being bequeathed the true fragment of the Holy Cross.'

'Yes,' said Sir Guy.

'And I fear that if, as I am inclined to suspect, the Poll Tax induces a widespread climate of resentment, the Church may find itself under attack.'

Sir Guy, cup raised to his lips, surveyed the abbot over its rim. 'Yes, I sympathise. So, too, will lawyers.'

The abbot was surprised. His plump white hands had been laid flat upon the table, his gaze fixed on the space between them, but now he raised his bright brown eyes to Guy's. 'Why so?'

Sir Guy thought with a touch of impatience, *Wake up, my friend.* How could a clever man, as Ralph undoubtedly was, be so obtuse, so blind? The priesthood had been too influential, too powerful, too self-centred, for too long.

He said, 'Ordinary people want only to be left to get on with their lives, but neither Church nor state will allow it. Both are seen to be rich, their riches exacted from the poor. This may not be altogether true but, for those who have to scrape a living, your beautiful new chapel at Stanwelle appears not only as an insult, but as a rejection of the fundamental tenets of Christianity. And where lawyers are concerned – well, it is men like myself who are directly responsible for imposing the weight of the law, even if we have had no hand in devising it. Churchmen and lawyers are increasingly hated, and I believe the breaking point may soon come. There could even be a general revolt.'

'Never!'

'If people are pushed too hard . . .'

Abbot Ralph, accustomed to a world in which lawful authority – which was another way of saying, his own – was never questioned, appeared to find this beyond his comprehension. Sir Guy wondered how he would react if confronted by an angry mob.

Slowly, the abbot answered the unspoken question. 'In this era of physical violence, as we go rushing towards the Day of Judgement, I have always been sheltered by the Church. I do not know how I would respond if I were to come face to face with aggression. I could not look on such a prospect with equanimity.'

Sir Guy placed his cup on the table and allowed his eyes to stray back towards his parchments.

There seemed nothing more to be said.

Abbot Ralph stared for a few moments into infinity, or perhaps eternity. Then, preparing to leave, he struggled to rise from his bench and Hamish – always there when he was wanted – appeared out of nowhere and lent him an arm. Sir Guy himself rose and bowed slightly. 'If I can be of any help in the future, in any way . . .' he said.

The abbot inclined his head graciously and sketched a cross in the air before him. 'Thank you,' he replied, and then, solicitously escorted by Hamish, made his way along the Great Hall towards the stairs.

3

In the meantime, Dame Constance had retreated to the Great Chamber, accompanied by the children and Alice, their chamberer.

Dame Constance stood by one of the windows – much larger here than in the older part of the castle, she had made sure of that – and tried to think, while the children scampered round and round, raising echoes and giggling happily despite Alice's attempts to quieten them.

After a few minutes, Dame Constance said, 'Children, this is not a playroom. Stop, please.'

'But it's such a lovely big space to run around in,' Blanche protested.

'You are not here to run around. You are here to learn.'

'Are we? What about?'

'About decoration and – er – taste. '

'What's taste?'

Dame Constance smiled faintly. 'You know how some food tastes good, some not so good? Yes? And some decoration looks good, some not so good. You must learn which is which, using your eyes rather than your tongue.'

'Oh. What fun!'

'Perhaps. Now let me think for a few minutes without interrupting me. Sit down on the floor and be quiet.'

'Yes, grandmother.'

She had been mentally scrutinising the possibilities for weeks and was less and less attracted to the idea of painted imitation tapestries, set against surrounding walls of red – or green! But young William Burnell had been right. There was no possibility of satisfactorily suspending real tapestries against the curved walls. And she felt that painted imitations would look tawdry and penny-pinching. The alternative of panelling the walls had the different disadvantage of being dull. The room was far too large, as Gervase had said, and small formal devices such as the Vine Regis bunch of grapes would simply look spotty. Perhaps if the lower part of the walls were wainscotted, the upper part would be more manageable . . .

She said, 'The artist suggests that he should paint imitation tapestries on the walls, large panels set against a coloured surround. Try to imagine what that would look like and tell me what you think.'

Eleanor looked shy and helpless, but Blanche, as always, had something to say, even if for once she said it doubtfully. 'Panels with pictures in them?'

'Yes.'

'Like the real tapestries in the Great Hall, with ancient heroes and battles and things?'

'Yes, that kind of thing. Although your father thinks Classical gods and goddesses would be better in here.'

Blanche was looking disapproving. 'Why do we have to have imitation tapestries? Why can't we have real, proper ones? We've *always* had proper tapestries. I don't see why we have to have imi . . .'

Patiently, Dame Constance said, 'We haven't *always* had "proper" tapestries. The ones in the Great Hall were new when you were a baby. Before that, our walls, like everybody else's, were painted in a plain, rough style, sometimes with pictures of people or animals. In fact, we were very much ahead of fashion when we installed our hangings – and still are! But we can't have them in here because woven tapestries are flat and the walls are curved. They would not hang well. There would be gaps behind them.'

Blanche said, 'Oooh, gaps we could hide in? That'd be good!'

'No.'

'Well, I still don't see why we have to have imitations. They'll look horrid. Why can't the man do proper paintings? Why can't he . . .'

Dame Constance laughed. 'Really, Blanche. "Proper" tapestries! "Proper" paintings! What do you mean by "proper" paintings?'

'I mean – ummm – proper *pictures*.'

It was clear that the child had something in her mind's eye, but it was necessary that she should learn to express it in words. 'Explain yourself.'

'Oh, pooh! I mean that, instead of squashing the gods into sort of squares, like pretend-tapestries, why can't he just make pictures like the ones along the bottom of the pages in my *Book of Hours*. People in open spaces rather than squeezed into boxes. That would look much better. Shall I fetch my book and show you?'

'No, I know what you mean.'

The child was right. Free-flowing paintings! Dame Constance thought about it, and liked the idea, though only if the paintings had the refinement to be found in tapestries – and, indeed, in *Books of Hours* – rather than the coarser style that so often marred traditional wall paintings. Plain panelling along the lower one-third of the walls, and gods and goddesses above, unrestricted by any formal framework. Yes.

'That is a very good idea, Blanche. Clever girl! Not *all* the way round the room, perhaps, but round most of it. What do you think, Eleanor?'

Eleanor, as always, thought as her sister did. 'That would be lovely.'

'I will talk to the painter about it and perhaps he might do some preliminary sketches. Let us hope he is as good a painter as I have been led to believe. And once that is decided, we can make up our minds where the joiner is to build the shelves and benches. It depended, before, on where the imitation tapestries were to hang, but we will have more freedom now. So – off you go, back to the schoolroom. Alice, a word with you, please.'

'Yes, Lady.'

As the children pranced off, Dame Constance remarked, 'I fear Blanche may be slightly above herself after that.'

Alice smiled. She had a lovely smile, a little shy. 'I can manage her, Lady.'

'I am sure you can. But there is something else. This Poll Tax. You have heard about it? Well, since you work for us and live here, Vine Regis will pay your contribution. But where your sisters are concerned, it is a different matter. Ask Hamish to explain it all to you tomorrow.' By which time Dame Constance would have revealed her tax-evasion plan to him and threatened him with the direst consequences if he ever allowed Sir Guy to find out.

'Yes, Lady. Thank you, Lady,' said Alice, dropping her a curtsey.

4

'So,' said Hamish, 'if your sisters continue at home, it'll cost your father a lot of money. Nine groats for the three who are of taxable age!'

They were out in the main courtyard of the castle, surrounded by the high walls of the building and filled, as always in the mornings, with so much bustle that it felt like a market place.

Their conversation was constantly interrupted by all the coming and going – of women from the village, grooms leading horses out from the stables, youthful squires learning to fight with wooden swords, pedlars selling ribbons and wooden nutmegs and other delights, kitchen boys drawing water from the well, clerks with their dark robes and white coifs and their burden of parchments. Master MacLeod knew and nodded to them all.

He was such a kind and helpful man, Alice reflected, taking time to explain everything to her. She liked him very much, and thought he liked her, too. She hoped that some day he might ask her to be his wife, though he had often said how much he valued his freedom. She could hardly tell him outright that she understood, that she would never try to limit his freedom to go *where* he would, *when* he would, at the Lady's command.

She smiled up at him. 'Yes, I see that it might be better for my father if they weren't living at home, but . . .'

'But where could they go? That's the question. Your father has a sister in the north, hasn't he?'

'Yes.'

'The difficulty is that if they went to stay with her *she* would have to declare them and pay for them.' He stopped abruptly, struck by an idea. 'Unless the collectors were doing their collecting *while* the girls were on their journey. How many days would it take for them to reach your aunt's on foot?'

'I have no idea. A great many.'

He wrinkled his nose thoughtfully. 'Aye, well, it's a possibility. While they were on the road, I shouldnae think they'd have any official residence. But they'd have to choose the right days to go on their travels, and we don't know when those would be.'

'They wouldn't *have* to go to my aunt's, would they?' she ventured. 'They could just go out and look for work.'

'To some place like the hiring fair at Woldesbury, ye mean? Well, the spring one's about due. By the time they walk there, and wait for an employer to decide to take them on, a fair amount of time will have passed.' His light eyes twinkled down at her from under their sandy brows. 'That's a good idea, lassie. But would they want to go and look for work somewhere else, when your father needs them at home?'

'Free labour,' she responded with a slightly lopsided smile. 'He doesn't pay them for all the work they do.'

'Perhaps he should just pay their Poll Tax after all!'

She giggled. 'Perhaps. But I think it would be good for them to get away from home. I myself have learned *so* much from working here at the castle and everyone is so kind! I would never wish to be anywhere else.'

Hamish came very near to uttering the fateful words but, as several times before, they stuck in his throat. He was not the marrying kind.

'That's good to hear,' he said. 'Now, I must go. The Lady wants me to ride over to Lanson with a message for the Lady Susanna.'

5

By the end of May, obedient to the command of the royal council to interrogate municipal and village authorities in order to track down arrears, Sir Guy had spent an unpleasant few weeks at Woldesbury summoning reputed backsliders before him to declare their taxable status under oath. Some incriminated themselves out of their own mouths, but it was clear to him that others had been denounced by neighbours or workmates as a way of settling old scores.

'You mean you do *not* go knocking on doors?' demanded a scandalised Dame Constance as they sat in the orchard one day, inhaling the sweet smell of growing things.

He grinned. 'Not even Weaver John's. You were wrong about the older girls being away from home, by the way.'

'Oh, was I?' Innocent though she sounded, she had already been entertained to learn from Hamish that the three older girls had flatly refused to leave home and walk for miles and miles and miles, just to save their father money.

Sir Guy went on, 'He paid up, grumbling bitterly. But not nearly as bitterly as Sim Walden.' Sim was the local bad character, lazy and surly. 'And you know those two brewers in Woldesbury . . .'

'You mean Jem Burden and Will Sothern? A thoroughly disagreeable pair, and their ale isn't very good, either.'

'We don't buy from them, do we?'

'Only as a last desperate resort.'

He grinned. 'Well, Burden wondered *very* confidentially if I knew that Sothern had an ancient grannie hidden away in the attic.'

'*Did* you know?'

'No. And I still don't. I am not prepared to participate in spiteful competition or in settling old scores. The royal council will have to do without grannie's three groats.'

'Tut, tut,' said Dame Constance, bending to pluck an unusually sturdy-looking daisy from under the pear tree. 'I must tell Master Robert not to buy any ale from Jem Burden for a while. I wouldn't like it to come spiked with something nasty in retaliation.'

He laughed. 'If that were the only problem arising from my chasing of tax arrears!'

She was surprised. 'Are you expecting others?'

'I have the feeling that the Poll Tax may be the last straw. There are likely to be local disturbances, no more than a few scattered outbursts, perhaps, although enforcing the tax seems to be making lawyers even more detested than usual. If there should be real trouble, it will be lawyers and the clergy who bear the brunt of it. Ordinary people are nurturing decades of resentment over the demands of the Church and the impositions of the state.'

Dame Constance, as accustomed as Abbot Ralph to deference from all quarters, merely remarked, 'Well, I cannot think we will have any serious trouble at Vine Regis.' Dismissing the whole thing from her mind, she twirled the daisy in her fingers and said, 'Now, where is Gervase? The painter has sent a message to say that he will be arriving soon, so I need to talk to Gervase about gods and goddesses.'

6

Summoned from the stables to attend his mother in the Great Chamber and tell her which gods he particularly fancied, Gervase said, 'We ought to show that fellow – what's his name? – the one with the leaves in his hair and a bunch of grapes in his hand.'

'Bacchus, you mean.'

'Do I?'

'He would be appropriate, I agree. And who else?'

Her son, becoming aware that her eyes were fixed on his boots and the stable straw they were distributing over the clean new floor, bent to pick up the divots and toss them into the great empty fireplace. Then, a trifle red in the face, 'Who do you suggest? Achilles, maybe?'

'Really, my dear! He was a hero, not a god.'

'Oh, yes. Of course.'

Patiently, Dame Constance led her son through Apollo, Mars, Mercury, Neptune and – with some hesitation – Pan, and the activities associated with them; they could not be pictured just standing around doing nothing. But at last Gervase admitted, 'No use asking me. I don't know any more. I'll have to leave it to you and the painter. But from anything I've seen in the king's manuscript of – what's his name? – Aratus, they all look very under-dressed. You'd better get the painter to put some clothes on them, don't you think?'

'If you wish.'

'Can I now get back to what I was doing?'

'Your horses can wait for a minute or two. There's something else I wanted to talk to you about. I don't know whether you have had any recent news from court?'

'Not for several days. Why?'

'You will remember that I have a cousin who lives in Kent.'

Gervase, spotting a wisp of straw he had previously missed, bent to retrieve it. 'That fool who recommended the builder to you?'

Dame Constance's lips twitched. 'I never had any very good opinion of Kentishmen before that. Since then I have whole-heartedly distrusted them and their judgement. But I had a message from him this morning, deliberately designed, it might be thought, to strike terror into my heart! He claims that the whole county of Kent is rising in revolt against the Poll Tax. He even claims that the rebels, *thousands* of them, are marching to attack Rochester Castle, and recommends me to look to the defences of Vine Regis in case the revolt spreads our way. I haven't yet mentioned it to Guy, who has enough on his mind. But it all sounds highly unlikely to me, and if you have heard nothing from court it may all be unfounded rumour.'

Gervase's eyebrows rose towards his hair. 'Marching to attack Rochester Castle! What with? Pitchforks?' He thought for a moment. 'No, it must be nonsense. We English don't go in for rebellion. A small riot now and then, maybe, but not much more. If there was real trouble brewing, I should have heard by now.'

'That is what I would have supposed. Now, go back to your horses – and send a groom up to sweep this floor!'

'Yes, mother.'

7

Next day, however, Gervase received a message summoning him back to court at Windsor. 'The king needs me!' was all he said to Dame Constance.

But to Sir Guy he said more. It seemed that there was a fear of demonstrations in London, and the king wished to be surrounded by men he trusted. His advisers regarded the situation as potentially dangerous.

'For the king himself? Surely not,' responded Sir Guy. 'Who *are* these supposed demonstrators, these rebels? Do we know? Peasants with pitchforks in the countryside, perhaps, but not in London.'

'There are always weapons to be had,' replied Gervase grimly. 'The mayor and aldermen have an armed force that could easily take care of a few score men with sticks and stones and even swords, but the rumour is of far more than that. The worrying thing is that many of the rebels said to be coming in from the countryside are not just illiterate peasants. Some are men who have served in village government – constables, bailiffs and the like – who are known to have a personal talent for leadership. It appears that, as my mother's cousin recently wrote, men from Kent and Essex are marching on London in their thousands. In the City itself, of course, they are likely to be reinforced by the poorer labourers and artisans and by the apprentices, who like nothing more than getting into a fight.'

They were in the armourer's workshop, Gervase supervising an adjustment to one of the pauldrons of his body armour, and the noise was deafening. It did not seem to affect Gervase, accustomed as he was to the clanging of steel, but Sir Guy found it impossible to concentrate. 'Outside,' he said, and dragged his stepson on to the landing.

Gervase said, 'Myself, I don't believe the danger is as great as it sounds. The really queer thing is that, even allowing for exaggeration, the trouble seems to have swelled to such proportions in such a short time. But if things *are* moving so fast . . .'

'Yes?' Sir Guy still found the changes in Gervase highly instructive. In earlier years, with no physical action in prospect, Gervase had always tended to go about the business of his estates without showing any sign of interest or enthusiasm; indeed, Sir Guy had infuriated Dame Constance on one occasion by telling her she was too competent, making her son feel inferior. But when it came to fighting, Gervase could now not only do it, but talk about it as well. He was in his own element, and very like – said Dame Constance – his domineering father, the late Lord Nicholas.

'In the improbable event of the trouble spreading towards Vine Regis,' Gervase said now, 'it would be best if I inspected the castle's defences before I leave for Windsor.' He paused, meeting Sir Guy's slight frown, then went on, 'Vine Regis has always been a good and considerate lord and landlord to those who live on the estates, and I know of only one reason why it might be attacked. And that reason,' he paused again and then went on, his voice laden with menace, 'that reason is you, Guy.'

Sir Guy's frown deepened. 'Possibly, but . . .'

Gervase interrupted. 'Royal government and the law have been intruding more and more into people's lives, enforcing labour laws and taxation, and it is Justices of the Peace who are the most visible representatives of that intrusion. The Church and its tithes and the government and its commissions are too often seen as having only one purpose – to rob ordinary hardworking people. The Poll Tax, however necessary it is to the wellbeing of England – and it is! – may prove to be the last straw.'

It was scarcely news to Sir Guy, who had said much the same to Abbot Ralph not so very long ago, but it confirmed to him that Gervase *had* learned a great deal at court. He could never in the past have imagined his stepson being so sensible and fluent. He had developed a good deal of authority in the last three years. Acting as equerry to the king had made him, not obsequious, as might have been expected, but the opposite. He now very often *did* know what he was talking about, instead of just pretending that he did.

Sir Guy said, 'I can see that, if this were to develop into a serious rebellion, the mob would be likely to leave a trail of destruction in its wake – looting and fire-raising and so on – but . . .'

'Yes, anyone living even in an ordinary manor house could be attacked, almost in passing, simply for being richer than members of the mob. Attacking castles like Vine Regis is more of a challenge, however. It would require organisation and discipline, which might only seem justified to any rebels if you as a lawyer were the target.' Gervase frowned heavily. 'No, don't flatter yourself that, because local people like you on a personal basis, you will be exempt from hatred of your official activities.'

Sir Guy had been wondering about that. Much would depend on the temper of the mob (if any) and its composition, the proportion of local people involved.

Strange though it was to be asking his stepson for an opinion, Sir Guy said, 'So? What do you suggest?'

'I've been thinking. You have that place up Northampton way. The trouble doesn't seem to have spread up there, or not yet. It would relieve any pressure on Vine Regis, and on my mother, if you were to take yourself off there for a while . . .'

From behind them on the stairs, a female voice asked dulcetly, 'And what are you two conspiring about?'

It was so unexpected that Gervase almost jumped out of his skin.

Turning to his mother, he repeated, 'Conspiring? What do you mean, "conspiring"?'

He looked a picture of guilt, and she said so.

Her husband, however, came to the rescue. 'We were talking,' he told her, 'about horses, what else?'

'Is that all? How disappointing. I was hoping you might be up to something more amusing.'

Gervase had recovered himself. 'Really, mother! You should be ashamed of yourself.'

She laughed. 'I am on my way to the carpenter's workshop to choose the wood for the panelling of the Great Chamber. If you would stand aside, I might be able to pass.'

8

The two men having tacitly agreed, on their way back down to the courtyard, that there was no need to worry Dame Constance with talk of dangers that would probably never threaten Vine Regis, she was quite unsuspicious when – her son having ridden off towards London with his armour blazing in the June sun – her husband also declared his intention of leaving Vine Regis to go off to Hervelock and inspect the work of his new steward there.

'When will you go?' she asked.

'Tomorrow, I think. There is no purpose in putting off.'

'And for how long do you expect to be away?'

'I don't know. A se'enight, perhaps. Perhaps more.'

She was mildly surprised when he set out next morning in

uncharacteristically dramatic style, trumpets blaring and pennants flying, accompanied by his full riding household and a score of retainers clad in blue livery. No one in the locality of the castle could possibly have been unaware that Sir Guy Whiteford, Justice of the Peace, was going to be away from home, and probably for some time.

Fond though she was of her husband and, within limits, of her son, there was pleasure in the prospect of having her life to herself, if only for a week or two.

Or would have been if the painter had not chosen that very morning to arrive, accompanied by half a dozen weary-looking apprentices, on foot, and with his equipment loaded in a horse-drawn cart spectacularly painted on each of its sides with a central image of an artist's palette, flanked by stripes in rainbow hues. Disappointingly, the canvas hood protecting its contents from the weather was undecorated. Instead, it was so lavishly coated with tallow against the elements that the smell of mutton fat was overpowering. Dame Constance hastily closed the window by which she was sitting in the Great Hall.

She welcomed Signor Alberti politely, small and volatile, with a nose more hooked than she remembered under his heavy black brows and hair. When Hamish offered to help him unload his cart and carry its contents up to the Great Chamber anteroom, which the painter referred to as his studio, his offer was rejected with the utmost scorn. The signor would not dream of trusting his canvases, his jars or his pigments to the hands of a vulgar ignoramus. His meaning was clear, even if his English was not.

Directing a meaning glance at Dame Constance, Hamish said, 'Well, I'll get a page to escort you and see that your apprentices dinnae lose their way in the castle. When ye've got everything settled, I'll show you where your workmen can sleep.'

Signor Alberti stared at him as if the concept was foreign to him. 'Sleep?'

Hamish tried again. 'I – me . . .' – he pointed a finger towards his chest – 'will show *you*' – his finger changed direction – 'where apprentices are to sleep.'

'*Si*,' responded Signor Alberti with a shrug.

Dame Constance had decreed that the painters were to sleep either in the village, or in one of the new and as yet unoccupied buildings in the bailey. 'And,' she said very slowly indeed, smothering her amusement, 'when you have settled everything to your liking, Signor Alberti, we must discuss what you are to do in the Great Chamber. I hope you will not object to what the Lord Gervase and I have decided. Briefly, what we would like is this . . .'

He listened, his eyes flicking back and forth between Dame Constance and the entrance to the Great Chamber. Finally, he bowed. '*Prego!*' and turned away towards his studio, over which it seemed he intended to preside while his apprentices did all the hard labour of carrying everything up from the cart. 'I tell where put things,' he added as he vanished through the doorway from the Great Hall.

Reminding herself that she had known there would be problems of communication, Dame Constance hoped he had understood, or even partly understood, what she had said – and what she was likely to say in the future. She needed that tall thin Venetian-bred girl Susanna had brought over last November. What was her name? – Flora something.

9

At that precise moment, the lookout's horn sounded again from above the Great Gate, blowing the series of calls that signified friends approaching.

Hamish glanced out of the window and saw a small group

of horsemen riding hard from the south. 'It cannae be, but,' he narrowed his eyes, 'it is.' He grinned. 'It's Abbot Ralph, and he's in a wee bit of a hurry!'

'Ralph in a hurry? Never!'

The abbot's progress, like his person, was apt to be imposing, even majestic. According to Sir Guy, this was of necessity since only a big Norman stallion or a Flanders mare would carry his weight – and not at anything even approaching a canter.

'No pennants, no trumpets and no more than a dozen men with him. Ye'd almost think he didnae want to draw attention to himself.'

'Very odd. I only hope there is sufficient space on the stairs to allow him and Signor Alberti's apprentices to pass one another.'

'They'll fall back before him,' said Hamish confidently.

It was several minutes before the abbot appeared, looking heated and breathing rather heavily, in the wake of the castle steward, Sir Walter.

Dame Constance rose to greet him and begged that he would be seated. A glance at Sir Walter assured her that refreshment would be brought at once.

Abbot Ralph sketched a cross in the air before her, then subsided on to a wooden bench. It reminded her that she must speak to the joiner about supplying cushions for the seating he was to build in the Great Chamber, and to Master Nicholas about the coverings for them.

Resisting the temptation to ask, 'To what do we owe this honour?' she tilted her head slightly, adopted an expression of polite enquiry, and waited, no more than mildly curious.

When he had recovered his breath, he launched into what he had to say without more ado. Neither voice nor expression diverging from those to which she was accustomed, he said, 'I have come, Lady, to ask for refuge. To throw myself upon your mercy.'

After forty-one years of life, Dame Constance had thought herself past the stage of being startled by anything. But she was aware of her mouth opening slightly of its own volition, and her eyes widening. 'You have . . . ?'

'I have come to put myself under the protection of Vine Regis.'

'Protection?' she echoed after a moment. 'Protection from what? From whom?'

A trifle distrait, he glanced around as if for support, but saw only the big Highlander who was Dame Constance's body-guard, perched on a window sill, whittling away peaceably at a piece of wood. Coming up the Hall with a tray of cups and flagons was a young page who, kneeling, offered the abbot a choice of wine or small ale.

Accepting the ale and sipping it gratefully, Abbot Ralph said, 'I had hoped to find Sir Guy or the Lord Gervase here.'

'Gervase has been summoned back to court, and my husband has gone to visit his estates at Northampton. So,' she smiled extravagantly, 'you will have to make do with me.'

Protection? What was he talking about?

He eyed her dubiously for a moment, never having become attuned to sarcasm. Then, 'You must know, I believe, of the rebellion against the Poll Tax that has broken out in Kent.'

She frowned slightly, still mystified. 'I had heard something of it,' she admitted. 'But I have been assured that rumour exaggerates.'

'No, no!' His voice suddenly lost all of its usual suavity. 'No! It does *not* exaggerate. This very morning a messenger arrived at Stanwelle to warn me that the constable of Rochester castle has surrendered it – surrendered *the castle*! – to the rebels. Worse than that. They have attacked Lessness Abbey and are now marching in their thousands on Canterbury. One cannot but fear for the safety of the Archbishop, who as chancellor of the realm is held responsible for the Poll Tax and hated accordingly. Fortunately, he is at present in London, but I am told on the best authority that the rebels' hatred for *him* places all other churchmen at risk.'

'Oh dear,' said Dame Constance, who didn't believe a word of it.

'And there has been violence! The rebels have actually dared to *execute* men whom they regard as traitors to the people.'

'Oh dear,' said Dame Constance again. It still seemed to her highly unlikely. Peasants simply did not go around executing people.

'As you will appreciate,' Abbot Ralph resumed, 'my peaceful abbey of Stanwelle has no military defences to withstand an attack by thousands of violent rebels. This is why I have come to you.'

He really was worried, she could see, so much so that he barely twitched at her nearness – thus depriving her of a private source of entertainment. Admirably restraining herself from asking how the abbey would manage without him, she said merely, 'But the revolt will surely be crushed before the Kentishmen come anywhere near Stanwelle – or Vine Regis.'

'If it were only so. The rebellion is, however, spreading widely and with alarming speed. It seems there are serious outbreaks in Essex and Suffolk, too. And violence and bloodshed are everywhere the keynote.'

Dame Constance tried, without success, to imagine Weaver John, or even Sim Walden, engaged in shedding blood. They might give someone a bloody nose, perhaps, but no more. 'Mmmm,' she said. 'Well, Vine Regis will of course give you refuge, if you so wish. May I ask if you are on any kind of diet at the moment?' Such as the bread and water which was a penance for licentious thoughts!

'No, no,' he assured her. 'I should be, but it would greatly inconvenience your kitchens if I were to insist on following it. I will be perfectly content to eat what you have the kindness to offer me. I can resume my diet when this sad business is over and I can return to Stanwelle.'

She summoned the lurking Hamish. 'Perhaps you would tell Sir Walter that Abbot Ralph will be staying with us for a while. He should have one of the chambers in the north-west tower.'

Then, turning back to her unexpected guest, she added, 'There are, I fear, a great many stairs up to the guest chambers. I hope they will not prove too much for you.'

'They will be a small price to pay for peace of mind,' he replied.

Chapter 3

1

Vine regis was well accustomed to guests arriving without warning – neighbours and acquaintances and distinguished personages on their travels – but never in such variety or such numbers as presented themselves in the next two days.

An exasperated Dame Constance, dragged away for what felt like the twentieth time from her attempts to communicate with the painter and the carpenter, greeted her uninvited guests with courtesy and listened patiently and with every appearance of sympathy to their reasons for coming to Vine Regis to ask for refuge.

Among the first to arrive was a merchant called Doggett, who brought his family with him and introduced himself as a liveryman of the Worshipful Company of Mercers. He was a short, fat, superficially jolly man with cold eyes and a florid complexion, expensively clad in the belted, narrow-hipped tunic of current fashion, which did nothing to flatter his ample stomach. His wife was built on unnervingly similar lines, with the same high colour and the same short white hair, and might at first sight have been taken for his twin. Strange as it seemed, the wispy flaxen-haired girl accompanying them turned out to be the daughter of this unprepossessing pair, while a dim middle-aged female was introduced as Master Doggett's sister. Attached to their party were four servants, eight horses, and two dogs.

They arrived, inconveniently, just after dinner, forcing the servants to duck around them while stacking away the boards and trestles. Master Doggett appeared to regard these necessary manoeuvrings as a personal affront, which did nothing to endear him to Dame Constance.

She rose, however, greeting him politely and then waiting for him to speak.

'How d'ye do, Lady?' he said and bobbed his head in a parody of a bow. 'I'll tell ye, we were set to visit her,' he nodded in the direction of his sister, 'over Amesbury way. And then we heard of houses being ransacked and set on fire, of cattle being stolen, and other criminal deeds. Ye'll understand that I feared for the safety of my womenfolk, so I thought to bring them here. I was reliably informed that Vine Regis has a reputation for hospitality and is well defended, and it's far enough away from the troubles for me to consider it a place of safety. I look forward to presenting my request for shelter to the Lord of the Castle.'

It gave Dame Constance pleasure to inform him, at her most gracious, that the Lord was away from home.

She could almost see him wondering whether there might be another castle nearby whose Lord was not away from home, but a faint moan from his daughter made his mind up for him. 'Yes, Hildy. That will do.' Then, turning back to Dame Constance, 'I take it ye've men here, though, who could defend the castle if need be?'

Even more graciously, she said, 'Of course. Let us hope the need does not arise.' She nodded, slightly purse-lipped, to Sir Walter, and concluded, 'My steward will see to your accommodation.'

And after the undesirable Doggetts came tenants from several of the Vine Regis manors, most of whom she knew and who were entitled to the castle's protection. And after them an assortment of strangers, who could not be denied hospitality. The main highways and the local roads were always busy with folk travelling from village to village or town to town – carriers of merchandise, officials either royal or ecclesiastical, pedlars, justices, small groups of minstrels, students making their way to or from college, traders, men seeking work. Few were accompanied by their wives, women being disinclined to forsake their domestic duties for the discomforts of travel. Country women were a sturdy breed and Dame Constance reflected that, if danger threatened their homes, most of them would be more likely to knock the rebels' heads together than to give in to their demands.

Then came Susanna, with the twins, their nursemaid, the nursemaid's maid and Susanna's two gentlewomen with their chamberer. Also Master William.

Susanna said, 'Piers thought we should be safer here, in case there was any real disturbance, but he himself doubts it and is staying at Lanson to defend it if the need should arise. I do hope it won't!' Lanson was not only Piers' and Susanna's home but where the Whiteford stud was located, and Dame Constance knew that Piers would never on any account leave his horses at risk.

She said, 'My dear, how well you look, and the babies, too! Haven't they grown! You are very welcome! Such an assortment of dreadful people we have, seeking refuge. You will provide some leavening. Ah, and Master William, too. I would have expected you to have gone back to Cornwall long since?'

'The barbary foals and then the prospect of watching your painter at work have kept me here, Lady,' said Master William cheerfully. 'And then, of course, I can scarcely leave while this revolt is building up. I am not myself of a bellicose disposition, but think how instructive it will be to see what happens!'

'"Instructive" is not the word I would have chosen. In any case, it is my view that the whole affair is being grossly exaggerated.'

Dame Constance turned back to Susanna. 'However, anticipating your arrival, I instructed that the chambers that were yours when you lived here should be kept empty and awaiting you. Otherwise, you would have found yourself in the guest rooms above the new Great Chamber, which are still unfurnished. The men are having to go in the rooms in the bailey, equally unfurnished and with the plaster barely dry.'

Susanna giggled. 'Sharing them with the pigs and the hens?'

'Certainly not! The livestock has not yet been moved in, only the straw for their bedding – which will serve perfectly well as mattresses for our uninvited guests.' Dame Constance's smile was mischievous. 'And give them more comfort than some of them deserve.'

'What's wrong with them?' William demanded.

'You will see.'

But worse was to come.

2

Dame Constance was still engaged with Susanna in the pretty apartment with its pale blue wainscotting painted with golden stars, hearing her latest news and admiring the chuckling twins, when Sir Walter came puffing up the stairs to announce the arrival of another refugee – 'a Large Person who claims to be a merchant of the Hanseatic League and is attended by some thirty mounted retainers and baggage ponies. He requires Vine Regis to provide him with lodging until the situation in the countryside quietens down.'

Dame Constance looked at him. '*Requires?* Not requests?'

'No, Lady. It rather took the form of a demand.' Even the normally imperturbable Sir Walter looked a trifle ruffled.

'And *thirty* followers?'

'Possibly one or two more or less than that number, Lady.'

Already irritated by the fact that many of the refugees had brought their attendants and retainers with them, not because they needed them or in the interests of their safety but as witness to their own status, Dame Constance's legendary patience came near to snapping.

'You may tell this Large Person that, while Vine Regis will be happy to offer him its hospitality, it is unable to accommodate more than five of his attendants. They may either share his chamber in the bailey, or else sleep on the grass in the outer courtyard. As for all these horses and ponies – where have we put the others?'

'When the stables filled up, we moved the sheep out of the west meadow to join those in the south meadow, and put the horses in the west meadow.'

'Excellent. In that case, this Person's horses *and* their remaining riders can join them. You may tell him so.'

'Yes, Lady.'

'And while I think of it, please make it clear to all our guests that their dogs are not permitted within the castle. I will not have them fighting and scavenging under the tables at mealtimes.'

'Yes, Lady. Where should we put them?'

'I have no idea. I am sure you will think of something. Tie the awkward ones up somewhere, otherwise there will be nothing but yapping and quarrelling. In this weather there is no need for them to be kennelled under cover.'

'No, Lady.'

As Sir Walter departed, Dame Constance smiled wickedly at Susanna. 'That ought to strain his ingenuity!'

Susanna said, 'Why should people have brought their dogs? And what *kind* of dogs?'

'All kinds. Mostly hunting dogs, though I would guess that few of our guests ever go hunting. But they feel that the dogs add to their status. And there are a few silly little lapdogs, too.'

Susanna said, 'I hesitate to ask, but how are you going to cater for all these extra people?'

'Master Robert is never at a loss, as you know! And, fortunately, Gervase and Guy took their riding households with them when they left, which means that, especially if we adhere more rigorously than usual to fast days, the kitchens should have plenty of food for everyone. Provided they don't stay for too long! We will even be able to seat most of our guests at meals.'

Very slightly embarrassed, Susanna asked, 'Would it help if I had my household's meals brought up to my chamber? My women could collect them.'

'Quite unnecessary. If I must have Abbot Ralph sitting on one side of me at dinner, I should prefer to have someone less ponderous on the other. I don't know why it is, but serious conversation at meals always ruins my appetite. Now, my dear, if Hamish helps you, can you settle yourself in without me? Before there are any more interruptions, I must get back to the Great Chamber and see what the painter is up to.'

3

Before she even reached the Great Chamber, however, she became aware, as she made her way along the corridor from the Great Hall, of heavy footsteps behind her and heard the raised voice of Sir Walter exclaiming, 'No, sir, if you please! You must observe the courtesies! I cannot permit you to intrude on the Lady without warning.'

She swung round. The owner of the footsteps proved to be a man who was not only large but gross, appearing to fill almost the entire width of the passage. The Hanseatic merchant, she assumed. Behind him, attempting to peer round his shoulder, was her steward, himself no insubstantial figure.

Coldly scanning the large man's face, she said, 'Thank you, Sir Walter. Let us return to the Hall, sir, if you wish to speak to me.' The prospect of such a massive personage striding along to the Great Chamber and probably demolishing the painter's studio on his way was too horrible to be contemplated.

To her relief, he succeeded in turning round without sweeping the plaster from the walls and trod back the way he had come, the new wooden floor creaking and groaning in protest.

Back in less constricted surroundings, she seated herself at her favourite table, waved the Large Person towards a wooden bench, and said with hard-held politeness, 'Now, sir? Please sit. And perhaps I may have the pleasure of knowing your name?'

He sat down with a reverberating thud, not on the bench but on one of the cushioned wooden stools. What a pity it was so sturdily constructed, she thought.

'I,' he announced, 'am Meester Pieter Koburg. I am a merchant of the Hanse and I am to the regional fair at Stourbridge travelling. With the disturbed state of the country-side, I haff need of shelter for myself and my servants.'

'Yes? And the reason why you wish to speak to me?'

'I haff seen the chamber it is suggested I should occupy, and I haff to say that it is not what I am accustomed to.'

'I don't suppose it is,' she replied with deceptive affability. It was a relief to note that he did not unfailingly place bits of his verbs at the end of his sentences, a European practice she had occasionally encountered before and one which she found thoroughly confusing.

'I wish for better. I *insist* on better.'

She met his narrowed eyes, her own sardonic. With foresight, she reflected, she could have instructed Sir Walter to put the man in one of the truly cramped and inconvenient chambers – the bakery, already equipped with its built-in bread oven, or the brewery next to it, with its malting floor, its mash tun, its copper and its casks. Too late now. 'You may insist all you wish, sir. Vine Regis, however, already finds itself having to accommodate – so far – well over fifty uninvited and unexpected guests, with their attendants, all seeking refuge from this rumoured danger of violence. Let me make matters plain to you. If you do not accept the room offered to you in the bailey, you will have to make arrangements for yourself and your servants elsewhere.'

The small, predatory mouth in the large, supercilious face tightened and the three deep furrows across his fleshy forehead deepened even further below the riot of short iron-grey curls. 'I am not satisfied. I demand to see the Lord of this place in person.'

'Then I suggest you retrace your steps to Windsor. He is there in attendance on the king.'

The beady eyes stared for a moment. Then, 'Leaving a woman to defend his castle? I believe it not.'

She rose to her feet. 'You may believe what you choose. Now, I have matters to attend to. I suggest you speak to my steward when you have decided what you wish to do.'

4

She had ruled over Vine Regis for fifteen years and found the task of controlling the whole intricate life of a great estate both interesting and absorbing. She was very good at it, and had quite forgotten what it was like to be dismissed by outsiders – as she had been at the beginning – as a mere female.

Hamish, coming downstairs from helping Susanna, took one look at her and said, 'Uh, oh! What's the fat man been saying to annoy you?'

She told him, her voice shaking.

His pale eyes regained their familiar twinkle. 'Ye're having a bad day, Lady. Him, and the man Doggett, too! But why let yourself be riled by a couple of common merchants who think they know everything but dinnae know anything? They'll learn.'

'I hope they're not here long enough to learn!' she replied tartly. 'But I would like you to tell Sir Walter that I want a guard – one of the squires, perhaps – to be set on the door from the Hall to the Great Chamber corridor. No one is to enter unless accompanied by me. The thought of our uninvited guests wandering in and out of the Great Chamber at their pleasure is enough to give me nightmares. The painter would have a fit!'

'Aye, he would that,' Hamish agreed, just as the lookout's horn sounded yet again, and she exclaimed, 'Not *more* refugees!'

Peering slantwise out of the window, Hamish said, 'I think it's that long thin lassie who looks like our Jinty on Mull. She's got three or four women and a boy with her.'

Dame Constance's temper took an immediate turn for the better. 'Well, that's an improvement. The long thin lassie who was brought up in Venice. *Just* the lassie I need!'

5

While Sir Walter took charge of Flora and her small party and installed them in one of the new apartments above the Great Chamber – the Lady having decreed that the more civilised, even if still unfinished accommodation should be reserved for female guests – Dame Constance herself at last succeeded in going to see what the painter was up to.

What he was up to was vigorously contesting his territory with the joiner.

Dame Constance's sharp, 'Stop this at once!' sufficed to draw the antagonists apart, but her demand for an explanation produced from the joiner, his fists still clenched, no more than a self-exculpatory mumble and from the painter a torrent of furious Italian that left her little wiser than before.

After laborious questioning, she discovered that the joiner had arrived to set up his table and his tools while the painter was absent from the scene, and that the painter, returning, had taken violent exception to the joiner's intention of doing his work on site.

'And the work is . . . ?' Dame Constance enquired.

'Well, I have to measure and saw and plane off the oak yer la'ship chose fur the panelling and the built-in window seats and settles and aumbry cupboards. I have to do it here, Lady,' he pleaded, 'or I can't be sure of a right fit.'

'Ha!' snorted the painter, just as if he understood.

'But that furriner,' the joiner resumed with a glare, 'says he won't be able to get at the walls with me in the way. Says a lot of other things I can't make out. Says he don't like my face, neither. Leastwise, I *think* that's what he says.'

'I do no more until he go!' yelped the painter, waving his arms about.

Dame Constance, pressing her fingers against her temples to

try and halt the headache that was building up, reproached herself for not having foreseen this difficulty. She had simply assumed that the two craftsmen would know what they were doing and would reach a satisfactory arrangement, if such were necessary.

She suspected, however, that there must be a good deal more to the painter's side of the story than had emerged from the joiner's narrative.

'I think, Master Thomas,' she told the joiner, 'that we should heed Signor Alberti's objections, for the moment at least. If you could take your tools and timbers back to your workshop, it would be advisable.'

The joiner scratched his head and wrinkled his brows. 'But, Lady . . .'

It was not difficult to anticipate what was coming next, so Dame Constance nipped his argument briskly in the bud. 'Yes, I appreciate that the result will be some delay in building the furniture and that you have other work waiting, but we can probably rearrange your priorities. As you will understand, I should prefer that the painter did not go rushing back to Italy in a rage, leaving me to find someone to replace him, which would not be an easy task.'

Reluctant though he was to have his plans disrupted, the joiner did not dare be surly to Dame Constance. 'If you say so, Lady.'

'I do.'

As he began gathering up his tools and timbers, she turned to the painter. 'Now, Signor Alberti . . .'

6

After this encounter, and having awarded herself an hour's recovery time for good behaviour, Dame Constance ascended to the bare new chamber higher up in the drum tower to ensure that Mistress Flora and her party were as comfortably settled as possible.

She said, 'As you will appreciate, Vine Regis has been unexpectedly inundated with guests fleeing this reputed revolt, just at the worst time for us, when our rebuilding and redecorations are by no means complete. So I fear that you will have to sleep on a mattress of bedstraw. If you lay your cloak over it, it should not – I trust – be too horribly uncomfortable.'

The luscious-looking, black-haired, and heavily pregnant damsel standing by the empty fireplace gave vent to something that could only be described as a snort.

Dame Constance glanced at her, eyebrows fractionally raised, and then back at Flora, who said in a harassed way, 'Yes, of course, I should make some introductions! Lady, this is Mistress Benedetta, my brother Stephen's wife. They were married last December. And this,' gesturing towards an elderly, vague-looking woman, 'is Aunt Edith, my late mother's sister. And here is Frederick, my younger brother. And my gentlewomen, of course.' There were two of them, both about thirty years of age, Dame Constance guessed, and better dressed than their mistress.

With a slight struggle, she recalled to mind the saga of Flora's papa and brothers – and of brother Stephen's dislikeable wife-to-be, who was no longer just 'to be'. And since she was here with Flora, the matter of Flora's inheritance from her mother seemed not to have been settled. A pity.

She smiled at Benedetta, who scowled back; at the aged and fluttery aunt; and at the small, impudent-looking boy who was Frederick, and then said, 'Flora, there is a matter in which I would value your assistance.'

'Of course, Lady.' It was said without a moment's hesitation.

'You will remember, perhaps, that when you were here late last year the decoration of our new Great Chamber was exercising my mind? The Lord Gervase has now decided what he wants – images of the ancient gods and goddesses, drawn in a free style – but I am not sure that the painter fully understands what I am asking of him. What he wants to do is paint the walls with panels *imitating* tapestries, which is not what *I* want him to do. He has also raised the strongest objection to having the joiner building furniture while he is working on his paintings, and I would like to know precisely why. He is Italian, from Florence, I believe, and his grasp of English is uncertain, while mine of Italian is even more uncertain.'

'So you would like me to translate for you? Shall I come now?'

This immediate and obliging response greatly improved Dame Constance's opinion of Mistress Flora. Gratefully, she said, 'Thank you. But not today, I think. Indeed, I have had more than enough of today. Perhaps tomorrow, after dinner, if that would suit you?'

'Of course, Lady.'

7

Next day at dinner, the Great Hall was as full as anyone had ever known it.

It was a very long and wide room, taking up almost the whole first floor of the east range of the castle. Its ceiling was high, its floors and rounded pillars built of masoned stone, its small glass windows deeply embrasured, and its lime-washed walls hung with tapestries showing the exploits of ancient heroes, mainly Achilles, who seemed to have been a very busy young hero indeed. Dame Constance sometimes thought that he could never have found time to sit down even for a moment.

The Hall was empty of furniture for most of the time, trestle tables being set up in it for dinner and supper. The head table reserved for family and honoured guests was raised on a dais set across the top of the room and below it, running the length of the room, were three tables for lesser mortals – which was to say, everyone else.

Today, there was a further small separate table at the side of the room, set up on Dame Constance's instructions to accommodate the women guests. In a castle normally housing up to two hundred men and only a small handful of women, the women's safety was a perennial source of concern. In ordinary circumstances, visiting ladies would sit at the head table, while their gentlewomen ate in their mistress's bedchambers, but these were not ordinary circumstances.

It would have been too much to hope that all Vine Regis's uninvited guests would sit down to table in an orderly fashion, even with the guidance of the castle's squires. And, of course, they didn't.

Gervase being away from home, the dais was not dignified with the blue-purple canopy of state at its centre, the symbol of authority and grandeur under which the Lord of Vine Regis seated himself to dine. Instead, Dame Constance presided, with Abbot Ralph and the castle chaplain on her right and the Lady Susanna and John on her left.

The first brief contretemps came as no real surprise, Meester Koburg inviting himself to the head table and plumping himself down on the stool intended for the castle chaplain. He had to be led away, bitterly displeased, by the Usher of the Hall.

And then it was the Doggetts, who else? Master Doggett having been seated at one of the long tables positioned at right angles to the dais, Mistress Doggett made a beeline for the

bench at his side, ignoring the women's table and waving im-
periously to her daughter to join her.

Susanna, sitting between Dame Constance and John,
murmured to the latter, 'Ugh, aren't they creepy?' But John was
too interested in the pretty daughter to respond.

Hamish, after a swift glance at Dame Constance, made his
way over to Mistress Doggett and said, 'Not there, mistress, if
you please. There is a separate table for ladies.'

She stared at him. 'Away you go, fellow! I cannot be separated from my husband.'

'Yes, you can,' Hamish told her bluntly. 'If you wish to enjoy
the hospitality of Vine Regis then you must abide by its rules.
This way, if you please.'

She looked as if she were about to argue, but then observed
that the Usher of the Hall was wondering where to seat the
Hanse merchant. So she rose to her feet to follow Hamish,
announcing loudly, 'Not because you say so, fellow. But to
give two important merchants an opportunity to talk.'

Meester Koburg showed no sign of being grateful as he
settled himself on the bench next to Master Doggett, while an
unruffled Hamish led the two Doggett females off to the
women's table.

As the soups, boiled capons, frumenty, and meat balls of the
first course gave way to the roast piglets, spring chickens, poult-
ry in almond milk, and the sweet fritters of the second, Dame
Constance took unobtrusive note of the behaviour of her uninvited guests.

Most of them were displaying exaggerated courtesy towards
the unknown neighbours with whom they shared their covers,
but it did not surprise her to see that the two merchants,
Doggett and Koburg, were wary of each other, rather like cats
sizing each other up, though not too wary to be diverted – if
Dame Constance was any judge – from being patronising to

their other neighbours. Not to mention depriving them of sustenance. The two men, helping themselves competitively from the serving dishes designed to be shared by four people, left very little indeed for their two fellow diners. No wonder they were so overweight.

Now and then, Dame Constance's eyes strayed towards the women's table, thoughtfully surveying those who sat there. Most of the visiting wives, she reflected, looked like tough old birds perfectly capable of taking care of themselves. But the three younger girls – Flora, Benedetta, and the Doggett daughter – were a worry. She hoped they would be sensible enough to recognise that they should be chaperoned at all times. The Doggett parents could presumably be relied on to look after their daughter, but Flora and Benedetta had no male guardian. Hamish would have to keep an eye on them.

Susanna, at least, had learned wisdom from past experience, having twice run into trouble during her previous prolonged stay at Vine Regis by venturing alone into the Bluebell Wood. Perhaps it would be sensible to remind her always to take John or William or Old Tom, her groom, with her when she ventured away from the crowd. Which, being Susanna and addicted to flowers and birds and all the glories of Nature, she would certainly do.

Conversation at the women's table looked as if it might be a little strained, since ladies could not fall back on war and horses, those perennial sources of gossip favoured by the men. It was to be hoped that Mistress Benedetta's very obvious pregnancy was not inducing too much talk of the hazards of childbirth.

Flora had asked that eight-year-old Frederick should be allowed to sit and eat with her, rather than at one of the long tables with the pages and younger squires, and he was making a thorough nuisance of himself, refusing this dish, demanding more of that, and complaining all too audibly, 'I'm a big boy now. Don't like all these women! Don't like sitting with all these women!' Flora tried to hush him, without success, and Benedetta, on his other side, finally boxed his ears, which caused him to raise a yowl that led heads briefly to turn throughout the Hall.

Only the Doggett daughter – whose given name, improbable as it seemed, was Hildegarde – showed a continued tendency to stare across the table at the Chandos contingent with unreadable pale blue eyes. She was a pretty girl, and knew it; delicately built, with a pointed face, a milk and roses complexion, a sweet little mouth, and very fine, fair, exquisitely curled hair. She was dressed in pale blue gossamer silks and linens which must have cost her father, mercer though he was, a sizeable sum. She was about sixteen years old, Dame Constance thought, vain and not perhaps very bright.

Was Mistress Hildegarde, Dame Constance wondered, shocked by the Chandos' complete disregard for fashion? Although young Frederick was brightly, even dazzlingly, clad in a red doublet and blue hose, Flora herself still looked as if she had dressed all by guess, and her aunt was clad in a gown of a style that had been out of fashion for twenty years and looked as if it had been worn every single day throughout those years.

8

Hildegarde, as it happened, was congratulating herself on the fact that Flora, the only other husbandless young woman in the Great Hall, was just a fussy old maid, and no competition.

Aware after a time that Flora was returning her stare, she gave her a limp little smile and transferred her gaze to the three long tables set at right angles to the dais.

Three long tables full of men.

She had been reared under the suffocating protection of her parents. Never had she been permitted to hold a conversation with, or even to see, more than a small handful of men, most of them elderly business associates of her father and inescapably dull. And now here she was in a Hall bursting at the seams with men – all kinds of men – and her parents in no position to prevent her from talking to any of them, short of tying her down! What she wanted more than anything else in the world was a husband, and she was tired of waiting for her father to find a suitable one for her.

It did not matter what kind of husband he was, as long as he had money. Youth, good looks and rank would also be recommendations, of course, but were hardly to be hoped for. She smiled with deceptive shyness at Dame Constance's handsome son John, seated at the table on the dais. He smiled back merrily, but she knew him to be a younger son and therefore unlikely to be rich. Or not on his own account. Though living in a castle, even one that was not his, had much to recommend it. She must think about it.

Vine Regis was truly grand. Hildegarde had never seen anywhere so large and splendid, not even the London Guildhall which, said her father, was no longer worthy of its role in the commercial life of the City and was soon to be rebuilt.

The Doggetts' own home in the street known as Westcheap had always seemed quite substantial to her, but it was only a black-and-white house built of wattle and daub, looking just like its neighbours. A castle was in a very different category. When she found her rich husband, she would have tapestries on the walls and shelves of gold platters and bowls and jugs, just like Vine Regis.

In the meantime, she concentrated on the long tables, the nearest of which was presided over by the castle steward, Sir

Walter Woolston, and appeared to accommodate the higher-ranking diners, including those whom she took to be the senior household officers, the comptroller, the chamberlain, and a learned-looking man whose role she could not guess at. She had smiled winningly at all of them individually before dinner, but to no useful effect.

At the other tables was a mixture of refugees and men in the grey castle livery with its bunch of purple grapes embroidered on one sleeve. Men wearing livery were, she assumed, unlikely to be rich and one of the pages had helpfully told her that most of them had homes of their own, left in charge of their wives when they were on duty at the castle.

Hildegarde therefore scanned the castle's non-liveried guests hopefully, trying to match them with wives at the women's table. It was not an easy task, and those who appeared not to have wives with them showed no signs of being rich and were in general, apart from the poor students and pedlars, rather old. Not that that was necessarily a disadvantage. Marrying a much older man offered the pleasant prospect of an early and moneyed widowhood.

Thoughtfully she scanned the company. How could she identify a man who would take her away from the tedium of the black-and-white house in the noisy, smelly, dirty City of London, the house with the open stall in front from which her father had embarked on his lucrative career by selling silks and velvets and ribbons and buttons and the like.

Take her away, too, from the parents she detested?

9

Although Dame Constance knew what a hive of gossip the castle was, even she was mildly surprised to discover how much her uninvited guests had succeeded in learning about one another while they were cluttering up the Great Hall before, during and after dinner and the subsequent entertainment by some strolling singers who warbled dutifully on, unheard in all the clamour of talk.

There was no question of the Lady of the Castle *listening* to gossip, of course, but if she happened to overhear it, that was a different matter. There was little she did not already know about Vine Regis's tenants from such manors as Amerscote and Woodcote, but she had no objection to learning more about the detestable Doggetts and the even more detestable Koburg.

Meester Koburg, it seemed, had decided to put up with the chamber he had been allotted in the bailey but now complained to Sir Walter about the smell of new plaster and the fact that the lighting was by tallow dips rather than beeswax candles. The dips not only offended his delicate nostrils but were, in his view, a sign of too-economical (even miserly) housekeeping.

As it happened, Dame Constance had decided that, with the vastly increased and unforeseen demand for lighting because of the number of guests, and despite the long June daylight, economy must be exercised in case the castle's stock of beeswax candles ran out sooner than it would otherwise have done.

Sir Walter had fended off the man's complaints, but Meester Koburg had said he would speak to the Lady about them in due course.

She could hardly wait.

She overheard John murmur to Susanna, 'There you are, you see. Clothes don't make the man, or woman. Look at these Doggett people – the parents, I mean, not the daughter – a fortune on their backs but you can tell they're just shopkeepers. Whereas Mistress Chandos and her family, despite their appearance, obviously have breeding.'

'John!' intervened his mother dryly, 'Judge people's quality by their looks if you must, but if you think that having your shirt poking out from under your tunic and your stockings sliding down to your ankles are indicators of birth and breeding, allow me to disabuse you.'

Susanna giggled. She and John's sister Isabelle, who was now married and living far away on the Welsh border, had both been obsessed with tidying John up, and had failed dismally. John was determined to go his own way, and if that way involved rejecting what he saw as the pointless effort of keeping up appearances, that was too bad. He only paid attention when the irritation of his nearest and dearest was put into words by the voice of authority.

Only slightly abashed, however, he said, 'Yes, mother. No, mother,' and applied himself with enthusiasm to the roasted spring chicken that had just been set before him.

Dinner was over and Dame Constance was still, rather absently, listening to Abbot Ralph congratulating her on the quality of her catering and saying that, if Master Robert – her Clerk of the Kitchen – should ever fancy a change of scene, there would always be a welcome for him at the abbey of Stanwelle, when she overheard Susanna's voice complaining about something. It was a tone she only used when she was talking to William. What had the boy done now?

He had been gossiping, it seemed, and Susanna did not approve.

But he was not, of course, to be silenced, especially when something amused him. 'That huge merchant fellow! He's just lost his wife. His third!' He chuckled. 'Do you suppose he can have squashed them all to death?'

Susanna said, 'Really, William! That is a most improper thing to say to a lady!'

'I don't see why. You're a *married* lady, so you know what I'm talking about.'

'That doesn't make it any better. And do *please* keep your voice down.'

Turning, Dame Constance saw Susanna casting a meaning glance at the Doggett girl, drifting past them in a haze of gauzy gown and wide-eyed innocence. Drifting towards the nearest group of men.

But Mother Doggett called after her, 'Hildegarde! Where are you going?'

In her breathless little voice with its slack London accent, the girl called back over her shoulder, 'I'm just going to talk to pa!'

'Oh, very well.'

Was it coincidence, Dame Constance wondered, that Father Doggett, who had been conversing – with false bonhomie – with Meester Koburg, should have turned away just then to talk to someone else, leaving Mistress Hildegarde free to flirt her eyelashes prettily at the big Hanse merchant? Surely the girl could not be foolish enough to think that, having just lost his third wife, he might be in the market for a fourth.

Dame Constance shuddered slightly.

10

With dinner over, Dame Constance felt no disposition to linger in the Great Hall but, extricating herself neatly from the garrulous gap between Abbot Ralph and her chaplain, Father Sebastian, sent a glance over to Mistress Flora, who responded at once, dragging her small brother with her by the hand.

He was still complaining about being seated at the women's table and Dame Constance said, as she led the way to the Great Chamber, 'I think, Flora, that he would be perfectly safe and probably happier if seated with the pages in future? You should be able to see him from your table, if you want to keep an eye on him. Or he could share a cover with Master William and two of the younger squires. What do you think, Frederick? Would you like that?'

'I s'pose so. Better than all that women's talk about house-keeping and children and things. Oooh, I hate Benedetta! You'd think no one had ever had a baby before!'

'What a horrible brat you are!' his sister told him.

'No, I'm not. I . . .'

Fortunately he was distracted by the arrival of Blanche and Eleanor, whom Alice had permitted to slip downstairs to look at all the strangers in the Great Hall and who promptly attached themselves to their grandmother. With the children, for no good reason that anyone else could see, it was a case of hate at first sight. Blanche, having been introduced by her grandmother to the concept of taste, had been obsessed by it ever since – so much so that Dame Constance had found herself thinking, *Jesu, I must stop using the word, in Blanche's hearing at least!*

Now, Blanche took one look at Frederick's garish outfit, curled her lip, and said, 'Pooh, what shocking bad taste!' Frederick, perfectly capable of interpreting her attitude whether he knew the meaning of the word or not, glowered back at her and snapped, 'Pink! How girly!' The three children were of an age, near enough, to play together, but that was obviously not going to happen.

Almost at once, the little party was joined by the endlessly inquisitive William, who appeared to have a sixth sense that told him when anything interesting might be going to happen. He was sure, he said, that the painter would not object to explaining the techniques of his art to an enthusiast like himself.

In the anteroom which the painter referred to as his studio, two apprentices were busily engaged in grinding dry pigments on the porphyry slab, though it was hard to tell the colours in their dry state. William assumed – correctly, as he was later pleased to learn – that they would be more identifiable when moisture was added. A third apprentice was mixing some faintly yellowish but clear liquid in a large jar. Primer, or varnish? William did not stop to enquire but, afraid of missing anything, hurried on to catch up with the others in the Great Chamber.

Signor Alberti had not been wasting his time. There was a line drawn all round the room at the height of the projected wainscotting, and above it, between the windows, he was sketching in, with red crayon, the first of his figures of the ancient gods. The god was almost life size, half sitting, half lying, holding above his head what appeared to be a bunch of grapes.

The painter's other visitors were standing well back surveying his work when William arrived, Dame Constance frowning slightly, Mistress Flora raising her spectacles, Blanche dancing up and down, more interested in the spectacles than in the sketches, Eleanor placid as always, and Frederick staring interestedly around him.

William broke the silence by exclaiming, 'Is that meant to be Bacchus? *He* won't do, will he! He looks more like one of the twelve apostles. Apart from anything else, those leaves round his head look like a halo, and he's got far too many clothes on.'

Dame Constance, who had been reflecting that she must tell Sir Walter to instruct the household comptroller to have some old rush matting laid on the floor to protect the timbers against trodden-in crayon and paint, said kindly, 'Thank you, William.'

Then, turning to Flora, she explained, 'Lord Gervase felt that the ancient gods, as traditionally represented with little more than scarves to cover their – ah – their more intimate parts, might be considered under-dressed for gracing the walls of an apartment in general use. However, I see what William means

82

and I am inclined to agree with him. While figures from the past such as the apostles at the Last Supper are usually painted in modern dress, I feel that in the case of the Classical gods we need to aim at something in a more antique style. Perhaps you could explain this to Signor Alberti?'

'Certainly.'

Everyone had thought Mistress Flora a quiet young woman, but in the next few minutes they discovered that she was not at all quiet when engaged in a full-blown Italian argument. Everything became very heated, with a great deal of screaming and shouting and gesticulating by both participants.

William enjoyed the exchange very much, while even Blanche stood speechless, with her eyes wide and her mouth agape.

In the end, Flora turned back to Dame Constance and smiled. Dame Constance was taken aback.

Flora – *smiling*! It didn't transform her into a beauty, but it did make her look far more attractive. Dame Constance, remembering how dull-witted the girl had appeared on her first visit to Vine Regis last November, began to feel much happier.

'It's the only way, I'm afraid,' Flora said, the smile still in evidence, 'but I think he understands now, although he claims that achieving some compromise between ancient and modern will be difficult. But he has agreed to sketch in all the figures in outline, and when you are satisfied he will treat the walls with linseed oil, which has to be purified first, and begin painting when it has dried.'

'Tell him to use bright colours,' said Frederick. 'I like bright colours.'

'Why don't *you* tell him to?' Blanche demanded pertly.

'Can't. Don't speak Italian. But I'm very good at French 'cos I was born in Paris.'

Dame Constance said, 'Thank you, Flora. That sounds satisfactory. Now, perhaps you could ask him why he objects to having the joiner working here? All I could discover was that he thought Master Thomas was going to get in his way.'

'It'll be the sawdust,' William said helpfully.

And indeed it was.

Signor Alberti, enquired of, showed a renewed tendency to wave his sinewy arms about as if it should be clear to the meanest intelligence that all that sawing and planing would fill the air with dust, which would cling to the walls and the paint and ruin everything. Not to mention that the flow of his art would be sadly impeded if he were forever to be tripping over the piles of timber laid out for the wainscotting and furniture. And the constant presence of that coarse fellow, the joiner, would certainly interfere with his, Signor Alberti's, artistic inspiration.

He seemed set to go on forever, but Flora at last cried, '*Basta! Basta!*' and – smiling again! – explained it all to Dame Constance.

'Yes, I see,' said Dame Constance thoughtfully. 'Thank you, Flora. I hope I may call on you again if further difficulties arise, since I do not have anything approaching your fluency in the Italian tongue?'

'That's a good word!' contributed William, who was not an admirer of Flora's. He suspected her of being clever, and being clever was *his* prerogative. 'Can I come and listen next time Flora is being fluent at the man?'

Flora's smile vanished into primmed lips and she raised a hand and tossed back her hair. There was a brief, disapproving pause before William, undaunted, resumed, 'I'm really interested in how everything is done, you know. And I wouldn't mind learning some Italian myself.'

'Not from me,' Flora retaliated.

Frederick said cheekily, '*I* want to see how they make the colours. *I'm* good at drawing. *I'd* like to be a painter. *I* like bright colours. Flora doesn't. She always looks dreary.'

He was not the most appealing of small boys.

Dame Constance, smiling conspiratorially at Flora, said, 'I think we have had a sufficiency of art for the present. Let us leave Signor Alberti in peace. Blanche, Eleanor, come along!'

'It was *my* idea that he should paint the gods like that, not squeezed into squares,' Blanche told William proudly. 'Grandmother said it was very clever of me.'

'But it was me who suggested the walls should be painted, instead of trying to hang tapestries on them,' replied William truthlessly.

'Painted *imitation* tapestries! Pooh!' said Blanche scornfully. 'That was a horrid idea.'

'No, it wasn't. Anyway, that wasn't what I suggested. It was . . .'

Dame Constance sighed quietly.

11

Meester Koburg was waiting to pounce on her when they returned to the Great Hall.

She had always thought Abbot Ralph to be as large as it was possible to be, but Koburg surpassed him. Abbot Ralph's heavy robes both emphasised and disguised his bulk, but Meester Koburg, like the merchant Doggett, seemed to prefer fashion to flattery. The line of his tunic, which should have been long and thin, was long but far from thin, and heavily belted round his huge hips. Over it, despite the warmth of the June weather, he wore a fur-trimmed *houppelande*, a loose full-length gown in heavy silk, with a high collar and long, funnel-shaped sleeves. And all in tasteful shades of red, peach and yellow.

Just giving her time to stalk past him and seat herself at her table in the window alcove, he remained standing and launched without preliminary on what he had to say.

Sir Walter had warned her what to expect, so that she was able to approach this, her second encounter with the Hanseatic merchant, with her sense of humour fully alert, dancing around and waving its little arms in the air – just like Signor Alberti, she thought.

Meester Koburg began, 'It is to me regrettable that the Lord of the Castle is away from home, Sir Guy Whiteford also. I understand that I haff to address myself to you on all things to do with the castle, and I haff to say that economical house-keeping is good but miserliness is not good. I am therefore wishful to supply you, while I am here, with the more refined necessities of life,' he paused significantly, 'at cost price.'

Her sense of humour stopped prancing around. She dropped her eyes to her folded hands so that he should not see the gleam in them. How dared the man? How *dared* he!

'So kind,' she murmured.

'For example, I will let you haff beeswax candles to replace the tallow dips. French wines in place of Vine Regis's own which, I haff no doubt adequate in their way, cannot be thought to compare. Sugar, always better than honey. And spices, *natürlich*, which I haff found very lacking in the dishes provided by your kitchens at dinner. All these superior materials will greatly improve the quality of hospitality at Vine Regis.'

'So kind,' she murmured again, reminding herself to try and be amused. 'Do you always carry such luxuries around the countryside with you?'

'Always wine and spices, though not always in quantity. They are necessary to my comfort. So, also, is the feather bed that travels with me efferywhere. The larger stocks of various goods that on my pack horses are carried will at the fair at Stourbridge be traded.'

'I am surprised,' she said, her eyes widening innocently, 'that someone as grand as a Hanse merchant should trade in person at our little local fair, rather than sending someone more lowly.' And that had struck home, she was pleased to see.

She didn't wait for an answer, but smiled charmingly. 'However, that is by the way. Perhaps I should explain that at Vine Regis we always have our food as fresh as possible and therefore have neither the need nor the desire for spices to cover up rancid tastes and unpleasant smells. But if your palate is not accustomed to the luxury of fresh food,' she paused and smiled even more charmingly, 'I suggest you supply my clerk of the kitchen with such spices as find particular favour with you, and he will ensure that the dishes served to you while you are our guest will be as liberally spiced as you may desire. And if you prefer your heavy French wines to the lighter wines of Vine Regis, my suggestion equally applies.'

As for beeswax candles, Vine Regis was certainly in need of a supply, but nothing on earth would have induced Dame Constance to buy them from Meester Koburg even at 'cost price'. Sweetly, while glancing over at Abbot Ralph, still standing gossiping nearby, she added, 'We normally have our candles from Stanwelle monastery and I hope to have further supplies soon.'

She had spoken in a deliberately carrying voice throughout and Abbot Ralph nodded majestically back, while Hamish, standing beside him, grinned approvingly.

Meester Koburg might be graceless but he was not stupid. His 'Danke schön,' was spoken abruptly and carried no conviction, and his massive back was rigid as he made his way down the Hall. Even his riot of short grey curls looked offended.

'Such a conceit of himself as that man has!' Hamish remarked later. 'And that silly Doggett lassie has her eye on him. Just look at her watching him. Aye, well. She's probably desperate for a husband, which ye can understand, but Koburg would be a bad bargain.'

'Just as long as she doesn't set her sights on John! He's too susceptible to a pretty face.' Dame Constance sighed. 'Oh, how I wish we could be rid of all these people! I still cannot believe in this so-called rebellion that terrifies them so.'

12

The 'silly Doggett lassie', perched on a windowsill inexpertly and unenthusiastically trying to coax something resembling a musical note out of her recently acquired cittern – which her father thought it would be ladylike for her to learn to play – was more interested in watching Meester Koburg stride off down the Hall and wondering how to find herself accidentally in conversation with him. Then she could say that she did *so* agree with him about the lack of spicing in the dishes at dinner. She might not know much about gentlemen, but she did know it was always necessary to agree with their opinions.

The small plectrum ('ivory it must be; nothing but the best!' pa had said) slipped from between her fingers and fell to the floor. By great good fortune, the younger son of Vine Regis happened to be passing at that moment and heard her exclamation of dismay. His bright grey eyes followed hers and he bent to pick up the little implement and return it to her.

'Thank you, Master John. You are so kind.'

'It's too lovely a day to be indoors, don't you think?' he said with his cheerful grin.

'Yes. But would it not be dangerous to go out!'

He couldn't at first think why. Then he said reassuringly, 'Not at all. We're not threatened here. If you are worried, I would be perfectly happy to escort you on a stroll in the outer courtyard.' Misreading the change in her expression, he added flippantly, 'We could run like lightning back into the shelter of the castle if any rebels appeared on the horizon.'

'Run?'

She was diverted. Ladies did not run, and she herself took care to avoid rapid movement of any kind, just as she avoided venturing outdoors when there was the faintest breeze, or, even worse, a hint of moisture in the air. How she looked was of the greatest importance to her. She spent much time before her mirror, testing out her smiles to see which made her appear at her prettiest, observing the effect of wide open or modestly lowered eyes, tweaking the neck of her gown to achieve the most attractive and seemingly innocent display of bare skin. But her hair had a will of its own. It was not only very fair but very fine. It submitted to being ruthlessly curled in the morning, but took pleasure in trying to betray her for the rest of the day. The merest zephyr of a breeze was enough to ruin the flattering arrangement of her curls, and if there was even a trace of dampness in the air the curls gave up entirely, leaving her with thin straight wisps of hair flying off in all directions. She was not vain. It was just that, while her father and her mother lived – which might be for many years yet – her looks were all she had.

Master John grinned at her, thinking what a pretty little thing she was, even if she couldn't see a joke. 'I don't think we'll have to run,' he said. 'If there were any rebels in the district, we'd have heard of them by now.'

She slipped down gracefully from the windowsill and glanced around. Her mother was nowhere to be seen and her father was deep in conversation with a large, noisy-looking man. 'I don't think I have to ask permission,' she said. 'I should be happy to stroll outside the castle as long as I have you to protect me.'

John offered Mistress Hildegarde his arm and she rested her little hand upon it. Together, in a state of mutual euphoria – followed by the maid who was her inescapable chaperon – they descended to the outer courtyard, Hildy prattling artlessly and John guiding her steps with infinite care.

13

Chaperonage! Dame Constance thought. At least Mistress Hildegarde would come to no harm from John, and John, his mother hoped, susceptible though he was, would come to no real harm from Mistress Hildegarde. Her parents did not appear to be concerned, thinking – it seemed – that to have her maid always, or nearly always, trailing along behind, was chaperon enough.

As for the other girls . . . Susanna knew to be careful. It seemed that Benedetta proposed spending most of her time in bed 'resting', which, Flora said, was not only predictable but highly desirable. And Flora herself regarded Frederick as an adequate chaperon, even if he had a tiresome knack of vanishing, as if he were deliberately trying to avoid her. But Dame Constance had put Hamish on guard.

She had wondered how all her uninvited guests would pass the time, but had not expected them to stay cooped up indoors – as they did. Most of them, strangely nervous considering that the roads on which they customarily travelled could never be regarded as anything like safe, seemed to have an irrational fear of the supposed rebels. They might venture into the outer courtyard for an occasional breath of air, but not for long.

Indoors, they seemed to be sorting themselves into groups based as much on income as occupation. The poorest – the pedlars, the students, the minstrels, the men seeking work –

struck up an informal alliance. The clerks, the justices and the messengers, who shared the dignity of officialdom, also shared a bond that united them, temporarily regardless of rank. In the case of the traders and merchants, however, the rules of precedence appeared to be less flexible. But all of them stood around, cluttering up the Great Hall, talking interminably about horses, about the war with France, about prices, about the Poll Tax.

By the morning of the third day, though they had still not talked themselves out they were all patently bored. As a result, Master Edward, the household comptroller, was not altogether surprised when one of the minstrels approached him and began by speaking admiringly of the quality of Vine Regis's musicians who enchanted the guests after supper. 'But of course,' the fellow went on, 'they have other duties at other times. We therefore wondered whether you might permit me and my fellow minstrels to mount an entertainment during the day to take our fellow guests' minds off their worries?'

Master Edward, after a few moments' consideration, said he would be prepared to put this proposal to the Lady.

The Lady, who had the strongest dislike of pointless and perpetual noise, shuddered. It was bad enough already with everyone talking at once and shouting to make themselves heard over everyone else.

'There are acrobats,' Master Edward tempted her. 'And mummers, and jugglers. Jesters, too.'

'And, no doubt, harpists and drummers and singers of part-songs warbling two or three entirely different songs simultaneously?'

'I fear so,' mumbled Master Edward.

Dame Constance told him forcefully, 'I will not be driven out of my own Great Hall by the noise. I will agree, but *on conditions*!'

'Yes, Lady.'

'No drummers.'

'No, Lady.'

'Mummers only if they keep their dramatic excesses under control and do not scream and screech and fling themselves about all the time.'

'Yes, Lady.'

'But, above all, they must ensure that their audience is prepared to pay attention. Singers and mummers trying to perform while everyone else goes on talking is not to be borne. The minstrels will have to sort that out before they even begin. We will of course pay them if, and only if, they make sure of that.'

'Yes, Lady. I will make it clear to them.'

'Is it too much to hope that the jester is funny?'

Master Edward felt he should have known. He wrapped his lips more firmly round his teeth, muttering, 'I don't know, Lady.'

'Well, we shall find out.'

The minstrels, having been warned about the penalty for doing no more than adding to the general noise, were soon to be seen scuttling from group to group of the guests, who did not immediately fall silent but in most cases began to moderate their voices a little.

Dame Constance stayed for a while. The jester was not funny, but the acrobat was, to Dame Constance at least. It was a boy dressed as a girl – as Salome, it transpired – who after the usual display of cartwheeling and head-standing and hand-standing, went somersaulting across to one of the mummers, supposedly his mother, asking what he should ask as his reward for performing before the great Herodias. His 'mother' ran through the whole gamut of mummers' emotions, throat-clutching, head-clutching and shoulder-shrugging, before alighting, as a just reward, on the head of St John the Baptist.

There had been a time, during the designing of the new round tower, when Dame Constance had been faced with the possibility of having it garlanded with gargoyles – all in the form of St John the Baptist's severed head, which the builder had assured her could be got cheap. It had been son John who had wanted gargoyles. Now, she laughingly caught his eye, wondering if he remembered. But seemingly not.

After the acrobat came a motet for three voices in counter-point, one high tenor and two high alto, singing three differ-ent texts – a love song, a diatribe against hypocrisy, and a drinking song. 'Pleasure is my pain . . . Deception, treason and wickedness . . . Another round of wine, God give us one.' It was a pleasant enough overall sound, even if the words were, at best, confusing.

By the time the juggler appeared, the audience's attention had begun to wander and conversations were being taken up again. One all too audible voice said, 'We can do without any more of that singing stuff. It's just a distraction from sensible thought. Any road, it's not what *I* call music. Drums and bagpipes and hautboys, like we have for processions in the City, *that's* music!'

Master Doggett, as on the previous day, was trying very hard and not very successfully to do business. Sitting stolidly at a table in the Hall, with his wife at his side writing conscien-tiously, he was endeavouring to squeeze information out of Meester Koburg, though it didn't, according to the invaluable Hamish, whose hearing was acute, seem to be getting him very far.

The mercers nowadays, it appeared, were ambitious to expand from their traditional trade in silks and velvets into more general territory – the territory currently dominated in north-ern Europe by the Hanseatic League. Treading with elephant-ine delicacy, Master Doggett was trying to extract from Meester

Koburg an accurate idea of the percentage profit on commodities in which the League had for so long had a monopoly. Not bulky goods like furs and timber, but those that might be manageable on a smaller scale.

'Wine?' queried Master Doggett.

'Shipping costs are heavy,' replied Meester Koburg, maliciously unhelpful. 'Rhenish costs little in Rheinland itself. All profit or loss depends on what you must pay for shipping.'

'Mm. And spices?'

'The same. It is here a question not of weight and volume but of distance and the profit of the middlemen – the Arabs who bring spices from the other end of the world, sell them to the Venetians, who in turn sell them to the Hanse, who sell them on. It is not possible to talk of percentages unless you know in advance what profit the Arabs and Venetians will wish to take and, *natürlich*, how much private customers will be prepared to pay for their pound of pepper.'

'Mm. Sugar?'

'Is valued at twenty times the price of honey. The Genoese haff a monopoly and, as with spices, your costs depend on what profit they wish to take.'

'Mm.'

Hamish, witnessing the discomfiture of the Doggetts, found it highly entertaining. Though they were every bit as dislikable as their tormentor, Meester Koburg, it was in a different way, since it was not their physical wellbeing that obsessed them. Jolly though they might appear on the surface, they had an envious disposition which revealed itself in spiteful personal criticism of anyone who failed to pay the exaggerated respect they believed to be due to Master Doggett's elevated business and social status.

As Hamish remarked, 'And him only a liveryman, not even an alderman!'

14

Dame Constance soon discovered that it was not just the Doggett parents who were unhappy.

So, too, was the harmless-looking but, Dame Constance suspected, predatory Doggett daughter, who was distributing her limpid little smiles impartially between an appreciative John and a patronising Meester Koburg. The girl was not popular with everyone, and especially not, it soon transpired, with the normally cheerful and cherubic castle chamberlain, Master Nicholas.

Dame Constance's custom was to start the day with High Mass and follow it with routine conferences with her senior household officers, before breakfasting on bread, cheese and small ale in her favourite window alcove in the Great Hall. The household officers came to report, one after the other, on matters they themselves were perfectly competent to deal with but which they thought she would wish to know about. Normally, their reports were brief and to the point.

But on one bright early June day, Master Nicholas was unstoppably loquacious. He was not a natural complainer, and not very good at it. He did not even mention Mistress Hildegarde at first. Instead, he began by reporting that he had acquired a length of a pretty golden-green sarcenet which would admirably become Mistress Flora, whose lack of style and poor eye for colour were painful to behold. It was not his place to say so, of course, but he had been encouraged by the Lady Susanna to speak to Dame Constance about it.

Dame Constance guessed what was coming. 'I know! You are going to remind me of how you and Isabelle transformed the Lady Susanna herself from a girlish vision in pink and blue into a lady of elegance. Well, please don't. I quite understand how you feel, but Mistress Flora is a guest here, not a future member of the family, and much as I should like to see her given some style, I can hardly tell her that her appearance needs improving and that she should submit to your ministrations. I might contrive to drop a few hints, but no more than that.'

Yearningly, he said, 'But Lady, I have some other lovely sarcenets and linens that would suit her colouring perfectly . . .'

'I don't like to disappoint you, Master Nicholas, but no! It would be a sad reflection on our hospitality if we were to try to make our guests over to suit *our* tastes rather than theirs. Was there anything else?'

He sighed. 'Alas, yes. It's the other young lady, Mistress Hildegarde. I have tried remonstrating with her, but to no effect. I wondered whether perhaps you might have a word with her?'

Dame Constance raised her eyebrows questioningly, and he went on, 'With all these strangers in the castle, needing shirts and smallclothes laundered, the washerwomen are badly over-worked. But Mistress Hildegarde demands their constant atten-tion. And dealing with those costly tissues of hers is terribly time-consuming, because it's not a simple matter of washing and ironing but of the most delicate sponging of the surfaces and taking care not to catch or pull any of the threads. She has an eagle eye for such faults, I can assure you!'

'Has she, indeed?'

Encouraged, Master Nicholas went on, 'And that's not all! It isn't *only* what she has been wearing since she arrived here! Her maid has unpacked her clothes chests and she says she finds some of their contents sadly creased – as one would expect, of course. She wants *all* of them pressed. And I tell you, Lady, you should see some of them. There's a robe of Tripoli silk, no less, and a mantle of Indian silk embroidered all over with flowers and leaves and doves in gold and silver threads, which would take an eternity to press.

'I have explained the difficulties to her, but she says, "What must be done, must be done." And she says it very sharply. I fear the sweetness of her looks is deceptive. She is a very determined young lady.'

. The girl had never been anything but fawning to Dame Constance, but Hamish had said much the same as Master Nicholas – that Mistress Hildegarde's looks were misleading. Dame Constance had strong views on people who behaved badly to those they regarded as inferiors.

To Master Nicholas, therefore, she said, 'Next time Mistress Hildegarde demands the attention of the laundresses, I give you my permission to say it cannot be managed at this time. And you may refer her to me, if necessary.'

'Thank you, Lady. Thank you! That takes a load off my mind!'

15

Scanning the Great Hall at dinner next day, Dame Constance found herself wondering what other problems lay in wait.

She was soon answered.

Master Robert, the Clerk of the Kitchen, had assured her that the Hanse gentleman would be unable, now, to complain of lack of spices. 'Ginger, cloves, cinnamon, pepper, galingale, grains of paradise, all in quantity, in the capon pottage,' he had told her with a shudder. 'And everything else to match. It shames my kitchen, Lady. I can but hope that those who share his cover also share his tastes.'

Dame Constance therefore watched the faces of Meester Koburg and his neighbours with interest. Disappointingly, she could detect no sign of approval or disapproval in any of them.

What she did detect, from the women's table, was a very audible – deliberately audible? – discussion between the owners of two of the banished lapdogs, who were bitterly displeased at being separated from their little darlings. One of them thought they should complain bluntly to the Lady, perhaps even go and collect their pets and bring them indoors regardless of the ban; the other, fearing that some servant would be ordered to snatch them away again, favoured the more tactful approach of promising to keep the little darlings prisoned in their laps at all times. Dame Constance sighed and mentally scanned all the different ways of saying 'No' decisively but not too ungraciously.

But her attention was almost at once diverted by eight-year-old Frederick, who had been among the last to be seated at the squires' table and who now rose to his feet and trailed up the Hall to where the women were seated. Looking like a miniature adult in his mid-thigh-length red doublet and long blue hose, with a buckled belt over his childish hips and his hood pushed back from his brown curls, he whined, 'Flora, I'm tired. Flora, my head hurts. Flora, I feel sick.'

Sympathy was not his sister's first response. Indeed, she took him by the shoulders, shook him slightly, and demanded, 'Why were you late? Where have you been?'

Worry often showed itself like that, Dame Constance thought excusingly. Mistress Benedetta, who rose from her bed only for meals, gave no sign of understanding what was being said, and went on eating while the other women at the table, with the exception of Mistress Hildegarde, ignored the exchange and determinedly continued their conversations.

'Nowhere,' Frederick replied piteously.

'I wish you would stop vanishing in this huge place. Sit down and behave yourself. You'll feel better when you've had something to eat.'

'No, I won't. Got a pain in my middle. Oooh, I'm going to throw up.'

Flora studied him with narrowed eyes, then jumped to her feet and whisked off with him down the Hall, casting a glare at Meester Koburg who, as they passed him, remarked all too clearly, 'Spoilt child. Looking for attention. I haff experience of the signs.'

Dinner was over by the time Flora returned, alone and looking harassed.

'Is Frederick all right?' Dame Constance asked.

Flora gave her familiar gusty little sigh. 'Thank you, Lady. I think so. A touch of colic. I've put him to bed and Aunt Edith is sitting with him. He's never had anything like this before and I can't imagine what caused it. He says it's because Benedetta slaps him so hard when he annoys her, but that seems unlikely.'

'If she slaps him over the ear, it could upset his sense of balance and the rest of his system as well.'

'Do you think so? I didn't know that. Well, he'll be better in the morning, I'm sure.'

He was better by suppertime, even if the pallor and a certain lethargy remained. But he was hungry, which was a good sign.

Or would have been, if his sickness had not returned immediately afterwards. And so it went on for the next two or three days, until Flora asked to see Dame Constance privately in her chamber.

'I think,' she said nervously, 'that Frederick is being poisoned.'

'You think *what*?'

'I think he is being poisoned.'

'Yes, I heard you the first time.' After a calming moment, Dame Constance went on, 'It seems a rather dramatic way of saying that you think he has been eating something that happens to disagree with him.'

'I hope that is the cause.' Flora gave a gasp and sniffled, as if it was all too much for her.

'It can hardly be more. I take it you are not holding the castle kitchens at fault?' Master Robert would have a fit at such a suggestion and Dame Constance herself was none too pleased. Collectedly, she went on, 'Frederick shares the food in his serving dishes with three other boys, none of whom is having similar symptoms. And, even if it were a practical possibility to poison one and not the others, I cannot believe that you think someone is trying to poison the child deliberately?' Who on earth, she wondered, would want to poison an eight-year-old boy, however cheeky and objectionable he was?

Flora opened her mouth and closed it again, as if thinking better of what she had been about to say.

The corners of her mouth deepening into a faint but understanding smile, Dame Constance said kindly, 'I suggest you take Frederick to see the castle apothecary, who will discover what is wrong and what should be done to cure him. Let me know what he says.'

'Yes, Lady. Thank you, Lady.'

But before the apothecary could offer his diagnosis, other matters intervened to claim Dame Constance's attention.

Chapter 4

'THEY'VE occupied Canterbury and they're marching on London! Sixty thousand of them! Armed and murderous!' Abbot Ralph was showing no signs of recovering the imperturbability for which he had been famous throughout Dame Constance's long acquaintance with him.

She said, 'Are you sure?' and then thought what a pointless question it was. How could he be sure?

'My source and my messenger are reliable.' He stifled a moan. 'More than that I cannot say. But how I regret that neither Gervase nor Sir Guy is here, so that I might discuss the matter with someone whose judgement I can trust!'

Nobly withstanding the temptation to offer him Meester Koburg as an alternative, and shrugging off the implied insult to her own judgement, she said, not for the first time, 'But it is all hearsay, isn't it? Have we news from anyone who has actually *seen* the rebels?'

2

Her question was answered almost as soon as it had been asked.

She was standing with Abbot Ralph and Hamish on the high walkway over the Great Gate when they sighted a group of about a dozen people, poor and grimy in appearance, plodding across the summer meadow towards the castle. They wore boots and broadbrimmed hats and each carried a scrip and a staff.

Pilgrims.

Hamish turned to Abbot Ralph and grinned. 'Yours, I think.'

The abbot showed no sign of pleasure. Indeed, his voice was sepulchral. 'And women among them.'

'Do you have something against women pilgrims?' Dame Constance enquired a little tartly.

He did not look at her. 'We find them difficult to deal with. Too often, they fail to understand that it is not permitted for women to enter the monastery precincts even to worship at the shrine of St Edmund, for whom they have a particular reverence. There has arisen some rumour of his miracle-working, though I myself have seen no proof of it.'

'So what do ye do about them?' Hamish asked.

'We require them to remain outside the gates, and when they discover this they are inclined to give way to noisy pleading and howling. The more ecstatic of them sometimes fall down in a fit. It has a bad effect on my monks.'

Dame Constance could not resist. 'Might it not have a less bad effect if you allowed the women access to the monastery precincts?'

'It would be quite contrary to the rules of the Order. There has been a suggestion that women might be permitted to enter the chapter room and that various sacred relics might be brought to them there so that they might make their supplications and prayers, but this would require much thought and organisation, taking my monks away from their proper duties. I would also need to be sure that the women came not in a volatile, but in a pure and devotional spirit.'

Aware that Stanwelle possessed fifteen authentic relics of Our Lord and three of Our Lady, as well as assorted vestiges of another two hundred and thirty-four blessed martyrs, apostles, patriarchs, prophets and virgins, Dame Constance recognised that Abbot Ralph's problem of organising displays of the required sacred relics could be very real.

However, knowing also that he hoped the new chapel he was building to house a fragment of the True Cross would do wonders for the abbey's profits, she said innocently, 'Allowing women to enter the precincts would, of course, allow the abbey to benefit from the gifts and offerings they bring.'

It failed to cheer him. 'Indeed so.'

'Well,' Hamish remarked briskly, earning himself a gloomy stare from Abbot Ralph, 'it doesn't look to me as if you need to worry about the three women in this bunch being volatile and falling down in fits. They look as if all they want to do is sit down and put their feet up.'

'Let us go down to the Hall,' said Dame Constance, 'and wait for Sir Walter to bring their leader to me. I am quite prepared to feed them, but we cannot possibly give them beds, or even seats at table.'

The leader turned out to be a personable young man with reddish hair and beard and a friendly grin which was wiped off his face when he discovered that the large Cistercian priest confronting him was no less a personage than the abbot of Stanwelle, the place to which the pilgrims were bound.

Dropping to his knees before Abbot Ralph, he declared his

103

name to be Edwin Wey. 'I am making pilgrimage as proxy for my grandmother, who is too old and sick to make the pilgrim- age herself.'

'Yes, I see. And where have you come from, my son?'

'From Canterbury, Father Abbot, and the shrine of St Thomas Becket.'

Abbot Ralph's eyes flickered. 'How many days since?'

'Six, Father Abbot.'

Abbot Ralph took a careful breath. 'We have heard rumours that in Kent there is – ah – some kind of peasants' revolt against the Poll Tax. Did you see any signs of that?'

The young man had a vividly expressive face. Puffing out his cheeks and twitching his eyebrows, he replied, 'Yes, indeed, Father Abbot. Fortunately, we were a small party and they therefore thought us to be harmless, but we were stopped at Dartford and made to say we favoured the rebels' cause and swear that we would spread the message in our villages when we return home.' His eyebrows shot up into his hair and he added in an awed tone, 'The king's own mother was stopped, too, coming from Canterbury, and was dealt with roughly.'

Abbot Ralph had no interest in the Countess Joan, only in proving to Dame Constance that his information about the revolt was reliable, however much she might doubt it. 'And how many rebels do you estimate there were?' he asked.

The young man shrugged and opened his eyes wide. 'Hundreds, nearer thousands, all Kentishmen.'

It would have been beneath Abbot Ralph's dignity to glance triumphantly at the Lady, but she could feel him striving to refrain from saying, 'I told you so.' Considerately, she acknow- ledged the numbers with a smiling inclination of the head, even while she still privately doubted the violence.

She said, 'Thank you, Master Edwin. Now, if we may return to the immediate present. What do you wish to do? If you prefer not to go on to Stanwelle at once, Vine Regis can offer you hospitality in the matter of food but not lodging, except for the women among you. The men, I fear, will have to sleep in the open.'

'Thank you, Lady. You are most gracious. May I consult my fellow pilgrims before answering?'

'Of course.'

3

Some little time later, it occurred to Dame Constance to discuss with Hamish how they might gain access to swift and, above all, trustworthy news. Preferably from Gervase, whom they assumed to be in the thick of things and who would know if there was any real violence afoot. 'For we have still heard nothing of it.'

Hamish said reflectively, 'Well, we cannae send a human messenger. If the countryside *is* in revolt, that would be too risky. It's fine for Abbot Ralph. In ordinary times, I'd guess that his superiors send him instructions by relays of messengers, who'll be armed and used to defending themselves against robbers. But that doesnae mean the news they're carrying now is any more reliable than anyone else's. From what he says, the senior churchmen seem to be scared out of what few wits they have.'

'Hamish!'

'Aye, well . . .'

His pale eyes took on the faraway look that Dame Constance so much enjoyed even while she profoundly distrusted it. He had a romantic habit of improving on the facts, more for his own entertainment than from any desire to mislead her. It was a game which amused them both.

'An ancestor of mine,' he resumed after a moment, 'went on a Crusade to the Holy Land, and when he came back he was full o' new ideas. One was about the messenger pigeons they used in Baghdad – a bit like Noah's dove, with an instinct for finding their way home. That would be handy now, but it seems they need training.'

Dame Constance chuckled. 'I know your family is adventurous, but a Crusader?'

He twinkled back. 'Aye well, not within the usual meaning of the word, maybe. But he *was* body servant to one.'

She said, 'I think I've heard of messenger pigeons – homing pigeons. Perhaps you'd better give the matter some thought. You could have a word with Master Langland of Woodcote. He knows all about doves. He could tell you if it was possible to set up a messenger service between us here and Gervase at Windsor or Westminster.'

'Aye. I'll have a word. Apart from anything else, it would be useful to know what the laddie is up to.'

4

Two or three years earlier, the laddie would have been fretting over having to keep his sword in its sheath, but he had learned much as equerry to a youthful king whose concept of chivalry was showing signs of taking a literary and artistic rather than a physical form.

He therefore stood by patiently while the king travelled by barge to the Tower of London and listened to discussion of how the royal council proposed to deal with the invasion of the City by thousands of angry peasants. Gervase would not have expected the old men of the council to ask *his* opinion, and of course they did not. But he was aware of the king occasionally casting a questioning eye in his direction, and knew that, in due course, he would be expected to offer a view from street level. The members of the council were too old and too elevated to have any sense of what ordinary people were thinking.

He already knew that violence was what they were thinking.

Fortunately, when two days later the king on his council's advice went by barge to make a personal appearance at Greenwich, the thousands of rebels gathered on the bank of the river proved to be turbulent but not hostile. Or not to the king. It was his leading councillors whom they held responsible for all their woes.

They even produced a list of those whom they wanted to see not just dismissed but executed, a list that included those great men of the kingdom, John of Gaunt, Treasurer Hales, and Chancellor of the Realm Sudbury, who was also Archbishop of Canterbury. The king refused to surrender to their demand – and John of Gaunt was, in any case, far away on the Scottish Borders – and returned to the Tower, it having been agreed that he should meet the rebels with more formality next day at Mile End.

'Well?' he asked Gervase in the privacy of his chamber.

'They are furious, sire.'

'I can see that. What is not clear to me is why.'

'They hate anyone and anything connected with the law and its statutes, its assizes and commissions, which have seemed to take over their entire lives in the last few years.'

'I have heard nothing of this.'

'No, sire. The controls have been imposed by your council, believing them to be in your best interests.'

'And you think they were wrong?'

Gervase hesitated for a moment. 'It is not for me to criticise your royal council, sire.'

'It is if your king requires you to do so,' the blond boy said coolly.

'Of course, sire.' Gervase hesitated again, gathering his thoughts together. 'Then I should tell you that the council also believes that these rebels are all men from Kent and Essex and Hertfordshire, and the majority may indeed be so. But I have the impression that there are many Londoners among them. Disturbances like this offer a fine opportunity to settle personal scores with business competitors, grasping landlords, and the like. I believe your council underestimates the strength and determination of the rebels.'

'Yes, I see. What you are saying in a roundabout way is that we can expect not just ordinary peasant disturbances but serious, even dangerous, trouble?'

'I think so, sire.'

Later that evening, the fourteen-year-old king stood in a turret of the Tower of London watching the flames leap over his city as the rebels destroyed the buildings that were the all too visible symbols of the men and institutions they most hated – among them the Marshalsea prison, the priory of St John at Clerkenwell, and the Temple, home of England's men of law.

At last they reached John of Gaunt's Savoy Palace, the richest, most noble and most beautiful building in the entire country.

'*What* are they about?' the king wondered. 'I know they have a particular hatred for my uncle, but how much damage are they doing?'

'Would you wish me to go and observe, sire?' Gervase volunteered.

The royal eyes briefly scanned his equerry's parti-coloured green and white doublet and hose, and Gervase added, 'I will borrow common dress from one of the grooms in the stables.'

'Very well, then. Go alone and do not draw attention to yourself.'

He went by river in a small boat and, instructing the boatman to wait for him in the shelter of the river wall, made his way up to the magnificent gardens of the Savoy Palace with their orchard and fishponds and milling throngs of men intent on destruction. To the stinks of the river were added the stinks of smoke and burning and blood.

Jostled by someone in the crowd, he grasped the fellow by the shoulder and demanded, 'What's afoot?' The fellow, about to snarl back, met the tall young man's hard grey eyes and thought better of it.

It seemed that the ducal wardrobes had already been broken open and all the golden cloths and silken hangings had been taken down to the Hall of the palace and put to the torch.

'And all them gold and silver plates and bowls and jewels and stuff are being crushed in mortars and thrown in the river so they c'n never be used again. Any man found guilty of loot-ing is to have his head off. What we're after is truth and justice, we're not thieves or robbers. If ye're one of us, ye must know that.'

Gervase nodded but, even so, when he saw a looter being thrown into the flames together with the silver platter he had been carrying, his instincts were to save the fellow and his hand went to his sword. Luckily, he discovered that he had left it in the stables and was armed only with an ordinary dagger at his belt.

Elbowed by the throngs, deafened by their shouting, half blinded by the flames, discovering that, when the destruction was over, the rebels proposed to gather outside the walls of the Tower and riot the night away, he withdrew at last by way of the palace gardens to the river and the small rowing boat invis-ibly awaiting him in the shelter of the steps. Accustomed to the disciplines of war, he was deeply disturbed by the wild behaviour of the mob, even if its leaders seemed to be laying down some kind of law of their own.

Much of this he reported to the king, once more emphasising the participation of Londoners. The king, young though he was, already had a good grasp of political realities. He said, 'So you think it is the Londoners who must be negotiated with? It is they who know what it might be *possible* for them to achieve? Unlike the peasants, who merely *hope* for some kind of bettering?'

'Yes, sire. But it is your safety that concerns me. I wish you would not meet them again.'

The boy drew himself up to his slender height. 'I am the king,' he replied.

There was no more to be said.

5

Early next morning, the king set out for Mile End, accompanied only by his household and an armed escort, leaving behind in the safety of the Tower the senior councillors whom the rebels had designated as 'traitors to be handed over for punishment'.

It was a strange meeting, which Gervase and many others in the royal escort found shocking. For a horde of peasants to dare to negotiate directly with their anointed sovereign was bad enough. What was worse was that the king had no choice but to listen and make concessions.

It was not easy to listen, since the rebels seemed to have no single spokesman and there was much shouting back and forth. In the end it became clear that their demands could be boiled down to three – the surrender of 'traitors' for punishment, a general amnesty for their own actions, and emancipation from all forms of serfdom and labour service. Gervase was well able to understand the third. Indeed, his mother had put an end to serfdom at Vine Regis several years before and everyone was the better for it.

Evading the first of the rebels' demands, the king agreed to issue charters proclaiming an end to serfdom for the people of the counties represented at Mile End. Delay was not acceptable to them, so clerks had to be sent for and the wording agreed and copies made for each of the counties. Riding back and forth for hours between the royal party and the rebels, Gervase was constantly on the alert for any hint that the rebels were proposing to lay hands on the king and hold him as surety for the agreement.

But all went well. Once they had their charters, many of the Essex and Hertfordshire rebels set out for home, though the Kentishmen and Londoners remained.

It was only when the royal party was making its weary way back to the Tower after the long day that it saw a separate band of rebels prancing along towards London Bridge, bearing on pikes the severed heads of Chancellor-Archbishop Sudbury and Treasurer Hales, who had been caught trying to escape the Tower by the watergate. Nor was it the end of bloodshed that day. A number of Lombards and at least forty Flemings, who enjoyed special privileges in the textile trade, were caught and beheaded. By their London rivals, without a doubt.

But the Kentishmen were still not content. Having won something, they now wanted more. The charters did not, they claimed, even begin to satisfy their demands and it became necessary for the king to meet them yet again the next day, this time at Smithfield. Now they required that all lordly possessions should be held equally among all men, and that the whole wealth of the Church should be divided among the common people.

They had now had the sense to acquire a spokesman and a

111

leader, by name Wat Tyler, but there were two other rebels with whom Tyler found it necessary to consult, a recalcitrant preacher named John Ball, and one Jack Straw of whom nothing was known.

It could have been worse. Indeed, it *would* have been worse had the king not also received reinforcement in the shape of the mayor and aldermen of the City of London, who now stood by him in their robes of office – their pleated green tunics, amber cloaks and rolled-brim hats – backed by the City's forces of law and order.

Tyler's attitude was uncouth and threatening. He stood facing the king, tossing a dagger provocatively from one hand to the other, but the king signalled to his escort to remain steady in face of this. Then, just as Tyler was turning away, one of the royal attendants shouted an insult after him. Tyler flung round and made a dash towards the king and the mayor beside him. It was too much for the armed royal attendants, who at once gathered round the king while the mayor shouted an order for Tyler's arrest.

Tyler struck out at the mayor with his dagger.

He missed, but the mayor struck back and did not miss.

The situation hung desperately in the balance, and some of the rebels were already drawing their bowstrings when one of the royal esquires ran the injured Tyler through with his sword, not once but again and again.

'Marston, no!' exclaimed Gervase, trying to stop him, sure that the situation would explode.

But there was no one among the rebels prepared to take Tyler's place as leader, and they had lost the initiative to the mayor and aldermen and the loyal Londoners who attended them. The wounded Tyler was promptly dragged away and executed.

In London, the revolt collapsed.

The king was not slow to acknowledge the loyalty of those who had stood by him, and the mayor and several aldermen found themselves knighted on the spot. He also showed favour to certain of his attendants, including the Lord de Clair.

When Gervase begged permission to pay a visit to Vine Regis, 'which my lady mother is defending alone', it was granted.

6

The Lord Gervase's lady mother, if asked, would have welcomed reinforcements, though to defend her against those in flight from the rebels, rather than from the rebels themselves. Would the Doggetts and Meester Koburg, in particular, behave less objectionably if confronted by the Lord of the Castle in person? She very much feared that they would.

In the meantime, the Doggett daughter asked to see her so that the problem with the washerwomen could be sorted out.

'I like to look my best at all times,' the girl explained. 'It's not vanity. It is time I was wed, and gentlemen don't like ladies looking less than perfect.'

Dame Constance gave way to temptation. 'And certain gentlemen in particular?'

Mistress Hildegarde dropped her eyes. 'Well, perhaps.'

Briefly trying to decipher the girl's thought processes, Dame Constance could only conclude that she saw nothing out of the ordinary in admitting to her hostess that she wished to look her best in order to entrap her hostess's son. John had always been susceptible to a pretty face and his mother found this perfectly understandable, if occasionally regrettable. Living at home, as he did, he met very few pretty faces of the right age and marital status. There had been a spell two or three years ago, when he had become enamoured of the Lady Emilia

Buckton, who had come with her brother to dine at Vine Regis on one or two occasions. A shy and negative girl she had been, but John had been dreamy-eyed about her for months.

As far as his family knew, he had not quite reached the stage of dreaming about the Doggett girl, possibly because, the reality being ever-present, he had no need to dream. A demure smile from her was enough to summon him to her side – to escort her on a stroll in the dangerous outdoors, or show her how to achieve certain notes on her cittern, or even to disentangle her embroidery threads. It would wear off, his mother reflected, when the tinkling laugh and the artless chatter eventually began to grate on his nerves.

She herself took care to say nothing to him about Mistress Hildy, and smiled benignly when he extolled her virtues. Susanna, however, was not so reticent.

'I reminded him straitly,' she reported to a half-amused, half-exasperated Dame Constance, 'that Mistress Hildegarde is merely a shopkeeper's daughter and quite unsuitable on that basis alone. Believe it or not, he brushed it aside! He only took notice – I think – when I pointed out to him that daughters always grow up to be like their mothers. And how would he feel when dainty little Mistress Hildy expanded in size *and personality* into a version of her dreadful mama?'

It came as no surprise to Dame Constance, therefore, when John complained to her that Susanna was becoming very dictatorial these days, talking to him almost as if he were William. 'And I won't stand for it! I asked her what her own mother was like, but she just tossed her head and wouldn't answer. *And* she said Mistress Hildy was flirting with that big Meester What's-his-name as well as me, playing each of us off against the other. Which is just plain nonsense, as I told her.'

It was not, of course, nonsense. Dame Constance wondered

how long the girl thought she could get away with it. The Large Person, who seemed to take it as his due that a pretty girl well under half his age should constantly seek his company and hang soulfully on his words, had apparently not yet become aware that the said pretty girl was pursuing a much younger and handsomer man with equal diligence.

Now, returning to the matter of the washerwomen, Dame Constance said only, 'Well, if you wish never to look less than perfect, you will have to be extra careful not to mark those gossamer garments of yours. I know that you will not take it amiss when I say that Master Nicholas, my chamberlain, is having quite enough difficulty arranging for the laundering of all our guests' necessities without the extra burden of your own demands. Please exercise some consideration.'

It was said perfectly politely, but Mistress Hildegarde didn't like it at all. The pale eyes widened in her pointed little face, and she said cattishly, 'Well, the laundrywomen are hardly being overworked by such as Mistress Flora, are they? And I should point out . . .'

But Dame Constance merely smiled and held up a silencing hand. What a self-centred and unpleasant little madam Hildegarde was!

7

Hildegarde, impressed though she might be by Dame Constance's slender elegance and air of authority, felt that she was being badly treated. When, therefore, she soon afterwards found herself having to make conversation with Mistress Flora she was in no mood for being charming. Not that she would have been, anyway. Charm was wasted on women.

Following Hildegarde's routine enquiry about her small

brother's health, Mistress Flora said, 'Everyone is so kind here, don't you think?'

'In general, yes. But I am having difficulty with the chamberlain. He complains that his laundrywomen are too busy to keep my wardrobe in order. I don't imagine' – she surveyed Flora from head to foot – 'that you have the same problem.'

Flora was perfectly capable of recognising an insult when it was offered, especially by an empty-headed little miss whose only interest was in trying to snare a husband.

'I have no doubt,' she responded coolly, 'that Master Nicholas's staff are excellent, but I prefer to entrust the laundering of my personal linen and the like to my own gentlewomen.'

'Indeed?' said Mistress Hildegarde.

'Indeed!' said Mistress Flora.

8

Dame Constance had more important things on her mind than Mistress Hildegarde's laundry, notably the state of young Frederick's health, which varied unaccountably from day to day. The castle apothecary prescribed a salt-and-water emetic, which Frederick hated – 'I can be sick without *your* help!' – and then an infusion of cumin. Neither remedy did any good.

Dame Constance called a conference of Flora, Susanna, John, William and Hamish in her private chamber.

Flora was looking positively distracted. 'The apothecary says that Frederick *is* being poisoned, though whether by his food or some other agency he is unable to tell. It's Benedetta. It must be!'

The others stared at her. 'But why should anybody, even Benedetta, want to poison a wee laddie?' Hamish asked at last.

'Because the child she is carrying is a girl, and my father said that if Stephen has no sons then everything will be bequeathed to Frederick. That seems reason enough to me.'

William demanded, 'How do you know she's carrying a girl?'

'All the signs are there,' Flora told him dismissively. 'I should have thought even you would have known! She is carrying the child more towards the left side. Her complexion is pale. She had a nosebleed the other day and, as if that in itself were not indication enough, some drops of the blood fell in a bowl of water and sank to the bottom.'

Dame Constance, trying unsuccessfully to remember whether her own womb had been tilted to the left when she had been carrying her daughter Isabelle, said, 'But even if this is so on the present occasion, she looks like a fertile young woman and her next child may well be a son.'

Flora gave an impatient little sigh. 'Benedetta is not some-one who believes in taking chances.'

Dame Constance smiled wryly. 'We all know how much you and your sister-in-law dislike each other, but don't you think that accusing her of attempted murder is carrying things too far?'

'No, I don't. You must remember she is an Italian, and Italians are adept at the arts of the poisoner.'

Reflecting that, for such a rational girl, Flora seemed to have lost all sense of proportion, Dame Constance said judiciously, 'I know you are worried about Frederick and can quite under-stand it. You feel responsible for him and I don't doubt that you have been lying awake at night going over and over the possibilities so that you have become obsessed . . .'

It was enough, or almost enough, to bring Flora down to earth. 'Yes,' she admitted.

Profoundly unexcited, Dame Constance resumed, 'But before we leap to conclusions, I think we must make an effort to look at his sickness in a cool and considered way. It seems to me most likely that he is eating something – something he may never have tasted before – that disagrees with him. It must be something that affects him alone, since those who share his cover at meals are unaffected. How do we set about finding out what it is?'

If Frederick had consented to stay in bed on a diet of almond milk and frumenty, the problem might have been more manageable; he did improve when he was kept in bed. But the moment he felt better, he began tossing about and insisted on getting up and going wandering about the castle. Staying in bed was too tedious, he maintained, and there was no one to talk to except females – his sister and his aunt. The hateful Benedetta was often there, too, claiming to be resting for the sake of the child she was carrying.

The very presence of Flora herself seemed to arouse him to disobedience – 'You're always telling me what to do, and I don't like it!' – and since Aunt Edith was physically incapable of controlling such a sturdy little rascal and could, in any case, scarcely guard him every hour of the day and night, there seemed no alternative – short of tying him to the bedpost – to letting him have his way and go a-wandering, especially if that way removed him from what Flora considered the dangerous proximity of his sister-in-law.

Susanna raised her voice. 'Wouldn't it be best if we could ensure that he is *never* left alone, that there is always someone with him to supervise what he eats or drinks, not only at table but in his wanderings around the castle?'

'That would certainly be instructive,' Dame Constance said, 'but the obvious companions would be Blanche and Eleanor, who are unfortunately females both. And since it seems to me that William and Frederick have a distaste for each other, it would hardly be reasonable to ask William to undertake the boy's supervision.'

William by now was bouncing up and down, his hand in the air as if he were in the schoolroom.

'Yes, William? Do you have some suggestion?'

'It doesn't matter whether I like the boy or not – I don't, as it happens – but I'm sure I can discover the villain for you!'

'The *villain*?'

'The food or whatever it is. I mean, he's not being sick all the time. So we have to make some kind of connection, to work out which food is upsetting him, and why. It's a challenge. An intriguing one.'

'Y-e-e-s,' said Dame Constance doubtfully. 'Go on.'

Flora, standing by the window, tightened her lips but said nothing.

'We have to investigate *all* the ingredients in *every* dish,' William replied. 'There may be the same ingredient in two quite different dishes on two different days. So we have to monitor every single thing, and it's too much to ask of your Clerk of the Kitchen. Now, if *I* were in the kitchen I could follow *everything* Frederick eats or drinks all the way from pantry to table.'

Flora gave a nervous toss of her hair. 'And I suppose it would also prove whether it's the food that is affecting him or whether Benedetta – or anyone else – is deliberately trying to poison him, wouldn't it?'

William sighed explosively. 'Yes, but I still can't see *how* your evil sister-in-law could poison your brother without poisoning me and Joseph and Edmund as well.'

Dame Constance raised an enquiring eyebrow and William said, 'Joseph and Edmund are the two pages who share our cover.'

'Ah. That all sounds very rational. The other difficulty is that of ensuring that Frederick doesn't eat or drink anything out of hours, so to speak. Flora, can you warn him strongly

119

against eating or drinking anything at all except at table? No sweetmeats or the like, however friendly the giver.'

'I can try.'

She was obviously weary and Dame Constance suddenly felt sorry for the girl. At her age she should be enjoying life, not perpetually looking after a tiresome small brother. If only she could be brought to recognise that her disapproval of men frightened them off and deprived her of such innocent pleasures as strolling in the orchard with some attractive young man in this beautiful June weather . . .

William leapt to his feet. 'No time like the present. I'll take myself off to the kitchens, if you'll excuse me?'

'Of course.'

Catching Susanna's exasperated eye, Dame Constance suppressed a chuckle. There was nothing William could say or do without annoying Susanna. She herself found him quite disarming, liking his enthusiasm. He was clearly delighted to have an opportunity to learn all about food and cooking, just as he was about painting. Vine Regis would never be rid of him, she thought. But she didn't mind.

9

Master Robert, Clerk of the Kitchen, could not have been said to welcome William's advent, or his demands to have all the cooking equipment and processes explained to him. William himself was taken aback to discover just how much was involved but, applying his excellent mind to the subject, soon found a way of minimising the difficulties. Frederick and he, and the two others who shared the same cover would simply have to make do with fewer dishes than usual and only dishes which they had had in the last few days and which Frederick had shown himself reliably prepared, and able, to eat. These were, if William remembered rightly, pork meatballs, chicken blamanger with rice and almonds, plain fried trout, and wheat frumenty.

The basic ingredients of all these dishes were common enough in all kitchens, and if any of them disagreed with Frederick it would have been discovered long since. So, in the likely event of its being the special flavourings that were the problem, William decided it was important to ensure that herbs or spices were not duplicated in the dishes to be served. On enquiry, Master Robert assured him that there were only raisins of Corinth and the merest pinch of mace and cloves in the meatballs, nothing exotic in the chicken or trout, and no more than a few shreds of saffron in the frumenty.

William rolled up his sleeves, armed himself with a brace of cleavers and, a little gingerly, began reducing to mincemeat a cut of pork fished out at random from one of the stockpots.

It was a hot and exhausted William who sat down to dinner a few hours later and watched Frederick spooning pork balls and frumenty from the dish onto one of the bread trenchers that served all the ordinary diners as disposable platters. Only the people at the top table were supplied with proper plates.

'Taste all right?' William enquired. 'It was me who cooked them, you know.'

'Oh, was it? They taste just the same as usual.'

It was hardly a ringing endorsement, but William was too weary to care.

'Where have you been all morning?' he asked politely.

'In the mews, watching the hawks.'

'Was it interesting?'

The boy giggled. 'They're moulting and the falconer says it makes them awfully bad-tempered. It's really funny. They keep falling off their perches.'

Relieved, William thought, 'Well, he can't have eaten or drunk anything *there*, poisonous or not. The falconer would have made sure of that.'

The day passed, and Frederick was cross, thirsty, and complained of a 'nasty taste' in his mouth, but he was not sick.

Grateful that the youngest members of the household were permitted no supper beyond a morsel of bread and cheese, William braced himself for the morrow and another bout of smiting and hacking and chopping and pounding in the big arched stone kitchens.

10

No one was more surprised than 'my lady mother' when Gervase came cantering up to the gatehouse, complete with his riding household, looking like a small army in full plumage.

Her first thought was that the Great Hall was quite crowded enough without her son's household to add to it. Another thirty men meant an extra table for meals, which would lead to everyone being unbearably crushed, even if the small women's table were moved into one of the window alcoves . . .

'Gervase, my dear, welcome home! What a delightful surprise!'

'The king gave me leave to come back and defend the castle. Who *are* all these people?'

He glared round the courtyard which was, as usual, full of refugees who felt like a breath of fresh air but were not prepared to risk crossing the moat and leaving the immediate safety of the castle ramparts. Only Susanna, with her addiction to birds and flowers and all the glories of Nature, showed any inclination to go walking or riding, escorted by John when he could be detached from Mistress Hildegarde, otherwise by Old Tom, her groom, or, if Blanche and Eleanor insisted on accompanying her, by Hamish. As little as Dame Constance did Susanna fear attack by the rebels.

'How gracious of the king,' said Dame Constance, much moved. 'But I am sorry to disappoint you, my dear – we have seen no sign of any rebels for you to defend us against. "These people" are all refugees who have come to Vine Regis for safety, and I devoutly wish that they would go home again.'

'Are you charging them for their board and lodging?'

'Of course not!'

'Well, you'd better start. That'll shift them fast enough.'

She laughed. 'Come indoors and tell me what has been happening in the last two weeks. Though it seems *much* longer!'

He had to thrust his way through the idling crowd – many of whom seemed to have no idea who he was or, if they guessed, of the respect due to him as Lord of the Castle – giving a brisk nod to those he recognised as tenants of the Vine Regis manors. Reaching the Great Hall, he sat down with Dame Constance at her favourite table in the window alcove and irritably waved away everyone within hearing distance. 'I don't know how you stand this!' he said. 'I don't like the looks of any of them.'

'Nor I,' she agreed as the admirable Sir Walter appeared, negotiating a path for one of the pages bearing a supply of ale for the master.

The trouble with long rides in warm sunny weather was the dust. Gervase disposed of a cupful in one grateful swallow. His thirst quenched, his voice returned and his temper improved.

'You want to know what's been happening with this revolt against the Poll Tax?' he said. 'Well . . .'

He kept his tale to what he regarded as the essentials – the number of rebels involved, their general violence and the king's negotiations with them. 'Once things have fully quietened down, of course, he'll simply cancel all the charters proclaiming an end to serfdom.'

But he could not resist telling his mother all about the sacking of John of Gaunt's Savoy Palace. 'Your old friend Gaunt was fortunately on his way to Scotland at the time, in search of refuge. I wonder if he's got there yet?'

Old friend, indeed! Dame Constance having remarked once on what an attractive man the king's uncle was, she had never been allowed to forget it.

She said, 'All these people are anxious to know how things are developing. Some of them might even go home if they learn that the revolt has been crushed in London, at least. I suggest that you make a speech in the Great Hall after supper tonight, explaining the situation.'

'I'm not one for making speeches!'

'The alternative,' she pointed out gently, 'is to have dozens of individuals coming up to you and asking the same questions, again and again.'

He frowned. 'That's true, I suppose.'

After supper, the Usher of the Hall called for silence and Gervase rose to his feet under the blue-purple canopy of state that had been re-erected over the table on the dais. In the middle of telling the assembled company what he thought they needed to know, he suddenly remembered that Abbot Ralph would have a particular interest in the fate of Chancellor/Archbishop Sudbury and, turning towards him, said, 'Oh, by the way, Father Abbot, I think you would wish to know that the rebels executed the Archbishop of Canterbury and displayed his head on a pike on London Bridge.'

Trust Gervase! For a moment, Dame Constance thought Abbot Ralph was about to faint. But although he turned a ghastly white, he did no more than bow his head and cross himself, his lips beginning to move very slightly as if he were uttering a prayer for the archbishop's soul.

'Anyway,' Gervase concluded reassuringly, 'the revolt in London is over, and the barons in Suffolk and Cambridge and Kent, where trouble persists, are fully prepared to deal with it. You should now be able to go home or about your business in perfect safety.'

11

If he had expected a rush for the doors, he was disappointed.

There was certainly a buzz of conversation, but no more. After a few minutes, Dame Constance said philosophically, 'It's too much to expect people to leap to their feet and gather their belongings and their servants together so late in the afternoon; and then to set out for home or wherever they happen to be bound.'

'I suppose so, though I would have expected more response than this. I'll wager you've made them all too comfortable.'

His mother opened her mouth and closed it again, her eyes on Meester Koburg who was sitting there, expressionless, looking like a huge, expensively dressed sack. She hoped to be a witness when he had his first encounter with Gervase.

After another few minutes, 'Enough!' her son exclaimed, slapping one hand down upon the table and with the other gesturing to the Usher of the Hall for supper to be cleared away. This forced everyone to rise, while Gervase himself stalked off towards the stairs, followed by John and a little later by Dame Constance, who paused to express sympathy to Abbot Ralph over Archbishop Sudbury's shocking death and to apologise for Gervase's thoughtlessness in breaking the news of it in such a brutal manner.

Abbot Ralph smiled weakly. 'Thank you, Lady. But young men accustomed to war are rarely sensitive to tragedy.'

When she reached the courtyard, which was slowly filling up with people from the Great Hall, there was no sign of either of her sons. She found them in the orchard on the other side of the moat, Gervase wearing a heavy scowl and John trying not to laugh.

'He's not in the mood for polite conversation,' he said, nodding towards his brother. 'He just glowered at a couple of our refugees when they came up to him in the courtyard, and they fled without daring to utter a word.'

'What a pity.' Dame Constance's smile was bland. 'Perhaps all they wanted to say was, "Thank you and goodbye." Ah, Hamish, there you are. Have you any idea why Gervase's speech hasn't sent everyone packing?'

He grinned. 'It was a good speech, Gervase, nice and clear and informative. But the mention of Suffolk, Cambridge and Kent was a mistake. They'd all rather wait until the rebellion has been crushed *everywhere*. What if they happened to be passing the borders of Cambridge before one of the barons wades in and settles things? And so on . . .'

John said, 'I suppose even the people who want to get back to a peaceful London are frightened of what might happen on the way?'

'Aye. But at least Master Langland will be happy to get back to Amerscote, though he'd be grateful not to have to go till the morn, if that's permitted, and the tenants of our other manors feel the same.'

Gervase, his scowl lifting, waved an indulgent hand. 'Fine, fine! Now what has been going on at Vine Regis over these last weeks that I should know about? Other than the invasion of all these so-called guests, I mean.'

After a swift and highly selective mental review, Dame

Constance said, 'The painter has started work in your Great Chamber. I suggest we go and inspect it after breakfast in the morning.'

12

It was unusually warm as they walked along the passage to the Great Chamber, and when they entered it they reeled back from the blast of hot air that met them.

June it might be, but there was a huge fire roaring in the hearth with a cauldron hanging over it.

Dame Constance put a hand to her brow and murmured, 'Oh!'

'By'r Lady!' exclaimed Gervase.

Flora, present in her role as translator, said, 'Frederick, come away from there!' and dragged the child away from the stool on which Signor Alberti was perched on tiptoe (sweat pouring down his face), sketching what appeared to be a thunderbolt in the hand of a tall, looming figure in the background. Vulcan or Jupiter?

'But I want to watch!'

His sister ignored him. 'Signor! *Per favore!*' she said.

The painter turned, dashing a hand over his dripping forehead. '*Si?*'

And then they were off.

Dame Constance leaned against the wall as far away from the fire as possible, while Gervase stood with hands on hips and glared around him. It seemed to become hotter by the minute.

At last, Flora, distinctly pink in the face, reported that the cauldron contained linseed oil, which had to be boiled with water for four hours in order to purify it. When the time was up – in another three hours – it would be left to settle and clarify, and the fire could be allowed to go out.

'After that,' she concluded unhappily, 'there will be further batches that need to be purified.'

Faintly, Dame Constance asked, already knowing the answer, 'Is it absolutely necessary?'

Flora turned back to Signor Alberti, who shrugged his shoulders angrily and answered very briefly indeed.

'He says yes.'

'Oh, does he?' Gervase snapped. 'Well, we can't stand here in this heat for the next three hours or more, just for the pleasure of looking at his drawings. Why can't he sketch everything out smaller, on canvas or parchment, instead of directly on the walls, and then we could look at everything where it's cooler and get a general idea of what he has in mind?'

It turned out to be a matter of scale, of proportion and perspective. It would be difficult, possibly misleading, to reproduce everything, including the windows and the proposed panelling, in a size that could be accommodated on a canvas. Signor Alberti was not prepared to waste his time on such an exercise. The lord would just have to come back when the temperature suited him better.

'Where did you find this fellow?' Gervase demanded of his mother. 'Surely there must be a decent painter somewhere who speaks English?'

'I was assured that he *did* speak English. And he does, though very basically and not at all when he is immersed in his art.'

'Indeed! Well, anyway, thank you for your help, Mistress – er – Flora,' Gervase said. Then he offered his mother his arm to lean on. 'You don't look well. Come along, let's get back to the Hall.'

If Dame Constance had been her usual self, she would have

laughed. As it was, she did not need her son's arm. What she needed was a nice cool breeze.

13

She was still sitting fanning herself by the open window when William came hurrying along the Hall towards her. She eyed him a little warily. He had obviously been afflicted by some brilliant inspiration and she was not sure whether she was capable of contending with an inspired William so soon after an inspired Signor Alberti.

'Might I have a quiet word with you, Lady?'

Gervase had gone off to the stables, and Flora and Frederick had disappeared. 'Of course,' she said, 'as long as it's a *quiet* word.'

He laughed appreciatively. 'Well, I've been thinking . . .'

'No!'

'Yes. About Frederick. He's still looking a bit green, but Mistress Flora has been keeping him beside her most of the time and she says he's only been sick once since I took over the cooking.'

'Congratulations!'

William beamed. 'Yes, and it's been really interesting, though I wouldn't want to do the cooking every day for the rest of my life. The only thing is that it hasn't got me any nearer to working out which ingredient doesn't agree with the boy. Because the one time he was sick, he'd only had plain fried trout and chicken blamanger with rice and almonds. And there's nothing in either dish beyond the basic ingredients.'

Dame Constance would have expected William to look a little downcast, but he didn't. She waited.

He scratched the tip of his nose thoughtfully. 'Do you remember when we first talked about this? Mistress Flora was convinced that Mistress Benedetta was poisoning him and we all said that was impossible, because poisoning *him* would mean also poisoning the three of us who share his serving dishes – Joseph, Edmund and me.'

'Yes. But?'

'But I've realised it *wouldn't* be impossible.' He beamed again, sunnily. 'What you'd do would *not* put the poison in the food in the serving dishes. You'd only poison Frederick's bread trencher! Easy enough!'

Dame Constance surveyed him pensively. When the trestle tables were made ready for meals, the servants put the white cloths on and laid out place settings, each consisting of a spoon and a slice of two-day-old bread which did duty as a plate. Every diner carried his own multipurpose knife around with him, usually tucked in his belt. There was a pile of spare slices of bread somewhere on each table to supply replacements when the original trenchers became sodden.

'Yes,' she said. 'I see.'

'So it's *possible*, though I'm not sure it's probable, that Mistress Benedetta (or someone else – I can't think *who*) could wander innocently along before everyone sits down, and sprinkle some poisonous powder or liquid over the trencher at Frederick's place. It would contaminate whatever food was spooned on top of it.' He scratched the tip of his nose again. 'What do you think, Lady?'

She resumed fanning herself. 'I think the poisoned trencher could be prepared elsewhere and simply substituted for the harmless one. Less chance of anyone noticing.'

'Yes, you're right, of course! But you don't think I'm being silly?'

'On the contrary, I think you are being very ingenious. If we lived in Italy and if Frederick were an adult rather than an eight-year-old boy I might even give credence to the idea.'

William's face fell and she smiled at him consolingly. 'Flora's belief that her sister-in-law is trying to poison Frederick probably owes much to her own Italian background. But if you think about it for a moment – can you see a young woman like Benedetta carrying a vial of poison around with her at all times, in case it might come in handy? *I* can't.'

'No.' He thought hard, then, grasping at straws, essayed, 'But women use all sorts of strange preparations for their complexions and their hair. I remember something about arsenic in face powder. Might there be some ingredient in cosmetics that could be poisonous if – er – taken internally?'

'There might be. I don't know and neither do you.'

'I suppose not.'

'So how would you go about discovering whether the trenchers are responsible for Frederick's illness? He may have been sick only once in these last days, but he still complains of a headache and he looks to me as if he is losing weight. He is certainly not at all well.'

William replied promptly. 'I'd just take away the trencher at his place when he sits down and give him another one from the pile of reserves.'

She gave it a moment's thought. 'And what will you do with the *possibly* poisoned one?'

'Throw it away. It's a pity you don't permit dogs in the Great Hall; they're always fighting for scraps. You wouldn't consider withdrawing the ban for a day or two – in the interests of research?'

'No, I most certainly would not!'

14

'Mistress – er – Flora' thought that at least Lord Gervase might have managed to remember her name. But that was men all over.

131

He might, she supposed, be a perfectly pleasant person but, even if he *had* remembered her name, she would still have been resistant to his good manners. There was something impersonal about his formal courtesy, as if she, like everyone else, was an inanimate object of that courtesy rather than an individual human being. It might, she supposed – virtuously giving him the benefit of the doubt – have something to do with his spending so much time at court, which distorted people's values. In Paris, she remembered without pleasure, courtesy was laid on like a varnish, so that one could never believe anything anyone said.

She did not feel challenged, but she did not like being ignored, made to feel diminished. Not that it mattered.

She turned over, the straw of her mattress making a faint crackling noise. Frederick seemed to be deep asleep, snoring a little. Aunt Edith was making no sound beyond an occasional slight cough. Benedetta tossed and turned and sighed noisily, and Flora thought that, if she expended more energy during the day, she would have less difficulty sleeping at night.

Lord Gervase was quite a goodlooking man, in his long-boned, slightly haggard way. His brother John was a younger version, without the harsh edges. Neither of them was in the least like their mother. She wondered whether Dame Constance's undeniable beauty had eased her path through life. Or made it more difficult?

Chapter 5

1

GRACEFULLY, but treading more swiftly than usual, Dame Constance made her way through the crowd in the Great Hall towards the pillar by which Gervase was standing, hemmed in by the bulk of Meester Koburg.

She arrived just in time to hear Meester Koburg say, 'I haff been told that you the Lord of the Castle are.'

'I am.'

'I am Pieter Koburg, merchant of the Hanseatic League. I haff to say to you that I am grateful for the hospitality of the castle of Vine Regis, but I would haff expected higher standards. I wish to make complaint.'

Gervase, an inch or two taller than the merchant, said, 'Indeed?' There was no mistaking the disdain in his voice.

'Ja!'

Even Gervase, no linguist, knew what 'ja' meant but, 'In English, please,' he rejoined austerely.

Dame Constance, carefully positioned behind the fat man so that he was unaware of her presence, smiled beatifically.

'"Yes!", is what I haff said. I wish to make complaint. Your lady mother has ordered that the accommodation offered me should be mean and unworthy, unsuited to my status. It smells of new plaster and of mutton from the tallow dips, so that breathe I can not. I haff found it needful to supply your kitchens with spices the food palatable to make. My servants must sleep in a field. Also, there are so many people in this castle that I fear for the safety of my possessions . . .'

Bored, Gervase interrupted. 'Well, if you don't like it here, why don't you just go away?'

Dame Constance smothered a choke of laughter.

'I – I . . .' spluttered the merchant. 'I will go when I know it safe is.'

'London's safe enough. In fact, that fortified hall of the League's – what d'you call it? the Steelyard? – was safe enough the other day even when the rebels started massacring the Flemings and the Lombards. I'd recommend that you go there.'

Meester Koburg made an attempt to recover himself. 'That is good. But I wish not to London to go. It is to Stourbridge that I go – to trade, you understand – and it may be in the countryside between here and there that danger lies.'

Except in his colouring, Gervase might bear almost no resemblance to his mother, but he had long ago picked up her trick of raising one ironic eyebrow. He raised one now, and Meester Koburg read his own meaning into it.

His massive chest heaving, he demanded, 'Do you accuse me of being a coward?'

'No, no, of course not. Now, if you will excuse me, I have important matters to attend to.'

'Hah!' The big man, seething, moved aside, causing Dame

Constance to skip back hurriedly, but enabling Gervase to find his way clear, whereupon Meester Koburg, radiating fury, marched off up the Hall towards the staircase.

Dame Constance turned to her son. 'Well done!'

'He's a nasty piece of work, isn't he? I've a good mind just to throw him out.'

Yearningly, she said, 'I wish we could. But he has thirty attendants . . .'

'*Thirty?*'

'Or thirty-one or thirty-two or thirty-three. I'm not sure whether Sir Walter has ever counted them exactly. But throwing them out might well lead to a pitched battle in the courtyard, and I won't have it!'

'No, I suppose not,' Gervase agreed reluctantly.

It was several minutes before Dame Constance realised that, out of the corner of her eye, she had seen the merchant turn to go *up*stairs rather than *down*. She did not like the thought of him marching around the more private parts of the castle, so where, she wondered, had he been going? To the chapel, possibly, though he did not seem like the kind of man to seek solace in prayer. The only alternative was that he was heading for the walkway at the top of the castle walls, there to stride off his fury. That also seemed unlikely.

So *where* had Meester Koburg been going? Dame Constance frowned. She must tell Sir Walter to set a guard on the staircase from now on.

2

Meester Koburg had been so angry that, instinctively right-handed, he had scarcely noticed his automatic turn to the right rather than the left, so that he was going upstairs instead of down. It was only when his legs began to ache that he realised his error.

He stopped to lean against one of the arrow-slit embrasures and give his legs a rest, preparatory to turning and descending again, and was staring around him with an unfocused resentment when the Doggett wench came into sight round the curve of the stairs above.

She gave a little gasp and almost missed her footing.

He looked, and very nearly smiled. He needed an outlet for his frustration, and here was one presenting herself to him unasked, prettily packaged if by no means as fair of flesh as he liked his women to be.

'*Guten Tag, Fräulein*,' he said, moving to block the stairs.

Her maid should have been with her, the maid who was supposed to chaperon her at all times, but Hildy had told the girl, 'You don't need to come. I shan't be a moment. I'm only going upstairs to fetch my cittern.'

She eyed the man without speaking, inchoately alarmed. Desperate for a husband, seeing Meester Koburg as rich and needing a wife, she had made every effort to attract him. But she had never been alone with him – and now she was, and she realised that he was not the detached and supercilious personage he appeared to be in public, but someone to beware of.

Hesitantly, she began to turn, intending to slip upstairs again, but, 'Come here,' he said harshly.

It was an order. He was breathing heavily and, her instincts warring within her, she did not know what to do. To flee would be fatal to her hopes. But if she stayed she would have to let him kiss her, which she supposed was what he had in mind. It would be the first step towards sharing the marriage bed with him and she knew that, if she wanted a rich husband, then that was a price she would have to pay.

Her heart pounding and the colour rushing to her cheeks, she moved down a few steps to come within his reach.

But he didn't want to kiss her.

He pulled her to him and enfolded her in his arms. It was like being embraced by a huge peach-coloured pillow that smelled nastily of ginger and garlic. The top of her head scarcely reached his shoulder and she was already beginning to feel suffocated when his arms tightened and he clamped her close to him. Then he changed his grip to free one of his arms, and began to run a big pudgy hand intimately all the way down her back. She shuddered but made no sound, frightened that if she screamed she would buy rescue at the cost of embarrassment and shame.

Then he shifted his grip again and began smoothing his hand down her front – throat to bosom to waist and onward – but when the intrusive hand reached the curve of her stomach she realised how much she hated it, how repulsive the man was, and this time she did let out a shriek of fear and disgust.

He muttered, 'A virgin, yes? Even better!' His hand continued to move, very slowly indeed, and at last she began to struggle seriously, trying to free her own hand which still held the cittern, thinking she might hit him with it. But his grip was too tight. She stamped her foot on his, without effect.

Her shriek now became a fully fledged scream, loud and sharp with panic. She screamed again. And again.

Meester Koburg was quite undisturbed by her screams, as he was by her struggles. His hand moved relentlessly on.

'Help! Oh, help, someone, *please*! Help! Mary Mother, *help*!' Why did no one come?

And then, in freezing accents, Mistress Flora spoke from the stairs above. 'If I may be permitted to pass?'

Meester Koburg dropped the terrified Hildegarde like a hot coal and backed into the window embrasure.

'Thank you,' said Flora. 'Let us go down together, Mistress Hildegarde, shall we? I have been admiring your cittern in these last days and would like an opportunity to study it more closely.'

Hildy, her legs so weak that she doubted if they would hold her, said, 'Of course, Mistress Flora.'

The two young women proceeded down the staircase together, Hildy trying to suppress the sobs that threatened to choke her.

Mistress Flora made no mention of Meester Koburg, offered no expressions of sympathy. She said merely, 'I have been up seeing the apothecary in his eyrie at the top of the tower.'

'Have you?' Hildy gasped. 'I hope he was helpful?'

'He has compounded a new medicine for Frederick. I don't yet know if it will cure him.'

Hildy gulped. 'No. Oooh, I must look awful! I shall have to go and tidy myself up.' She half turned, as if to go back upstairs to the Doggetts' chamber, and then said, 'No, I can't, can I?'

After a moment, she gathered herself together sufficiently to begin patting her curls into place and to say, 'I hope you won't mention to anyone what you have just witnessed.'

'I have no intention of doing so.'

Flora thought what a silly chit the girl was. Nothing in her head but catching a husband. Well, it was to be hoped that she had learned a lesson this day. At least she *had* been struggling . . .

Belatedly, Hildegarde said, 'Thank you for coming to my rescue.'

'Someone else would have come, no doubt.' Flora did not add, *if you had screamed a bit louder, and had not encouraged the man in the first place.*

But Hildy guessed something of what she was thinking, and disliked her all the more for it.

3

'Well,' Gervase was saying, 'let's do something useful and see how the painter's getting on. My Chamber must have cooled down by now. Where's Mistress – er – Flora?'

Just then, Flora appeared from the staircase accompanied, to Dame Constance's surprise, by Mistress Hildegarde looking very slightly distraught.

Gervase, who had not so far encountered Mistress Hildegarde, murmured, 'God's bones! Who's that?'

'That,' Dame Constance replied, 'is the daughter of the Doggetts, the merchant couple, the Terrible Twins as John calls them.'

'Impossible!'

'Apparently not. It's a strange thing, heredity.'

And then, catching Flora's eye, Dame Constance gestured towards the Great Chamber – and discovered that Mistress Hildegarde proposed coming too. Next, John appeared, declaring that it was time he had a look at what the painter was up to, although his mother suspected that Mistress Hildy's melting gaze had something to do with his sudden interest. Then Mistress Hildegarde's vacant-looking maid joined them, almost immediately followed by an eager William, freed from his morning's labours in the kitchen.

A few moments later, Susanna emerged from the staircase and made straight for Dame Constance, saying, 'I have just found that enormous merchant fellow on the stairs. He shouldn't be there, should he? He was just standing by one of the windows and when I said, "What are you doing here?" he said he was lost. I told him he should know by now that the bailey was *down*stairs and he said, "*Danke*", or something of the sort, and I left him looking as if he were going to follow me down. I think Gervase should speak to him!'

Gervase, overhearing, said, 'Oh, that fellow! No, one thing

at a time. We're just going to look at how the painter is getting on. Are you coming?'

'Yes, please.'

It was thus quite a large party that left the Hall for the Great Chamber, and would have been larger had not Dame Constance told Alice firmly that the children were not to be allowed in, at any stage, to watch the painter at work. Blanche was desperate to see what was going on, and would have been a thorough nuisance both in the Great Chamber and out of it if she had seen any likelihood, however remote, of permission being granted. Even so, the patient Alice, Dame Constance knew, was becoming tired of repeating, 'Your grandmother says, "No", and you must obey her wishes.'

'I *know* we must obey her wishes – we always do! – but I don't see why we can't go in, just once, just for a peek.'

'You would disturb the painter, and just think what fun it will be – what a lovely surprise! – when we see it all finished.'

'Don't want a surprise. I'd rather see it now . . .'

Dame Constance had no difficulty in imagining what poor Alice had to put up with. Blanche was a very tiring child.

She smiled to herself and, again, approvingly at the squire who had been set to guard the entrance to the studio passage against inquisitive guests and was dutifully, if unnecessarily, scanning the face of every member of her party before standing aside to let them through.

Her approval did not last. Frederick, in the course of his wanderings around the castle, seemed to have slipped past the guard.

There he was, standing absorbed in the antechamber, watching the painter's apprentices pounding away busily with their pestles and mortars.

In reply to his sister's exasperated cry of, 'Frederick, what are you doing here?' he said, 'Just looking. They're grinding

140

what looks like earth, not like colours. Ask them why, Flora!'
He tugged at her hand, jumping up and down. '*Ask them
why.*'

Sighing, she asked one of the apprentices and was told they
were preparing a light tint to be laid over all the images before
the artist began his final painting. 'Does that satisfy you?'

Frederick frowned heavily. 'I s'pose so.'

The temperature inside the Great Chamber was now bear-
able and the linseed oil had been washed over the walls and
appeared to be drying well. Well enough, Flora translated, to
let the painter get on with the real work.

The outlined Bacchus and Vulcan had been joined by a
galaxy of other figures, identifiable by their symbols even if
their faces were as yet undefined. Bacchus was recognisable by
his grapes, Vulcan by his thunderbolt, Mars by his helmet,
Mercury by his winged sandals and serpent-entwined rod. There
were a couple of cherubs, and a few little satyrs, looking like
Cupids with horns, wafting around in the air above. The figures
were elegantly arranged, nicely balanced, relaxed and natural,
some lying, some half-lying propped on their elbows, some
standing, some hovering. There looked as if there were going
to be modest draperies where they were needed, assisted by
trailing plants.

Signor Alberti was good, Dame Constance thought with relief.
Much now depended on his not being too heavy-handed with
his colours.

William had a thoroughly enjoyable time, showing off his
Classical knowledge. While he was hesitating briefly over the
identity of one of the figures in the background, Dame Constance
took advantage of the momentary silence to say to him, 'I hope
that you no longer find the figures over-dressed?' She turned
to Gervase. 'Or under-dressed?'

The artist, busily brushing in grey shadows to give shape

and definition to the draperies, had not even turned at their entrance. Gervase said, 'They look about right to me. I didn't know the shadows were painted in first. I would have expected them to be last.'

The artist told Flora waspishly, 'Outlines first, then shadows to define for me the moulding of the larger shapes, then a wash of Cologne earth within the outlines, then I paint in colours with the final shadows to fit the colours.'

Dame Constance, with a sly glance at William, said, 'It would spoil our enjoyment if we asked who are the figures we don't recognise. What about the elegant lady standing between Bacchus and Mars? Ariadne, perhaps, since she stands a little closer to Bacchus than to Mars?'

'Only a very *little* closer,' William responded. 'I'd say Venus.'

As if the name of Venus had breached the language barrier, the artist swung round to survey his audience. After a moment, staring intensely at Mistress Hildegarde, he exclaimed, 'A face!'

Even Hildy had heard of Venus, the goddess of beauty and of love. 'Me?' she gasped, blushing. She had no interest in art but had followed Flora simply for safety, grateful to form part of a group, and now felt herself rewarded.

But Flora, a touch suspicious, enquired further.

Signor Alberti replied briefly and to the point. He already knew what Venus should look like, thank you, and it was not like Mistress Hildegarde. But the young woman had the kind of face he could use if he were painting an angel, and in the Classical context, he thought she would do as a model for one of the other figures, such as . . .

Flora closed her eyes for a moment, all too obviously suppressing a desire to laugh, then opened them again and said carefully, 'Not Venus. Signor Alberti sees you more as – as an attendant nymph.'

William gave a splutter of mirth and Dame Constance looked

142

at him reprovingly. 'That sounds charming,' she said. 'And when all the paintings are complete and the Great Chamber is in use, we will be able to tell people that we are personally acquainted with that particular nymph. How delightful that will be. Now, if we have all looked our fill, I suggest we return to the Hall.'

When they had entered the Chamber, Mistress Hildegarde's little hand had been resting lightly on John's arm. When they left it, Dame Constance noticed that it was Gervase's arm on which the little hand now reposed.

4

'No, really, Ger!' exclaimed John heatedly a short while later. 'I won't have you stealing Mistress Hildegarde from me!'

'Is that her name? And her second name is Doggett, isn't it? What a queer combination.'

'Yes, well, never mind that!'

His brother grimaced at him. 'I didn't *offer* her my arm, so don't get excited. She put her hand on it of her own accord, and I could scarcely reject it, now could I?'

'No,' John agreed glumly. It was just as well that Susanna had gone off to play with her twins – or bath them, or feed them, or whatever young mothers did with their infants – because he couldn't forget what she had said about Hildy playing him and the Hanse man off against each other. It had been nonsense, of course, but he could foresee that, with Gervase home again, Susanna would take pleasure in pointing out that Mistress Hildegarde would consider a rich lord a better match than a rich merchant, and either of them a vastly better match than a younger son.

Gervase patted him on the shoulder. 'She's a pretty little thing, I agree, but let's talk about something more important.'

He glanced round the Hall. 'How are we going to get rid of all these people?'

John allowed himself to be diverted. 'I don't know. You could always try telling them again that the danger is over and – er – hinting that the hospitality of Vine Regis is no longer – er – available.'

Dame Constance, overhearing, stopped on her way to the stairs and said, 'It sounds tempting, but what if some of the people we have sent away were to fall foul of a stray band of rebels fleeing from Cambridge or Suffolk or somewhere? I could not find it in my conscience . . .'

'Why don't we,' interrupted John wickedly, 'that is to say, why don't *you*, mother, persuade Abbot Ralph to set an example by going back to Stanwelle?'

His mother ignored the implication. 'Yes. Taking his pilgrims with him!'

'*Pilgrims?* What's he doing inflicting pilgrims on us?' Gervase looked suddenly thoughtful, as if trying to capture some elusive memory. 'Now, who's been talking to me about pilgrims lately? Oh yes, I remember. There's this fellow at court, name of Chaucer – he's a comptroller of Customs, or some title like that – who writes poetry. I know him quite well . . .'

He became aware that his mother and brother were both looking hugely amused.

'. . . and I don't see what's so funny about me being acquainted with a poet! Anyway, he was talking to me about pilgrims the other day. He's thinking of writing a long poem about them. I wonder if I should talk to Ralph's pilgrims? They might give me some useful information to pass on.'

Then, putting his mother in her place, he added pointedly, 'Your friend John of Gaunt is Master Chaucer's patron, and Chaucer is wed to the sister of Gaunt's mistress.'

It was too much. Dame Constance went off into a peal of

laughter, emerging at last to say, 'Why not send Hamish to find *our* pilgrims' leader for you? He's out there somewhere.' She waved towards the new courtyard between the castle walls and the bailey, where the thin grass was struggling for life against the assault of guests and their servants sitting or lying in the sun. 'Oh, how I *wish* they would all go away!'

'Yes,' said Gervase. 'I'll have to try telling them again that everything is safe now.'

5

There was one person who did not need to be told.

Benedetta.

She had heard Gervase's after-supper speech with a total lack of understanding and had later asked Flora what it had all been about.

Flora had given her the gist of it and Benedetta replied with her usual toss of the head and curl of the lip. Then she had said, '*Bene!*'

No more than that.

But she had been thinking, and now, almost two days later, announced to Flora that she did not like it here and that she wanted to go home to Stephen, the Lord Gervase having said it would be safe to do so.

Flora, her brain whirling, went off in search of Dame Constance and found her in Susanna's pretty chamber, discussing the desirability of a stroll in the Bluebell Wood.

The Lady said, 'Sit down and calm down, my dear. You would be delighted for Benedetta to go back to Coteley Valence, wouldn't you?'

Flora's answer was a heartfelt, 'Yes. Oh, yes!'

'But you yourself would prefer to stay here?'

'Yes, if I may?' She looked as if she were holding her breath.

'Of course! I should be grateful if you would. Susanna and I both take pleasure in your company – and you have been amazingly helpful in dealing with Signor Alberti. Indeed, I have no idea how I should get on without you.'

'I enjoy it so much! But . . .'

'There is not the slightest need for you to feel that, if Benedetta and presumably Aunt Edith go, you must go too.'

'Thank you.' Flora's relief was almost overpowering. She smiled shakily.

'But, you are thinking, we can't simply hoist Benedetta into her saddle, give her palfrey a slap on the rump, and wave them both goodbye.'

Flora laughed. 'No.'

'As you say, no. She needs more than her groom to escort her in safety. I will tell Hamish and probably John to go with her as soon as you like. And I am sure William would be delighted to join the party, if you approach him tactfully.'

Flora frowned. 'He doesn't like me, but he did say yesterday that he felt in need of exercise.'

'There you are, then. Everything is easily resolved with a little goodwill all round.'

Flora sniffed. 'Thank you. *Thank you.* You are *so* kind.'

'Not at all, just sufficiently detached from your problems to be able to think reasonably logically.'

6

Hildy was ensconced on a window sill right at the front of the Great Hall, her maid by her side and her eyes carefully averted from where Meester Koburg was sitting talking, with his most condescending air, to her father.

He had acknowledged her, in passing, with only the slightest nod of his head, and she was relieved, because he was a horrible man, so horrible that even his riches could hardly make up for it. She was innocent and she knew it, but the acute physical revulsion she had felt at their encounter had come as a severe shock to her. If she had previously considered the matter at all, she would have expected to feel not much more than a mild frisson of distaste, well worth suffering in the far more important interests of money and matrimony.

Her mind slipped sideways to Lord Gervase. His brother John was a pleasant enough young man, but as husbands went the lord himself had a great deal more to recommend him. She scanned the Great Hall for him without result, then, glancing absently out of the window, observed him perched on a low wall in conversation with a young man she had not seen before, a young man with his hat tilted back on his head, short red hair and beard, and a merry smile.

Gervase was saying, 'But surely, Master Edwin, you should have pilgrim medals hanging from your hat brim, shouldn't you? Souvenirs of the shrines you've visited?'

'I have only the one, my lord, from the shrine of St Thomas Becket at Canterbury; see, it is strung through my buttonhole. I'm not a regular pilgrim. This is my first venture and' – he grinned cheerfully – 'I hope it may be my last.'

Gervase was still dubious. The fellow didn't look like a proper pilgrim to him. 'Don't you carry papers to prove your status?'

'My *testimoniales*? Yes, I have them here in my scrip and will produce them for you willingly enough.'

'Unnecessary. So, why are you making this pilgrimage?'

'For my grandmother's sake. She had sworn to make it herself, but age and sickness prevented her and I promised to make it on her behalf. I fear she may have died while I have been on my way, so I must pray that she be released from her vow. And also, of course, for her soul.'

Gervase, thinking that Master Chaucer probably knew already about proxy pilgrims, was about to ask whether there was more virtue in walking than in riding – Master Edwin looked and sounded to him like the kind of young man perfectly able to afford a horse – when he raised his eyes and, glancing along the road that led to the village, gave vent to an explosive, 'By'r Lady!'

Then, jumping down from the wall on which he had been sitting, he strode swiftly along the south front of the castle, to reach the drawbridge just as the group of men shouting and waving spades and pitchforks arrived at its outer end.

Dame Constance, Susanna, and Flora, returning from a pleasant stroll in the Bluebell Wood with Hamish as escort, stopped dead in their tracks on the barbican rise, Dame Constance drawing a long, quavering breath. Susanna turned worriedly towards her, only to discover that her lips were tight, her eyes wide, and that she was trying very hard not to laugh. Susanna looked again at the rebels, and understood.

There were about a score of them, all clad in the peasant's hodden-grey tunic and footless stockings, and all wearing the kind of hood that fitted round the face at the front and tapered off into a waist-long tail at the back.

They also appeared to be wearing masks.

Susanna gave a hiccup of laughter just as Dame Constance gasped, 'Hamish, what are they shouting?'

'They're swallowing their words a bit, but I think it's, "All lord's possessions to be shared equally among all men!" Redistribution of wealth was one of the things the rebels were demanding of the king at Smithfield, Gervase says.' He grinned. 'From their timing, they seem to have noticed that this particular lord has arrived back home.'

Gervase was by now standing grimly, legs astride and fists on hips, at the castle end of the drawbridge, and the shouting and pitchfork waving began to become erratic.

The uninvited guests who had been strewn around the outer courtyard had vanished as if by magic into the shelter of the castle walls.

Gervase raised his voice. 'Yes? You have something you wish to say to me?'

Someone at the back shouted, 'We doan' like lords. We wan' our share o' yer goods!'

A pitchfork tossed from the same direction clattered against the edge of the drawbridge and fell into the moat. Gervase ignored it, but one or two of the men at the front of the group twitched nervously.

Gervase scanned the masked faces before him.

'I have no idea,' he said, 'why you should think I wouldn't recognise you if you wound the tails of your hoods round your faces. Take 'em off!' He stabbed a finger at one of the men. 'Weaver John.' Then at another. 'Sim Walden.' And another. 'Jem Tripp.' Then, 'Will Knapp.' And so he went on, until he reached the agitators at the back. 'I don't know you three, but I'd guess you're from over Elborough way and I suggest you get back there, fast.'

Then he surveyed the villagers once more and, scorn in his voice, went on, 'You're a bit late in the day with your demonstration. You're a bunch of witless, mutton-headed, dozy, lie-abed scroungers, but I think you've been misled by all this talk of revolt. If you've got a genuine grievance, it isn't against me but against the royal council. *I* can't do anything about the Poll Tax or the pressure of the new laws. If you have the sense you were born with, you'll just go back to work, and you and I can behave as if this encounter never happened. Now, off you go!'

149

They shifted uneasily, each hoping that one of the others would make the first move.

Ostentatiously, Gervase smothered a yawn.

The villagers muttered among themselves.

'I said, "Go!"' Gervase repeated.

But still they hovered indecisively.

Dame Constance murmured, 'A little encouragement required, I think,' and picking up her skirts began to move down from the barbican rise towards the drawbridge.

The villagers fell back to let her pass. She smiled and acknowledged them, still masked as they were. 'Sim. Weaver John. Will. Jem . . .' They ducked their heads as they always did, and her smile deepened.

It was enough. By the time Dame Constance and her little party had crossed the bridge, they had turned and begun to drift away, though not until they were almost back at the village did they unwind the tails of their hoods from around their faces.

Gervase stood and watched them go, one corner of his mouth creased in a derisive half-smile.

7

Inside the Great Hall, the people struggling to peer out of the windows had seen nothing to amuse them about the encounter. All were talking at once and there was no doubt in anyone's mind that, whatever the Lord Gervase had said in his speech after supper a couple of days earlier, the rebellion was not over. They had seen proof of it with their very own eyes and the proof lost nothing in the telling. The limited view some of them had been afforded had given them no accurate idea of the numbers involved and exaggeration inevitably followed.

They crowded round Gervase when he returned to the Hall, babbling questions and failing to listen to his answers. Eventually he threw up his hands in disgust. 'You're making as much noise as the menagerie in the Tower. It was only a few of our local villagers making a demonstration, no more, no less. Now, if you'll excuse me, I have important matters to attend to.'

As he turned to stalk away, a breathy little voice at his side murmured, 'So *brave!*'

Hildegarde, from the vantage point of the window in which she had been sitting at the start, had seen most of what had gone on. 'I watched you stand *alone* against all those men,' she explained. 'So *brave!*'

No more than any other man was Gervase proof against being admired by a pretty girl. His hard features relaxed a little as he looked down into eyes that were twin pools of innocent blue and said, 'Thank you. It was nothing. Would you . . .' But then he became aware of John's gaze on him and changed what he had been about to say. Instead of proposing a stroll outdoors so that she might see how safe it all was, he went on, '. . . will you forgive me if I resume my interrupted conversation with Master Edwin?'

'Of course,' she said. 'May I come, too?'

Gervase was far too courteous to utter a simple, 'No', and his assurance that she would find it of little interest had no effect.

'Who,' she wondered, 'is Master Edwin?'

'The leader of the pilgrims.'

'Oh.'

Casting a slightly harassed glance at his brother, Gervase made for the stairs, moving a little too fast for Hildy's comfort. But she was still clinging to his arm when they reached the relatively empty inner courtyard to find Master Edwin in conversation with Dame Constance, the Lady Susanna and *dreary*

Mistress Flora. They all, with the exception of Mistress Flora, were looking amazingly cheerful.

Hildy, who in her mind had been rehearsing the light chat with which she had intended to charm the Lord Gervase, was annoyed.

Dame Constance greeted them with, 'I think Master Edwin is one of those rare people who carry merriment around with them!'

Master Edwin grinned. 'Well, it's better than gloom and despondency, isn't it, Lady?' He turned to Gervase. 'Was there anything else you wanted to ask me about making a pilgrimage, sir?'

'Yes.' Gervase removed Hildy's hand from his arm, looking vaguely unsure of what he should do with it until she took it back and patted her hair with it. Then he laid his own hand on Master Edwin's shoulder and said, 'Yes, I wondered whether you are all as impoverished as you look?'

'Of course not. We are a small band, and looking poor is as good a way as any of ensuring that we don't attract the interest of thieves and robbers.'

'I see. I also wondered about the level of virtue achieved by walking instead of riding. Let us go and sit . . .'

Flora broke in. 'I should be obliged to have a word with you, Lord Gervase, at some convenient moment. Fairly soon, if you please.'

Surprised, he said with a perfunctory smile, 'Just after supper, perhaps?'

'Thank you.'

He turned away, leaving Hildy seething, Susanna looking inquisitive, and Dame Constance as tranquil as always.

With unconvincing solicitude, Hildy enquired of Mistress Flora, 'And how is your dear little brother today? Has the apothecary's new mixture been of benefit?'

152

Flora's arched brows rose. 'Thank you for your interest. I don't yet know whether the medicine is beneficial or not. He is able to keep his food down, but that may be due to Master William's efforts in the kitchen. His complexion is still grey and his temper erratic.' Her voice changed and she addressed the empty air. 'And *where* can he have got to now? He has begun to regard supervision as something to be deliberately escaped. Pure defiance, in fact!'

Dame Constance said consolingly, 'Small boys are always like that. Now, shall we go and sit in my garden for a while?'

There was no hint of dismissal in her manner or tone, but it was clear to Hildy that 'we' did not include Mistress Hildegarde. So she said, 'I have been too long in the Hall, and am in need of fresh air. I shall go and stand on the drawbridge for a few minutes and gaze into your lovely clear moat.'

The Lord Gervase and Master Edwin were almost bound to pass close by when they had finished their conversation.

8

Dame Constance's garden was her private refuge, an enclosed corner of the central courtyard consisting of little more than a pair of wooden benches surrounded by sweet-smelling herbs and flowers – thyme and rosemary, mignonette and pinks. It was enclosed in such a way that, from the outside, no one could have guessed what lay within. It looked like just another outhouse.

As Dame Constance opened the gate, Flora exclaimed, 'Oh, how lovely!' Then, '*Frederick!* What are you doing here?'

He emerged from behind the gate, looking very slightly guilty. 'Just 'xploring.' He was twirling a sprig of southern-wood in his fingers. 'This smells nice but it tastes nasty.'

Dame Constance said sharply, 'Have you swallowed any of it? Have you tasted any of these plants before?'

He stared at her, wide-eyed, but his primmed lips and shrugged shoulders could have been taken to mean either yes or no.

Flora snapped, 'The truth, Frederick, if you please.'

But Dame Constance was shaking her head. 'I doubt if southernwood could harm him, though it is not a herb to be taken internally. We use it mostly, as I am sure you know, to repel insects on the floors or in the wardrobes. But one forgets how readily children will put almost anything in their mouths.'

She frowned slightly, turning towards Hamish, who was hovering behind them. 'It has never been necessary before, but I think we should have some kind of lock on the gate. Can you construct something? Not too obtrusive . . .'

He grinned. 'Aye, Lady. An invisible latch, or a lock with a wee light key, since you will have to carry it around with you. I'll do it today.'

Flora began apologising, but Dame Constance said absently, 'No, Hamish will enjoy it. He is an expert at carving, and likes a challenge.'

But she was reflecting that far more dangerous than any of the herbs in her garden, and far more difficult to guard against, was the pretty but highly poisonous golden rain tree, the laburnum, in the far corner of the orchard. The new season's pods were probably not yet sufficiently developed to be tempting, but she suspected it would be wiser not to draw them to this undisciplined child's attention. So she said only, 'Frederick, you *must not* chew bits of plant or anything of the sort. Your health is better than it was, but you want to get properly better, don't you?'

'I'm not being sick any more, but I don't *feel* better.'

'That will improve if you are careful and do as you're told.'

Susanna intervened, a little impatiently, 'Why don't you go away and play?'

'No one to play with.'

'Why not Blanche and Eleanor?'

'They don't like *me* and I don't like *them*. If they're not play-ing with dolls, they're playing with spinning tops. I've never had a spinning top and I can't make it go round, and they laugh at me, and I don't like it.'

'If ye'll come with me,' Hamish said self-sacrificingly, 'I could take you along to the Master of the Henchmen. He's teaching the pages knightly pursuits and how to fight with swords – wooden ones, so ye wouldnae get hurt. I'm sure he'd be blithe to teach you, too.'

The boy curled his lip. 'Makebelieve fighting! Don't like fighting and we're only here for a few days so he won't have time to teach me much. Even though I pick things up quickly!'

Hamish said, 'Come on, laddie. It'll make a change.'

After a hesitant moment, the boy went with him.

9

When they were comfortably seated, inhaling the aromatic delights of the garden, Dame Constance said, her voice care-fully neutral, 'Flora, have you ever thought of employing a nurse or tutor for him?'

Flora sighed. 'He is too old for a nurse and Stephen main-tains that he is too young for a tutor. So I teach him at home.'

Not for the first time, Dame Constance reflected that the girl had too many responsibilities, and that they were weighing her down. She was still wondering whether to say something of the sort when Susanna again intervened.

'Flora, I have been meaning to ask whether you have found out anything more about the inheritance from your mother?'

'Would I be here with Benedetta if I had?'

'I suppose not.'

Remorsefully, Flora said, 'I'm sorry, Susanna, I didn't mean to snap. But no, I am no further forward. I have no idea what the inheritance consists of. I didn't know my mother well. She had – er – little interest in her children.'

'That's not unusual. My own mother is wonderfully kind and considerate, but I have no idea whether *she* has any estate to bequeath to me. There may be mention of something in my marriage contract with Piers but I have never asked. I have never felt the need to know. Of course my brothers will inherit Cernwell.'

Dame Constance, her mind elsewhere, said, 'If the inheritance consisted of landed property, might not Stephen agree to let you go and manage it? It cannot be comfortable for him to have his sister and his wife living with him and perpetually at odds.'

'I doubt if he has even noticed.'

Susanna, thinking *Can Stephen be as bad as all that?* exchanged a glance with Dame Constance and then said, 'It surprises me that he didn't come here with you. Or is he like Piers, and prefers to stay at home and defend it if necessary?'

Flora gave a bitter little half-laugh. 'He was too lazy to *come*, though if Coteley Valence were to be attacked he would not be too lazy to run away!'

Susanna exclaimed, 'How can you say that about your *brother*?'

'Family feeling, you mean? I know of no law, human or divine, which decrees that you have to like someone just because he happens to share your parents.'

There was no answer to that but, following a natural process

156

of thought, Susanna asked after a few moments, 'Do you *really* not want a husband? Don't you feel the *need* to be married?'

'No, I don't,' Flora replied composedly.

'But people *expect* a woman to be married. If you're not, they assume no man wants you, which is unflattering, to say the least.'

'Perhaps. But I had rather no husband than marriage to a man not of my choice. There must be many women who feel as I do. If only they would make a stand!'

Dame Constance, emerging from her abstraction, remarked, 'You want, in effect, to change society? Well, I suppose it might be possible – but not in our lifetime.' Then, in a lighter tone, 'Ah, it sounds as if our guests are deciding to hazard their lives in the great outdoors.'

10

The noise in the courtyard had been gradually increasing as people began to descend from the Great Hall and venture out onto the grass. Among them was John, who arrived at Mistress Hildegarde's side and received a perfunctory little smile just as Gervase and Master Edwin reappeared round the corner of the Buttery Tower.

Seeing them out of the corner of her eye, Hildy moved slightly, so that it was impossible for them not to stop, or not without downright rudeness. It was pleasant to be surrounded by three handsome young men even if only one of them was eligible. Her smile at once limpid and opulent, she said, 'I was just thinking how quiet it is here . . .'

Master Edwin chuckled. 'Save for chattering guests and villagers with pitchforks!'

She giggled. 'That wasn't what I meant. I meant that in the

City it is church bells all the time. I live in Westcheap, close to St Peter's, St Mary Magdalen's, All Hallows and St Mary le Bow. There's St Vedast's nearby, too, and St Paul's. It is *very* noisy.'

Obligingly, Lord Gervase remarked, 'It is indeed. I have noticed it myself. There are more than a hundred churches within the City, which makes me grateful that I spend most of my time at Westminster or Windsor.'

'I envy you. Because when the bells are not tolling,' she resumed, 'there's the constant singing of chantries, prayers for the dead, which sound dreadfully melancholy.'

'The only consolation,' suggested Master Edwin cheerfully, 'must be that you have a perfect view of all those gorgeously clad processions passing just under your windows.'

'Oh yes!' She smiled brightly, then found it desirable to add, 'And my father takes part in many of them, all dressed up in his robes of office as a liveryman of the Worshipful Company of Mercers. He is fond of getting dressed up. So am I. I really like clothes. I have quite a lot of them. I even have a blue velvet robe that took twenty men and nine women thirteen days to embroider! I wear it on special occasions with a matching chaplet of silk entwined with pearls.'

Her companions were kind-hearted, even if not impressed.

'How interesting,' Gervase said.

'Matchless, I should think,' contributed Master Edwin. 'There can be no one in the processions to compare with you. How lucky that everyone's always so busy singing and dancing that they don't have time to be envious.'

'Yes, everyone enjoys themselves. My pa loves taking part, though he doesn't sing or dance, of course! That's only the people gathered to watch.'

'Oh, I see!' rejoined Master Edwin teasingly, his narrowed eyes gleaming against the sun. It suddenly struck Hildy that, with his reddish hair and beard he looked rather like a marmalade cat. She liked cats. Her affectations briefly vanished and there was a trace of mischief in her shy little smile.

Gervase, tiring of this interlude, said briskly, 'Well, we have no processions at Vine Regis and few bells, only the Vox Domini in the village and those of Stanwelle monastery, which we mainly hear when the wind is from the south. Normally, it is indeed quite quiet. Now, if you will forgive us, Mistress Hildegarde, there is something I have to discuss with my brother. Come, John.'

'In a minute,' John said, hanging back. Gervase shrugged, and went.

Mistress Hildy had barely acknowledged John's presence, and he was hurt. He had been half in love with her, and had thought she was beginning to respond.

Susanna had been wrong – he *knew* Susanna had been wrong – to claim that Mistress Hildegarde had been flirting with him and with the big Hanse fellow at the same time. John knew perfectly well that any young woman was bound to be on the lookout for a husband, but it was unthinkable, indeed repellent, to contemplate Koburg in that role. 'Mercenary!' had said Susanna scathingly, but *No*, thought John. There were limits.

Being a forthright young man, he decided he ought to talk to her, which was not easy, since she and Master Edwin were now flirting happily. He appeared to be telling her an amusing tale about his experiences and saying how grateful he was that his grandmother had not chosen to make Jerusalem the objective of her pilgrimage.

'That's a long way, isn't it?' Mistress Hildy said. 'And over the sea, too. Oh, I wouldn't like that.'

'Nor I!' agreed Master Edwin with a grin. But as he opened his mouth to continue, he caught a chilly look from John and interpreted it – correctly – as a request to take himself off. His brows shot up towards his hair over laughing eyes, and he raised his shoulders a fraction, touched both hands lightly to his chest and then opened them in a gesture of submission. He bowed to Mistress Hildegarde – and went.

Breezy though he might be, Master Edwin seemed to John to be far too impoverished to be accounted a likely suitor for any marriageable young lady. What concerned John was his fear that the young lady had other fish to fry.

He said to her politely, 'We have had little opportunity to talk during these last days. Since my brother's return home, in fact.'

'Yes.'

'I have noticed . . .' *How should he put it? Should he put it at all? Oh well, in for a penny, in for a pound.* 'I have noticed that your acquaintance with Meester Koburg has – er – cooled since then?'

Her chin went up. 'It is no business of yours, but I have found him to be a very unpleasant person and not someone I choose to be acquainted with.'

'I'm pleased to hear that. I would be even more pleased if I did not have the impression that you were avoiding *me*, too.'

She pouted. 'Why should I avoid you? I don't dislike you.'

Well, of all the . . . He frowned. 'And you don't dislike my brother, either!'

His sarcasm was wasted.

Pretending to be mystified, she said, 'I don't know him.'

And that went too far. 'It's not for want of trying!' he snapped.

The blood rushing to her sweet little face, she exclaimed spitefully, 'Oh, you are *nasty*!'

'No, just truthful. Go on, admit it! All you want is to catch a husband and my brother is easily the most desirable *parti*.'

'I don't know what a – a *parti* – is, and there's nothing wrong with wanting a husband, or not that I know of. Though I wouldn't marry *you* for a fortune!'

160

He did his best to laugh sardonically. '*If* I were to ask you, and there's no chance of that.'

It was one of those conversations that had nowhere to go but down, so it was fortunate that, at that moment, Gervase reappeared from the staircase.

'Are you coming, John?' he demanded. 'I'm tired of waiting for you.'

'Yes, my lord,' John responded. 'Certainly, my lord. Whatever you say, my lord.'

11

'A charming girl, John, I have no doubt,' remarked Gervase as they made their way back up to the Great Hall. 'But her conversation is – what's the word? – limited.'

'Not when it comes to listing her local churches or the number of her embroiderers,' John agreed morosely.

Gervase clapped him on the shoulder and grinned. 'When I go back to court, you'd better come with me and we'll find you a really nice lady to fall in love with.'

'You don't seem to have found one yourself!'

'Too busy.'

'You mean the ladies you fancied didn't fancy *you*?' John retorted. 'Or vice versa, of course!'

Gervase, who had never been very good at seeing a joke, brushed this aside. 'Now tell me,' he said. 'All those idiots in the Hall who thought our villagers were genuine rebels – have they gone back to being too frightened to leave?'

'I'm afraid so. After you went marching out – at your haughtiest, even with Mistress Hildy hanging on your arm! – the general feeling was that people's attitude to danger is a comparative thing. You're used to it, they're not. What seems to you a minor threat that can easily be dealt with, seems to them much more worrying.'

'Fools!'

'No, be reasonable, Ger. They're civilians, not warriors. There's no use just telling them again that all's safe. I don't think we're going to be rid of them until they've forgotten today's little episode. Let's just hope that nothing else happens to cause them concern.'

12

Frederick having been despatched early to bed in the care of Aunt Edith, whose primary concern was overseeing the packing for her and Benedetta's departure next day, Flora presented herself before Gervase just after supper when the tables were being cleared away.

'Ah – er – yes,' said that gentleman. 'You wanted to talk to me. Would you prefer to go outdoors, where it is quieter?'

'If you please.'

It was still June, still perfectly light, and the air smelled sweet as they walked along the west wall of the castle, across the small bridge over the moat, and into the orchard where there were half a dozen benches scattered around.

'Here, I think,' said Gervase, gesturing towards one under an apple tree.

Flora sat down, but he remained standing. Not one word had the girl uttered since they left the Hall, and his mild curiosity had given way to a less mild irritation. What was it all about? He suspected something of importance to her, but not to him. He waited, looking politely interested and showing no sign of the impatience he felt; he had been well trained, both at home and at court.

To her own surprise, she found him less intimidating than she had found Dame Constance at first encounter. Perhaps it was because what she had to say now was not personal and indecisive but something about which she knew a good deal.

She began, 'I think you know that I was raised in Venice, which is why I speak Italian. You may not, however, know that my father was a municipal councillor there and an astrologer of some repute.'

'No.' He felt a vague stirring of curiosity.

'A few years ago,' she went on, 'he was invited by the king of France to go to Paris as court astrologer. He accepted, of course. But long before the king died last September, it was clear that his heir, now a boy of twelve, would be saddled with two regents and that factions would develop at court. My father foresaw that he himself would lose influence – and possibly his life. He therefore sent me and my brothers back here to England for safety. In Paris, I should explain, I was enabled by his connections at court to receive an exceptionally good education, in which he encouraged me.'

'How very unusual!' Gervase wasn't at all sure that he approved. Clever women were the devil – with the exception of his mother, of course.

'Yes, I was extremely fortunate.' She paused to disentangle her hair from the back of the bench and to draw it forward over her shoulder. 'I am telling you all this for one reason, and one reason only – so that you will understand that I am not just an ignorant female, but that I know what I am talking about, especially on the subject of astrology.'

'I would never have thought you an ignorant female,' he replied with automatic courtesy.

Flora's lips tightened. He made her feel again as if she were not a real person but merely a target for his good manners. 'Thank you,' she replied a little grittily. 'Now, as I am sure you know, the science of astrology has two branches, the natural and the judicial . . .'

He did not know, nor wish to. He compromised. 'I have never been entirely sure which is which.'

'Most people,' she replied with a slightly superior smile, 'share your uncertainty. *Natural* astrology is concerned with the general character of planetary influences in fields like agriculture and medicine, which is why the astrologer-physician is always much respected. *Judicial* astrology applies – or endeavours to apply – these influences more directly. War, epidemic and famine can be foretold for a city or country, while the destiny of individuals, which is more complex in some ways, can similarly be foretold. The truly expert astrologer can predict the most propitious moment for any undertaking one may have in mind.'

Without thinking, he exclaimed, 'You are saying that the stars and planets are as influential as God!'

'No, no. God is the first cause, and the stars are the second, operating by divine permission.'

'Hmmm.' Gervase wondered what Abbot Ralph would say to that.

Flora took a deep breath. 'The reason I wished to speak to you is that I have been consulting my almanac and I believe you should be warned.'

Tired of standing, Gervase sat down on the grass. 'Warned?' he repeated.

'According to the planetary conjunctions, Vine Regis is destined to witness two affrays. One is minor, and I take that to be the villagers' demonstration which occurred today. The other is of more moment and likely to occur two, or perhaps three, days hence. Everything suggests that you should prepare yourself for a defence of Vine Regis, not against odds that might be described as insuperable, but certainly against a force greater than you would expect.'

He was looking dubious, so she added, 'I will give you details of the conjunction of the planets if you so wish, but . . .'

'No, no. You understand them, but I would not.'

Was she right? *Could* she be right? His mind began racing, trying to assess the source from which any danger might come. Short of attack by a full army, he had no doubt of Vine Regis's ability to defend itself, but being specifically forewarned was valuable. Mentally scanning the defences, he found himself analysing the weak points and allotting the senior members of his household to the charge of them.

She watched him, his eyes narrowed in thought, and wondered, *Did he believe her? Was he clever enough to believe her?*

To his own surprise, he found that he was not doubting her. She spoke with the voice of knowledge and of authority, which he knew better than to doubt.

Suddenly aware of the silence, he rose from the grass and held out a strong, long-boned hand to help Mistress Flora to rise.

Another man would have smiled his appreciation, but Gervase smiled rarely. His expression softened a little, however, the harsh lines of his face seeming smoother and the grey eyes brighter under their prominent brows.

'Thank you,' he said. 'I am grateful.'

And meant it.

13

When they returned to the Hall, they found William and Abbot Ralph standing at the entrance to the Great Chamber corridor, talking to the squire who was on guard.

William greeted them anxiously with, 'I'm dying to see

how the painter is getting on but this man says I'm not family so I can't go in on my own. I thought perhaps Abbot Ralph . . .'

'He's not family either,' retorted Gervase with a grin, 'though he does lend an aura of respectability.'

Abbot Ralph accorded this sally no more than a majestic nod.

'Very well,' Gervase said. 'Let us all go in, but we must be quick because I have much else to do.'

Despite the grey tint delineating the shadows and the earth wash over the images, the basic outlines of Signor Alberti's nude sketches were still visible. Abbot Ralph looked very slightly shocked.

However, there was something else that troubled him more. 'I am disappointed, Gervase, that you should choose to have such impious imagery on your walls. Is not the Christian tradition sufficiently rich for you?'

Gervase's jaw did not quite drop, but very nearly.

'Young people today!' the abbot went on. 'Alas, I fear for the future of mankind.'

Daringly, William interjected, 'What there is of it! I thought the Day of Judgement was due any minute now?'

'It is,' the abbot confirmed reprovingly. Then he startled everyone very much indeed by addressing the painter in perfectly workmanlike Italian.

It should have occurred to Dame Constance that Abbot Ralph, in the course of elevation to his present level of authority in the Church, must have visited Rome many times before the schism in the papacy, and that the Latin in which clerical discussions were conducted would not see him very far in the context of everyday life there. But it had not occurred to her and, if it had, she might have hesitated to ask his help in communicating with the painter. Or, as she admitted to herself when the truth was revealed, she might have seen it as a golden opportunity to tease him.

Flora was annoyed, though not surprised, to discover that the painter was considerably more respectful towards Abbot Ralph than he had been towards her, and more informative in his replies. He even offered to show the abbot the colours being ground by his apprentices in the studio.

'Yes, *please*, Father Abbot,' said William excitedly when Abbot Ralph translated this offer.

So they all moved back into the antechamber to watch the apprentices at work, busily grinding the pigments with oil. It should be nut oil, Signor Alberti told them, but the process of purifying nut oil in a cold country such as England when it required to be set out in the sun for a goodly time was not reliable, so linseed oil had to be used instead.

'And as little as possible,' Abbot Ralph reported, 'because too much makes the colours less brilliant when dried.'

'What's that?' demanded William, pointing at a small container. 'Father Abbot, please ask what that is!'

It was quicklime, always added in small quantities when walls were being painted.

'And that?'

It turned out to be ground glass, mixed in to hurry up the drying of the lake colours and others that dried slowly in oil.

William sighed happily.

The bell for Compline rang out from the village church, and Gervase had to wait for Abbot Ralph to cross himself and murmur his *Ave Maria*s before saying, 'I have no more time to spare, and I anticipate' – he gave Flora a nod of acknowledgement – 'I anticipate being much occupied in the next two or three days.'

Then, taking pity on William, he added, 'Father Abbot, would you be so kind as to tell the painter that this young man has

167

my permission to come and watch him at work? Though he will either have to remain silent or come accompanied by Mistress Flora or, if you feel so inclined, by yourself.'

'Thank you, *thank* you!' William was ecstatic. 'And you will . . .'

'Yes, yes. I will remember to tell the squire guarding the door from the Hall that you are to be allowed through. Now, let us go.'

Chapter 6

1

A S THEY returned to the Great Hall, the lookout's horn sounded the series of calls that meant, 'Friends approaching'. Gervase reminded himself to make sure that not only the lookout but everyone else in the castle would recognise the signal for 'Enemy approaching', which Mistress Flora's almanac suggested might be needed. It was a signal which never before, in Gervase's memory, had sounded over Vine Regis.

In the meantime, marching briskly but without obvious haste towards the stairs leading up to the top of the gate tower, he wondered who in the world could be arriving so late on a lovely June evening. The sun was going down, more to the north-west than to the west at this time of year, and the approaching party, a substantial one, seemed to be riding straight out of it. It took him a few moments to adjust his eyes and recognise the pennants and the liveries.

The portcullis, lowered at curfew only a few minutes earlier, was already being raised again to allow Sir Guy, with his riding household and retainers, to enter.

Dame Constance, warned by the invaluable Hamish, stood there waiting, smiling a welcome. She had missed him desperately. He was more than husband, more than lover; he was the only person she could talk to, laugh with, be understood by. He was the other half of herself.

Dismounting, he strode in under the portcullis and greeted her with a formal 'My lady', before raising her hand to his lips.

It was the correct way for a returning lord to greet his lady in public, and only the two of them were aware of the light in their eyes and the erotic quiver of lips and hand.

'My lord,' she replied equally correctly.

He nodded to Gervase, Sir Walter and Hamish, standing close by, then, glancing round the courtyards which were, as usual, full of refugees who felt like a breath of fresh air before retiring, he frowned and demanded, 'Who *are* all these people?'

He sounded so exactly like Gervase on his return from London – even his words were the same – that Dame Constance burst out laughing.

Neither Gervase nor Sir Walter knew what was amusing her, but Hamish's grin spread from ear to ear.

Sir Guy said, his dark eyes dancing, 'I feel that I may have been missing something. Shall we go indoors and you can tell me about it?'

'By all means,' responded his wife cordially. 'And you can tell us what you have been up to in this last three weeks.'

'I have been staying out of your way, as instructed by your son.'

'You have *what*?'

2

Gervase had the grace to look very slightly embarrassed but, some little time later in Dame Constance's private chamber, he convinced himself all over again – in the process of explaining his reasoning to his mother – that it had been perfectly sensible to save Vine Regis from possible attack by ensuring that the rebels, if any, would not be attracted to it by the presence of one of the justices of the peace they so hated.

'At any rate,' he concluded, 'it's all over now.'

'I'm afraid you are out of touch, Gervase,' Sir Guy told him mockingly. 'The revolt may be all over in London, but there is still trouble throughout the eastern counties. I have been close enough to hear a good deal of local gossip. It seems that the redoubtable Bishop Despenser put a brisk stop to a rising in Cambridge a few days ago and is on his way to Norfolk to do the same there. But there is still violence in Essex, Leicester is under threat, and St Albans is virtually in the hands of the rebels – though I believe there is a royal commission pending there which is causing some of the more nervous of them to disperse. We met two or three small groups on our way home today.'

'Well, they can't disperse to the east unless they fancy swimming the North Sea,' Gervase said thoughtfully, 'or to the south where they'd run straight into the royal men-at-arms, and they're unlikely to go north if Despenser is in their path. So – cross-country?'

'Westward, yes. I believe so. And since we are almost on a line with St Albans, it is to be hoped that the various small bands do not converge into a large one or we might have trouble on our hands.'

'Yes, we might,' Gervase agreed, thinking of Mistress Flora's almanac. 'Let's talk more about this in the morning. I'm sure you and my mother would like to be left alone.'

'*So* considerate of you,' murmured his mother.

When he had gone, she turned to her husband. 'Welcome home,' she said.

3

Next morning, his mind not entirely adjusted to almanacs, conjunctions of the planets and the like, Sir Guy listened patiently to what Gervase had to tell him.

They were in his stepson's bedchamber high in the north-west tower, a starkly simple apartment panelled in oak, with a painted ceiling, and most of the floor space occupied by the big curtain-hung bed. There was a small shrine in an alcove, but no other hint of decoration whatsoever.

Gervase had been inhumanly austere even as a boy, Sir Guy recalled. Perched painfully on a corner of the clothes chest, he reflected that the sooner Gervase's Great Chamber was finished the better. There were to be cushioned stools in it, Dame Constance had assured him, so that it would be possible to sit down in something approaching comfort.

Gervase concluded his report of what Mistress Flora had told him by saying, 'She's a clever young woman, isn't she?'

'It seems so, though I can't judge on a personal basis. I have not yet had the pleasure of meeting her.'

'But you were here, weren't you, when she first came over with Susanna on a visit – last November, was it?'

'I was otherwise engaged that day.' It did not mean that he had failed to be informed about the long hair and drab clothes. And the spectacles. 'Though I remember hearing that she *looked* very clever.'

Gervase's brows drew together. 'Y-e-e-s. It's a pity, that.'

Faintly amused, Sir Guy watched him weighing up brains

172

against beauty. Gervase's mother had both, and so, too, had his lovely but lethargic sister Isabelle. Any young woman who hoped to attract Gervase's interest would have a lot to live up to.

Sir Guy had as yet no idea whether or not Mistress Flora hoped to attract Gervase's interest. He must ask Constance, who was dedicated to the need to find a new wife for her son. It was a challenge, she maintained whenever Sir Guy questioned what seemed to him to be becoming an obsession. Mistress Flora, from what little Sir Guy knew, seemed unlikely to be a candidate. He was open-minded enough, however, to look forward to meeting her and judging for himself.

Gervase shook his head as if to clear it. 'Well, I hope the girl, Mistress – er – Flora is right. Because we are going to have to organise a defence and dole out basinets and pauldrons and everything else from the armoury. We're going to look pretty foolish if they're not needed.' He frowned heavily. 'Have you any idea of how big an attacking force we might have to face? *If* it comes to that.'

Sir Guy shrugged. 'Not more than a hundred, even if the small bands do coalesce. There might, I suppose, be more if the St Albans men converge with others en route, but Vine Regis is certainly strong enough to withstand them. We can simply drop the portcullis, stay indoors, shoot off a few arrows, and wait for them to go away.'

Gervase was shocked, even insulted. 'Wait for them to go away!' he repeated. 'Certainly not. It is our clear duty to teach them a lesson.' Then, turning from the window and studying the other man's face, he said accusingly, 'I see. You were trying to take a rise out of me, weren't you?'

Sir Guy sighed inwardly.

'Weapons?' Gervase resumed.

'Bows and arrows, a few swords.'

'Pitchforks?'

Sir Guy laughed. 'Not a one. Or none that I saw'

'Anything else?'

'No siege engines, of course, although if there are carpenters with military experience among them, they might be able to build a primitive mangonel or trebuchet. However, it seems unlikely.'

'Were they mounted, the bands that you saw?'

'Yes, surprisingly enough. In fact, there were very few real peasants among them. My impression was of men such as village constables, minor officials and the like, the kind of men who would have – or could beg, borrow or steal – a horse. The horses, I may add, looked as if they were approaching exhaustion, so they would either have to be rested, or their riders might have to steal fresh mounts.'

'Hmmm. It doesn't sound as if they should cause us any trouble. We have well over a hundred trained fighting men in the castle – more, now you're back – and I have already decided who should be put in command where.'

Sir Guy grinned. 'And who were you thinking of putting in charge of those uninvited guests of ours? Indeed, *where* were you thinking of putting them? From what I hear, they're likely to be a godforsaken nuisance, tripping over one another trying to stay out of the line of fire.'

'God's bones!' Gervase slapped himself on the forehead. 'I hadn't thought of that. They'll get in *everybody's* way!'

'You could lock 'em in the dungeon,' Sir Guy suggested temptingly.

His stepson thought about it for a moment, but only for a moment. 'If we were to put Master Doggett and Meester Koburg in there, and add Abbot Ralph for good measure,' he retorted, 'we couldn't even squeeze a mouse in. But you haven't met the first two yet, have you?'

'No. I have, however, already heard a good deal about them!'

'I'm sure you have. Meester Koburg has been a sore trial to my mother.' Then he added, in tones of such concentrated loathing that Sir Guy could not help but laugh, 'Wine! Sugar! Spices!'

It seemed to Sir Guy that there were one or two associated problems that might also have slipped Gervase's mind. 'Our guests' horses?' he murmured helpfully. 'And their dogs?'

Gervase glowered at him. 'You *have* been busy!'

'Well, it would have been hard *not* to notice as I came home last night that two of the five-acre fields had been turned into paddocks. And the dogs, of course, spoke for themselves.'

Gervase groaned. 'We had to move them further away from the castle a few days ago, because whenever one of our refugees sent a servant over to see that his animals were all right, every last one of them started barking. I suppose,' he went on thoughtfully, 'we could set 'em all loose if we were attacked.'

'Good notion! A few score dogs jumping and yapping at a mounted body of men would certainly have a demoralising effect. But we will have to put a strong guard round the paddocks. We would not like our uninvited guests' mounts to be stolen, would we?'

'Why not?' Gervase retorted. 'It wouldn't bother *me*!'

4

The morning passed and nothing happened.

Or nothing except that Gervase's determination to be un-obtrusive about his military preparations – low-voiced consultations, an air of abstraction, much quiet but purposeful striding about – led to a perceptible increase of tension among the refugees.

175

Sir Guy, meanwhile, took the opportunity to survey and assess them, his maturity and air of authority quelling any tendency on their part to argue or complain, as they had shown an increasing inclination to do with Gervase who, Lord of the Castle though he might be, was considerably younger than most of his guests.

However, arguments and complaints there were in plenty when dinnertime came, Dame Constance having decreed that, with the return of Gervase's and Sir Guy's riding households, there were far too many people to be accommodated at one sitting. With her most charming smile, she had instructed Sir Walter to allocate the guests to two sittings, and Sir Guy was entertained to see his own earlier impressions confirmed as the self-important ones thronged round Sir Walter demanding, as their due – indeed, as if it were a confirmation of their social status – that they be allocated to the first sitting. But Sir Walter – wily old bird that he was – managed very well in his majestic way. Aware that any reliance on the principle of first-come-first-served would without doubt have led to a vulgar scrimmage, he ignored those who had seated themselves without waiting to be invited (among them Meester Koburg) and gestured towards others of the guests to sit at the places to which he pointed with his carefully manicured hand. Sir Guy suspected that the chosen ones were those who had not previously given him offence in one way or another.

Those favoured by inclusion in the first sitting had of necessity to remove themselves from the Great Hall when the second sitting convened, and betook themselves to the fresh air of the outer courtyard. There they were ultimately joined by most of those who had been allocated to the second sitting.

And still nothing happened.

When Dame Constance and Sir Guy returned to the Great Hall from where they had taken refuge in Dame Constance's private chamber, they found it unnaturally peaceful. There were a few gossiping groups down at the far end overlooking the road to the village, and Mistress Hildegarde was perched on a windowsill trying in a desultory way to make music with her cittern. She smiled delightfully at Sir Guy, but even as he thought how lonely the poor girl looked his wife's voice said in his ear, 'Take no notice. It's just habit. She'll smile at any personable man, even at any man not so personable, if he's rich. She was doing her best to play John and Meester Koburg off against each other, but is now hoping to lay siege to Gervase.'

Sir Guy laughed. 'Well, I suppose one must give her full marks for trying.'

All the tables had been cleared away except for the women's table which was occupied in solitary splendour by Mistress Flora, who was frowning in concentration over a roll of vellum, a hand's-breadth wide and long enough to overlap the table at both ends. The little ink-horn which normally hung from her belt was carefully propped up on the table to her right and in her hand was a fine metal stylus with which she was making notes on a separate, much smaller piece of parchment.

She glanced up as they approached and said to Dame Constance, 'I hope you don't mind the table not being put away, but it makes such a difference having a table to work on.'

'No, of course I don't mind. What is that, may I ask? The long roll with the drawings and writing.'

'Have you not seen one before? It's a kind of summary of Time and Nature, a cosmological diagram. The points of this big lozenge, here, show earth, water, air and fire, and in the ring around it are the signs of the zodiac. Further down, here' – she pointed at the lower end of the roll which had come to rest in her lap – 'is my almanac. I have to update it year by year, otherwise it would give me all the wrong answers.'

Dame Constance smiled. 'I heard of one astrologer who fore-saw that some royal personage, I don't remember who, would live to be eighty-five. Unfortunately, the prince in question died at thirty-three . . .'

'And the astrologer was discredited and dismissed!' Flora shook her head disapprovingly.

Sir Guy said, 'I see you use a metal stylus, which must be rather inflexible. Why not a quill?'

'The stylus is slower, but it writes finer and smaller, which is important when space is limited, as it is when I am bring-ing the almanac up to date.'

She sighed, removed her spectacles and laid them on the table, then rubbed the bridge of her nose wearily. 'What I am trying to do at the moment, using this scrap of parchment for my calculations, is work out Frederick's immediate destiny. I am very worried about him. He is still far from well, and I have just calculated that some danger threatens him, probably tomorrow. What *kind* of danger, what *level* of danger, I can't tell.' She sighed again. 'I don't even know where he is at this moment. Trying to escape supervision as usual, I suppose. But *where?*'

Just then, while Dame Constance was endeavouring to think of something useful to say, Susanna appeared, followed by Gervase with Blanche hanging on to his right hand, Eleanor on to his left, and a smiling Alice behind. The contents of the impressive roll of vellum had to be explained to the new-comers and not even Alice noticed that Blanche was a great deal less interested in cosmology than in the spectacles lying on the table. When she was sure that no one was watching, she slyly picked them up and went dancing off with them, trying to perch them on her small nose and squealing, 'Oooh, doesn't everything look funny!'

There was a moment's horrified silence before Dame

Constance snapped, 'Blanche!' and Flora cried, 'Take care, take care. Don't drop them! *Please* don't drop them!'

Gervase was quick. Four strides were enough. He plucked the spectacles from Blanche's hand before she knew he was there, then wagged a reproving finger at her, and brought the lenses back to Flora, presenting them to her with a slight bow.

She gave an almost tearful gasp, her gratitude threatening to overpower her.

Mistress Hildegarde, watching this exchange from her perch on the windowsill, had to make a conscious effort to prevent her sweet continual smile from hardening on her lips. Where any other girl might have nibbled on a fingernail while she wondered how best to approach the problem of charming the Lord Gervase into paying attention to her, Hildy was far too conscious of her grooming to make such a fundamental error. Instead, nibbling on her ivory plectrum, she concluded that no good purpose would be served by competing with others for the lord's attention. She would wait and catch him in a quiet moment.

Unfortunately, Gervase seemed to have no quiet moment, being too preoccupied with matters of organisation to have time for anything else. Nothing happened for what remained of that day except that Mistress Benedetta and Aunt Edith rode off home to Coteley Valence, an event that would have been of no interest to Gervase if Dame Constance had not instructed Hamish to go with them on guard duty.

'Straight back, Hamish!' Gervase exclaimed. 'I have things I want to talk to you about, arrangements to make.'

'Aye, aye, laddie.' Glancing at the two women, Hamish added thoughtfully, 'It's going to be a slow journey, I can see, so maybe John had better come, too. Then, if it's getting late, I can get back here myself and leave him to it.'

John having been dug out of the armourer's workshop and

told what was expected of him, Hamish was at last able to say, 'Now, are we ready to be off, ladies?'

Flora, Frederick and Dame Constance stood on the draw-bridge and waved the little party goodbye, Frederick dancing with glee and Flora having a struggle not to do the same.

It had been a normal, peaceful-seeming day and everything, too, seemed peaceful the next morning, so that Gervase had to remind himself, and other people, as they sat down to the first service of dinner, that *this* was the day when trouble might be expected.

5

Frederick was eight years old and had no one to play with, but he was used to that. He had never had anyone to play with.

All the time it was grown-ups saying, 'Frederick, do this – don't do that – where have you been? – what have you been doing? – pay attention – come here – sit there – be quiet – behave yourself . . .'

And since they had come to Vine Regis there had been added, 'Frederick, how do you feel today? – better? – worse? – you must not eat this – drink that – you must swallow this medi-cine – you must stay in bed – you won't get better unless you behave yourself – behave yourself – behave yourself . . .'

And when they went back to Coteley Valence, Flora would go on making him construe Latin and Greek and learn about geography and the stars and other boring things.

He had never had anyone to play with, so he had learned to amuse himself by deliberately annoying Flora.

Now, he stood in the great gateway and thought that escap-ing her supervision and making his way to the barbican rise on the other side of the moat would really annoy her. But although he was feeling a bit better and hadn't been sick for two days, his legs were still wobbly, so that getting across the drawbridge without being seen – and chased – was easier said than done.

He was still thinking about the problem when the answer obligingly presented itself in the form of a big open cart with basket-woven sides and huge wheels. Drawn by three horses harnessed in a line ahead, it was rumbling along the road from the direction of the village and, folded back at the rear end of the cart, there was some kind of canvas covering that could be pulled protectively over the mountainous load if it started to rain.

It was a salt wagon.

Frederick watched as the cart stopped with its tail end just past the entrance to the drawbridge. Then it waited. Someone came out of the Buttery Tower and ran over the bridge and started arguing with the driver about who was going to carry the great chunks of salt indoors. After a while, the driver angrily gave in and yelled at two men who had been snoozing peacefully among the folds of canvas. Then with some swearing and much cracking of whips, the three horses, with the three men at their heads, were slowly backed up so that when cart and horses came to a halt again, they were neatly positioned on the bridge and the salt could be unloaded from the back of the cart and carried indoors with comparative ease.

Just as well the horses weren't poled rather than harnessed together, Frederick reflected, but they and the driver were probably used to awkward manoeuvring, though the horses didn't look as if they much liked going backwards.

The castle seemed to use an amazing amount of salt. During his wanderings Frederick had found himself in the kitchens and had asked what that man was pounding away at with a pestle and mortar almost as big as himself. 'That's the yeoman powderer', he had been told. 'Our salt is delivered in big lumps and he has to break it down into grains so that it can be used for salting beef and pork to preserve them, and for flavouring dishes, and so on.' The yeoman powderer, Frederick thought with a giggle, was going to be kept hard at it from now until the time for the autumn slaughter almost five months hence. Lucky him!

The unloading completed, the three drivers buried their noses in mugs of ale someone had brought out from the kitchens. Also, it was dinnertime and only those castle guests doomed to the second sitting were strolling about, their minds on their empty stomachs rather than on what small boys were getting up to. Frederick knew he would never have a better chance. Once he was sure that no one was looking, he heaved himself up into the now empty cart and hid under the canvas. All three men would be occupied leading the horses back on to the road and by the time the two lazy ones decided to resume their snooze, he would have slipped out again onto the grass verge on the other side of the moat.

It worked like a dream and, once across the moat, Frederick didn't care who saw him. He wandered up the slope of the barbican rise and surveyed the landscape from an unfamiliar angle. Everything was violently green and lush and looked very peaceful. He wandered on. He had been out for more than an hour and had gone quite a long way when he turned back to look at the castle.

It was very odd. The outer courtyard, which had been full of hungry people when he left, now seemed to be full of horses. It took him several minutes to work out that the servants must have led them there from the fields that had been used as paddocks close by the Bluebell Wood.

Soon after, he felt the ground begin to vibrate slightly under his feet and, looking to the open country to the east, saw a solid body of horsemen in the far distance, riding fast. At the same moment the lookout's horn rang out from the castle's Great Gate tower in a series of calls Frederick didn't recognise but that were unmistakably urgent.

He turned back and began to run, stumbling, towards the distant drawbridge and the safety of the castle.

6

Pushing his plate away and jumping to his feet, Gervase snapped, 'That's the call for Enemy approaching! Let's see what they look like!'

But even as he reached the window, Mistress Flora was halfway to the stairs, exclaiming, 'Frederick! Oh, no!'

Gervase caught up with her just before she reached the court-yard. 'What's he doing out there? Leave him to me. It looks as if he can't move very fast, and he's too heavy for you to carry.'

Mistress Flora paid no attention, just hitched her skirts up a little further and broke into a run. Gervase gave a sigh of exasperation.

Then he saw that one of his grooms was just outside the stables, fitting the new saddle Gervase had ordered for one of his favourite coursers. Casting a swift glance over the saddle, girth straps and harness, he raised questioning brows at the groom and then gathered the reins, put one foot in the stirrup, swung the other leg over, and was off, shouting as he went to Hamish, 'Get everything moving. You know what to do. I'll be back in a minute!'

As he raced across the bridge past Mistress Flora, he was aware that she had stopped running. Sensible girl.

He reached the boy within seconds, rode on past him and

then wheeled round, scanning the oncoming horsemen with a cold, perceptive eye. They were still almost a mile away. He took one foot out of the stirrup, shouted, 'Frederick, can you put your left foot in the stirrup and reach up to me with your hands?' The boy understood and did as he was told, so that they were on their way back to the drawbridge with minimum waste of time.

The minute they were across, Gervase yelled, 'Right!' and the men stationed there for the purpose hauled on the ropes to swivel the bridge away from the outer side of the moat, and then on another set of ropes to bring it to the castle side and lay it flat against the vertical bank.

Meanwhile, the uninvited guests were being shepherded up to the walkway round the castle roof, as far out of the way as possible. It was a slow process, hindered by John being too polite to them and Gervase's deputy Master of the Horse, Roger Lestrange – who was better with horses than with people – trying loudly to bully them.

Gervase merely nodded when Mistress Flora thanked him politely for delivering Frederick safely to her, then sprinted up to the Great Hall.

7

'This is ridiculous,' Dame Constance was saying. 'How many of them are there – sixty, eighty? They can't possibly be intending to attack the castle. Why should they?'

'Horses,' Sir Guy told her kindly.

'Oh? I thought it was Justices of the Peace they didn't like? And *why* must they ride straight through the flax field like that, just when the crop was coming along so nicely?'

Since it was as clear to her husband as it was to Dame

184

Constance herself that Gervase was repressing an explosive, 'Women!' Sir Guy stepped nobly into the breach. 'They are anxious to put as much space as possible between themselves and royal justice. They must need fresh horses, and not just half a dozen or so.'

'Yes, yes, yes. And castles contain a goodly number of people, which means a goodly number of horses. I am quite capable of working that out for myself, thank you.'

Susanna exclaimed, 'Oh dear, I'm so worried. What if they passed Lanson? What if they saw the stud? What if they stopped? There are far too many of them for Piers to deal with! Oh dear! I hope he's all right.' She looked as if she were about to burst into tears.

Sir Guy said reassuringly, 'Don't worry. I sent him a message yesterday warning him to be on the lookout.'

'Oh, thank you!'

'They're almost here,' Gervase snapped. 'Mother, will you please go up to your chamber out of harm's way! And take Susanna with you. The arrows will soon be flying.'

She cast him a chilling look and stalked off, with Susanna dutifully trailing along behind, just as the lookout's horn gave a brief double toot.

The two pages who had been left in charge of the dog compound heard it and obeyed, flinging the gate of the field open and then diving for cover.

The dogs ran out in a barking, yelping, snarling torrent, straight into the path of the rebel riders, whose mounts, rearing and whinnying, took violent exception to their incursion. Several of the horsemen were thrown, while the others had to struggle hard to regain control.

Gervase shouted, 'Hamish!' and Hamish, stationed on the stairs from the Great Hall, shouted back, 'Aye, aye!' and then directed his voice up the stairs and let out a bellow of, 'Three!'

The lookout's horn gave a triple toot, whereupon all Gervase's men-at-arms, stationed inside the castle's windows, let fly with their arrows.

Gervase, grinning happily, told Sir Guy, 'Come on!' and they both raced into the Great Chamber and over to the window.

'Oof!' exclaimed Sir Guy. 'Why is it so hot in here?'

'It's that painter fellow,' responded Gervase, cranking up his crossbow. 'He's been boiling up his linseed oil to purify it. Four hours it takes before he lets the fire go out, and the cauldron goes on radiating heat for the rest of the day.' His mind on more important matters, he took careful aim at the exposed rear of a grounded horseman, released the tension lock and, seconds later, grunted with annoyance. 'Missed him! It's these new bolts. They're poorly balanced.'

'Not too many dead bodies, if you please,' requested the Justice of the Peace at his side.

'No, don't worry. I've told all my men to disable but not to kill.'

'Well, that's something. But I'd rather you put that devilish instrument of yours away. It's too likely to be lethal.'

'Oh, you lawyers!' Gervase complained. 'They're thieves, so we're entitled to kill them.'

'What you mean is, we *think* they *may* be thieves.'

Gervase sighed heavily, but propped his crossbow down against the wall and reached for his longbow instead.

'Ah!' he said. 'They're beginning to disentangle themselves. Looks as if they have ropes to use as halters and there's a fellow there – do you see him? – who seems to have some authority. I think – I *think* – he's telling them not to unsaddle until they're sure of replacement mounts.'

'Very wise.'

'Ho, hum,' said Gervase, taking aim. 'And where did *he* come from?'

The 'he' in question was a lithe young man who had found his way across the moat and was trying to scale the outer wall of the bailey.

'Upriver,' Sir Guy replied succinctly. 'He looks wet. Must have swum across the river above the weir or found the stepping stones.'

The man was still wearing a coif which had become rucked up on top of his head. Gervase neatly shot it off and its owner ducked hurriedly down behind the protection of the wall.

But suddenly there were another half dozen men scaling the bailey wall and sliding down over the roof into the outer courtyard, two of them clutching arrow-struck parts of their anatomy but all of them, reaching the courtyard, protected by the horses surrounding them.

Gervase, turning his head to glance out of the window at the back of the castle, swore suddenly and said in shocked tones, 'Would you look at that!'

Sir Guy looked and saw one of the rebels trying to force an unwilling horse, a big chestnut with a touch of Andalusian in his ancestry, to swim the moat across to the vineyard. No amount of hauling on the makeshift halter or kicking the animal's haunches was having the slightest effect. The man obviously had no idea of how to handle the animal.

Gervase, exclaiming, 'Mother will kill me if I let them trample the vines!' took careful aim and let fly. The man grabbed at his left buttock and dropped the halter. The horse kicked up its heels and made a hasty exit from the scene.

Sir Guy was just fitting another arrow into his own longbow when he became aware of a small, dark figure materialising at his side. He glanced down.

The figure, which had a streak of bright blue on one cheek, said, 'Signor, you want boiling oil, yes?'

Sir Guy stared at him. 'I'm sorry, what did you say?'

'I say, you want boiling oil, yes? I have a-plenty here in ze cauldron. Ees not boiling no more, but ees still ver', ver' hot.'

Sir Guy continued to stare at him disbelievingly for a moment but, when the sense finally penetrated, it was too much for his gravity. Trying with no success at all to smother an outburst of laughter, he waved a helpless hand in Gervase's direction.

The painter, with a grimace, poked Gervase in the ribs and repeated his offer. 'You want boiling oil, yes?'

Gervase said, 'What? No, of course I don't want boiling oil. Don't bother me with idiotic questions. This is England. We don't pour boiling oil over people here. Go away, you silly little man.'

The painter, with a justifiably offended toss of his dark head, marched off across the room and disappeared into his studio.

'He can understand English when he wants to,' snorted Gervase, taking another arrow from his quiver. Twang, hiss. 'Got him!'

'He can paint, too,' responded Sir Guy, with a swift glance round the walls.

'Yes. Pay attention, Guy! Can you reach that fellow down there on the left? You've a better angle than I have.'

Sir Guy duly obliged, and the fellow on the left sat down abruptly, clutching his shoulder.

After a while, Sir Guy asked, 'What about the faces? Are they going to be portraits of the lord and his family?'

'Don't know.' Twang, hiss. 'Mistress Hildegarde is going to be a nymph, though. That I *do* know.'

Sir Guy grinned. 'And if you stayed with your crossbow, you could be Jupiter with his thunderbolts.'

Gervase missed the point entirely. 'I'm getting tired of this,' he said. 'It's about as exciting as target practice.' He ducked aside as an unusually well aimed arrow looked as if it might reach his window. 'Can you see how many of the fellows there are in the courtyard?'

'About a dozen.'

'We're not going to tempt any more in, are we?'

'I shouldn't think so.'

About fifty of the rebels were still grouped where they had halted originally, hiding behind their horses and occasionally kicking out at one of the dogs still leaping and snarling about them. The other dozen or so had penetrated the outer court-yard, and seemed to be arguing the possibility of getting the castle horses over the bailey roofs and across the moat. A steady flight of arrows had discouraged them from trying the exposed vineyard route.

'Mmmm,' said Gervase. 'I suppose we'll have to make do with the ones in the yard. They'll fill the dungeon nicely and we can chase the others later.' He raised his voice to a bellow. 'Hamish!'

'Aye, what now?'

Gervase told him and, after a moment, they heard the heavy, creaking sound of the portcullis being partially raised and saw twenty men-at-arms marching out to arrest the rebels.

The main group outside kicked a few more dogs, then hurriedly remounted and fled. While a faint cheer rang out from the observers who had been confined to the walkway on the castle ramparts, Gervase watched irritably, knowing that Guy was right and that trying to arrest and detain the whole group was beyond the castle's capacity. It didn't mean that Gervase had to like it.

Guy had said, 'We can arrest the ones in the courtyard for attempted theft. I've been a witness to that. But the others have committed no crime of which I have knowledge. Our system of justice requires proof of ill-doing, which *may* exist in St Albans or wherever they've come from. That means they must be returned there for trial.' He had raised a cynical eyebrow at a protesting Gervase. 'Can you spare a hundred men to escort them?'

'No.'

'I thought not.'

8

The uninvited guests gradually descended the stairs, chattering busily, the bravest and loudest of them even venturing down as far as the courtyard and shouting for their servants, who had sensibly taken cover inside the bailey buildings.

Sir Walter, ably assisted by John and Hamish, began overseeing the return of the horses to their paddocks and the dogs to their compound, discouraging the owners from arguing about which horse or dog belonged to whom.

John said to Hamish in astonishment, 'Some of them don't even recognise their own animals! It's just as well the dogs, at least, know their masters!'

'Aye, they know the smell of them. Most of these folk have never gone hunting in their lives, but they think it looks impressive to have two or three hunting dogs always at their heels. Poor beasts. I think it's sinful.'

Gervase and Sir Guy, emerging from the dungeon staircase with a list of reluctantly revealed names, addresses and occupations, found themselves waylaid by Mistress Hildegarde.

Gazing up at Gervase, she murmured throbbingly, 'So *brave*! So *clever*!'

Gervase gave her a smile that was no more than a slight curve of the lips and a deepening of the creases that ran from the corners of his mouth to his nose, and said, 'Thank you. I hope you were not unduly distressed by all the excitement?'

His eyes wandered beyond her. 'Ah, if you will forgive me, I must have a word with Mistress Flora.'

Mistress Hildegarde watched him go, her pretty mouth pursed up. 'Such a dull and dutiful girl,' she breathed to Sir Guy. 'She thinks of nothing and no one but her little brother.'

'I believe he has been ill,' he replied neutrally.

'Mmmm, yes.'

Luckily, at that moment William appeared. 'Oh, there you are, Sir Guy. I wish I hadn't been sent upstairs with everybody else. I'd have learned a lot more down on your level.' He stopped. 'That sounded a bit insulting, didn't it? It wasn't meant to be.'

'I didn't think it was,' Sir Guy said amiably. 'Now, if you will excuse me, I wish to talk to my wife so I will leave the two of you together.'

An expression of stark horror appeared on both faces, and he chuckled inwardly as he went off to Dame Constance's chamber.

9

Gervase, meanwhile, was congratulating Flora on the accuracy of her predictions.

She said defensively, 'You make it sound like fortune-telling! I don't tell fortunes. Astrology is *science*!'

He agreed hastily, and she could see that he was impressed. It gave her an unexpectedly warm feeling inside, the knowledge that her cleverness was appreciated. It made no difference, of course, to her general view of men, but this one did seem quite tolerable.

Frederick, temporarily resigned to Flora's firm grasp on his hand, had already decided that he approved of Lord Gervase, who had dashed to his rescue when he was frightened. It was interesting that, when Lord Gervase told people to do something, they did it without arguing. And it wasn't only because he was a lord. It was something else. Frederick thought that if he followed Lord Gervase around, observing closely, he might learn the trick of it, though he would have to be careful in case Lord Gervase noticed and chased him away.

Gervase was saying, 'Is it hard to learn? It all seems very interesting.'

Flora thought for a moment. 'You have to have the right kind of mind, a feeling for precision and organisation. But I suppose you yourself must have those. It seems to me that everything that has happened today has been admirably controlled, as if you knew how those men would behave and how you could best deal with them.'

'Experience,' Gervase replied modestly.

She thought for another moment. 'Partly, perhaps, but not wholly. Experience is useless unless you learn from it. You need experience *and* judgement.'

'And time.'

'Yes, if you are talking about learning astrology.' She smiled at him. 'Concentration, too. It also helps to be young, of an age when learning comes easily.'

'Like Frederick here?'

Frederick spoke for himself. '*I* don't want to learn astrology. *I* want to paint pictures!'

The grownups ignored him. As usual.

Lord Gervase said, 'I suspect I do not have the necessary qualifications. We must leave the science of astrology to you, Mistress Flora.'

'I am happy to have been of help, and I hope I will continue to be so' – her voice was slightly pensive – 'for as long as I remain here.'

He said, 'I have to go off to St Albans tomorrow with our prisoners. I hope you will still be here when I get back.'

She had no idea whether it was just his ingrained courtesy speaking, or whether he was being truthful.

10

'That Doggett girl!' snapped Susanna. 'If, just one more time, I hear her telling people that you are really rather dull because you care so much for your little brother that you have no interest in anything else, I shall be very rude to her indeed. She means your clothes and your appearance, of course.'

She waited expectantly for Flora to react. She had asked Dame Constance's opinion and the Lady had said thoughtfully, 'It *might* work, I suppose, since you won't appear to be criticising Flora directly, but I don't need to advise you to tread delicately.'

'No. Might we go into your garden to talk?'

'For privacy? Yes, of course.'

And now Flora was sitting staring blankly at her, not reacting at all. Frustratedly, Susanna drew her fingers up a sprig of southernwood and sniffed the pleasant lemony fragrance of it.

Flora watched her but said nothing. She had already been feeling unsettled without quite knowing why, but nasty little Mistress Hildegarde had given shape to her unease. She could see herself dwindling into a cleverer version of Aunt Edith, doomed to the perpetual looking-after not only of Frederick but of Stephen and Benedetta's children when they had them. It was not what she wanted. She wanted a life of her own, a life where she could be useful to others if she chose, but *only* if she chose.

She knew perfectly well that, if she said as much to Susanna, they would be off again on the subject of husbands.

Better to be a wife than an Aunt Edith? She didn't know. Better to be *neither*, but in possession of a household of her own! If only – if only! – she could find out more about her mother's legacy.

Susanna asked tentatively, 'Do you ever give thought to your appearance?'

Startled out of her abstraction, Flora shook her head slightly and raised a hand to toss her hair back. 'Not really,' she admitted. 'I never seem to have time. As long as what I am wearing is comfortable, I am content. I am no beauty and never will be.'

And what, Susanna wondered acerbically, am I supposed to say to that?

She compromised. 'You have lovely hair, but keeping it long and straight is *so* unflattering. It's as if it pulls your mouth and eyes down to match and makes you look depressed even when you aren't. And it must be a nuisance, surely? When you are poring over your almanac, I mean, don't you find it falls forward and gets in the way?'

Incurably honest, Flora replied, 'Yes, it does.'

Susanna tilted her head consideringly and tried to look as if it were an idea that had just occurred to her in passing. 'You could plait it, I suppose, but have you ever thought of cutting it shorter, perhaps to a level with your chin, and getting your women to curl it under?'

Mistress Flora clearly did not fancy curls, but Susanna persevered. 'I don't mean *curls* exactly,' she explained, 'just the ends smooth and turned under, rather like a man's. You could wear a gold fillet round your forehead and a gold-trellised coif to hold it all in place. When we go indoors again, I could hold your hair up and show you in my mirror what it might look

194

like. It would give a tremendous lift to your features and your whole appearance.'

'Thank you.' It was said without enthusiasm.

Susanna hesitated. One thing at a time? Should she leave it there? But she might never have another opportunity, so she went on, 'And a little bit of colour in your dress, perhaps?'

Flora was not deceived. 'Are you trying to make me over to suit other people's tastes? Why should I care what people think of my looks?'

Susanna almost gave up. How blind and stubborn was it possible to be? 'I should have thought – for your own satis- faction – vanity, if you like – it would be good to know that you are making the best of yourself . . .'

'As Mistress Hildegarde does?'

It was what Piers would have called a 'home thrust'. After a moment, Susanna said, 'She must work awfully hard at it. Those pretty blond curls are certainly not natural. And she gives her complexion a helping hand, undoubtedly.'

'Are you saying that, without all her hard work, Mistress Hildegarde would be just as plain as I am?'

It was, of course, exactly what Susanna had been saying, but she stammered, 'No, no, of course not. But whereas, when she has made the most of herself, she achieves only an empty- headed prettiness, you could achieve something much more interesting. You could have *style*.'

Flora looked thoughtful. However unintentionally, Susanna had made Mistress Hildegarde sound as if she were deliberately posing a challenge. Flora might have disregarded it if the girl had not been so insulting – indeed, impertinent – but Flora felt strongly that she needed to be put in her place.

'I wonder,' Susanna resumed as innocently as if she had not already enquired, 'whether Master Nicholas – the castle chamberlain, you know? the fair, chubby young man – might have some fabrics that might suit you. He's a shocking magpie. If he finds some material that particularly appeals to him he can't resist acquiring it, even if he has no special purpose in mind for it. It means that he can nearly always produce what you want, even if you didn't know you wanted it! And he has excellent taste. I remember when I first came here that I always dressed in very girlish pinks and blues, but Dame Constance's daughter Isabelle and Master Nicholas between them completely changed my colour palette and the way I looked. I was not pleased at the time, but now I am grateful.'

Flora said, 'You always look elegant.'

Once, Susanna would have preened herself at the compliment, but now, knowing it to be the hard-won truth, she gave a little laugh and said, 'None of my doing! Even now, I always come to Vine Regis to consult Master Nicholas before I have any new gowns made. I wish Isabelle were still here. She has the most unerring eye.'

'As well as the family's good looks?'

'Oh yes. Her colouring is different – I believe she takes after her father – she has hair the colour of cinnamon and usually wears spicy colours to emphasise it. But you, with your chestnut hair – amber tones would suit you in winter, but a fresh green in spring and summer would be lovely. I wonder if you could wear pink?' she tilted her head consideringly. 'Perhaps, though red would be better. But *not* blue.'

Flora said nothing.

Susanna wailed, 'Don't look so disapproving! Trying out all the colours would be such fun. Just by draping a bolt of something over your shoulders, we can tell what would suit you.'

'I'm not looking disapproving. I'm just not sure that I want to be made over. Besides, I have no right to take up Master Nicholas's time – or his fabrics.'

'Don't worry about that. He'll enjoy himself hugely – you'll see! But perhaps you'd prefer it if we proceeded one stage at a time?'

It had only at that moment occurred to Susanna that, however desirable the final result, it might not be the wisest course to transform Flora too suddenly and dramatically. If Gervase returned from St Albans to find Flora changed as if by magic into a smart and stylish young woman, he might very well wonder why. And although he certainly needed a new wife, he might react badly if the change in the girl was too glaringly obvious. No more than any other man would he like the sensation of feeling entrapped into marriage, especially with a castle-full of people watching and whispering.

Droopily, Flora said, 'Oh, very well. Though I still don't see why my looks should be of interest to anyone except me.'

Susanna would have liked to explain the facts of life to her – that if a lady went to the trouble of making herself attractive, gentlemen were much more inclined to be attractive back. All this nonsense about Flora having no time for men! The truth was that, if Flora chose to look dull, she would be seen as dull. Susanna had noticed with surprise and some pleasure that Gervase was taking an incipient interest in Flora, but her matchmaking instincts told her that they both needed help. If anything were to come of it, Flora must be turned out more becomingly. Brains were all very well in their place, but she could certainly never go to court in her present depressing garb. Susanna knew it, and Gervase knew it. Flora would just have to learn.

Susanna would have liked to say, 'Hair first,' because that would be the key to the whole new look, the most radical and striking element in the transformation. Instead, she made do with, 'A little colour in your dress, to start with.'

11

Dame Constance, meanwhile, was taking a less obtrusive hand in Flora's destiny.

The sky was clouding over as she and Sir Guy stood just within the Great Gate and studied the trampled grass of the outer courtyard, now that the horses had been returned to their paddocks and everything had been swept up that could be swept up. 'We need a good downpour,' she said, glancing skyward, 'to turn all that residue of manure into fertiliser that will encourage the grass to grow again. Though at least it will have the benefit of discouraging our guests from coming out and cluttering up the courtyard when the sun shines. I know that Gervase enjoyed his little battle, but in my view we could well have done without it. I feel as if our guests will never leave!'

'Don't worry,' her husband told her. 'Some of the hardier souls are talking of going very soon. They saw that the rebels were defeated even before they reached here, and that their only interest was in finding fresh mounts. So they think the danger to honest citizens has become minimal.'

'And what about the *dis*honest ones?'

Sir Guy laughed. 'You mean the ones with baggage worth stealing, like Meester Koburg and the Doggetts?'

'Precisely. I must ask Flora whether her almanac can forecast peace as well as problems. It would be nice to know when we are likely to return to normal. Which reminds me,' she added astringently, 'now that you have deigned to return home, there is something you might do to help the girl.'

'*I?*'

'You may remember – oh, surely, Guy, you *must* remember? – I told you about her father sending the family back to England from Paris with some vague reference to an inheritance from

Flora's mother. He has not been in touch for over two years, which gives me no very great opinion of him. I suspect him of being one of those men who gives an order and simply *assumes* it will be carried out by someone or other with no further effort from him.'

'A common failing among men of high position,' Sir Guy agreed. 'Kings and senior officers of the crown are particularly prone to it.'

'Anyway, it seems to me that, if the man is still alive, he must be brought to a sense of his duty to his family.'

'And – er – ?'

'And, er,' she grimaced at him, 'I am sure that, war or no war, you know some fellow lawyer in Paris who might investigate on our behalf. The official court astrologer can hardly have disappeared without trace. There must be *someone* who knows where he is or what has happened to him!'

He had a great deal of overdue business to attend to, but he smiled wryly back at her. 'I will see what I can do. There have been violent disturbances in France and I would be reluctant to put a private messenger at risk, but I think Gervase might be able to help when he gets back. There are royal heralds going back and forth between England and France all the time . . .'

'Are there?'

'Of course! Our own royal council sends Norroy or Surroy king-at-arms with a few *pursuivants* to the court in Paris, saying, "We've won the war, why don't you admit it?" And they send him back with a message saying, "Pooh! Nonsense!" And a few weeks or months later, the same thing happens in the opposite direction. They send Mountjoie king-at-arms to us and we say, "Don't be ridiculous!" and so it goes on.'

'I didn't know that!'

'No reason why you should. Anyway, the heralds' tabards

more or less guarantee them safe passage, and I would guess that Gervase is well enough acquainted with one of our heralds or *pursuivants* to arrange for a message to be conveyed on a private basis to the right address. There is at least one of my fellow lawyers there who owes me a favour.'

Dame Constance looked at him admiringly.

'Just remember,' he concluded, 'it's not only a matter of the journey there and back. It's *when* a herald is due to set out, and *how long* he is kept waiting on the whim of the young French king's council. Whatever happens it will take weeks, perhaps months, before we have a result, if any.'

'Yes,' she said. 'I won't mention it to Mistress Flora until we know more.'

Chapter 7

1

FLORA prided herself on never losing her temper, which she considered a very juvenile thing to do, but when, two days after her consultation with Susanna, feeling self-conscious in the bright leaf-green kirtle her women had just made for her and which she was doing her best to hide under her everyday mud-coloured surcoat, she came face to face with Mistress Hildegarde, she lost her temper as if she had been doing it all her life.

They met in a shady arbour in a corner of the orchard. Hildy had no male arm to lean on, John (after their disagreeable encounter) being no longer at her beck and call, Meester Koburg staying as far away from her as she did from him, and Lord Gervase (of whom she still had hopes) having gone off somewhere with his prisoners. She was reduced to such an extremity of boredom that, taking only her maid for company, she had decided she might as well go and find a tree to sit under.

She was in the mood for trouble.

When, therefore, she encountered the dull and dowdy Mistress Flora strolling along the path towards her wearing a bright new gown, she reacted accordingly. Her eyebrows rising and her lips forming themselves into a neat little rounded 'O', she waggled her shoulders saucily and gave a suggestive little smile.

With a surge of unfamiliar fury, Flora raised a hand and smacked her smartly across the face.

Mistress Hildegarde shrieked, staggered back, and sat down with a thud on the grassy walk.

She went on sitting there for a moment, legs spread, mouth open, looking remarkably silly, but when her twittering maid ran to help her up she proved to be of sterner stuff than she looked. Inches shorter than Flora she might be, but she rushed at her and grabbing at the long chestnut hair with both hands, pulled at it for all she was worth.

Flora in turn let out a shriek and slapped furiously at the hands while Hildy raised a foot and began kicking her ankles. Flora tried to push her away but despite her superior height all that happened was that Hildy wound her fists more tightly into the long chestnut hair and tugged even harder and more painfully. Flora smacked her face again. And again. Then she tried to hook a foot round Hildy's kicking ankle, but Hildy promptly returned her own foot to the stability of the ground.

Slap, scratch, tug, kick, push, shove, gouge – and all, after the first shrieks, in a grim silence. It was a private fight and shockingly unladylike, and Hildy, with her social ambitions and despite her fizzing rage, was still conscious of the need not to attract attention from the small groups of men scattered talkatively at the far end of the orchard.

It seemed to go on for ever, though Flora later thought that it could not have been more than five minutes, and it was the weather that won in the end. Not the downpour that Dame Constance had been hoping for but a faint smirr of rain, the kind of rain that was little more than a dampness in the air but which Hildy knew to be fatal to her curls. With a gasp of horror, she abandoned her grip of Flora's hair and fled sobbing back along the path towards the castle.

Flora, her temper cooling rapidly, watched in astonishment as Mistress Hildegarde ran off, followed more slowly by her mystified maid.

Heads were turned as Hildy ran, but not until she reached the other end of the small bridge over the moat did anyone show any concern. And then there appeared as if from nowhere a young man holding out open arms to stop her.

It was Master Edwin, the pilgrim. 'What is wrong, Mistress?' he asked worriedly. 'You are sobbing as if your heart would break!'

Hildy could feel her curls uncoiling themselves to fly in thin straight wisps around her head, but he didn't seem to notice. 'It's nothing,' she gasped. 'I – er – I twisted my ankle, and it hurts. And it's raining and I don't like getting wet.'

At that point, hurried along by the sight of her mistress being accosted by a *man*, the maid caught up with them. Master Edwin, sufficiently reassured by Mistress Hildegarde's response to revert to his normal merry self, held out his hand to the maid, pointing at her scarf and, when it was given to him, draping it delicately over Hildy's head against the rain. He offered her his arm to lean on, 'to save pressure on your ankle,' he explained. 'Is it swollen? Does it hurt badly? Let me help you back indoors.'

'No, it's nothing, thank you, though I would be grateful for an arm to lean on.' She smiled artlessly at him. He was a lovely young man. What a pity that he was just a poor pilgrim. If only he had been rich!

2

Hildy made it abundantly clear to her maid that any talk of what had happened would lead to instant dismissal, if not worse.

Flora did mention the initial confrontation to Susanna, but not the fight that had followed; she did, however, become more amenable to the idea of having her hair cut. Indeed, she wanted it done now, today, not tomorrow or next week or next month.

Susanna, who had privately worked out a timetable for Flora's transformation, was alarmed. Gently, gently, she thought. Compromise.

'Why don't we,' she said, 'try the overall effect first, and see how you like it?'

'How?'

'Well, rather than cutting it immediately, which would be a bit – er – irrevocable, we could try dividing it into two long plaits and coiling them round your ears. The effect would be of shorter hair, but you wouldn't be committed.' No fillet or coif yet; those could come later. And with luck, Susanna thought, everyone – including Gervase, if he even noticed, for he could be remarkably obtuse about such things – would assume that Flora was simply tidying herself up rather than restyling herself.

'Mmmm.' Flora, though mystified by Susanna's seeming retreat from what she had been so decisive about only three days ago, felt the need to persevere with her own declared lack of interest in the whole process of being made over. She said, 'We could try, I suppose. But as I've said before, I hate being uncomfortable and if the plaits have to be wound tightly and anchored with pins . . .' She would then have a perfectly valid excuse for having it cut after all.

'Yes. But if you like the *general* look we can go ahead with the cutting!'

Both felt satisfied at having achieved their objectives – Flora of agreeing the likelihood of having her hair cut, and Susanna of having delayed it until a tactically better time.

Contentedly, Susanna said, 'Now, let us go and see what fabric Master Nicholas suggests for a light surcoat to go over that leaf-green kirtle, whose colour suits you wonderfully well!'

3

The rain having cleared again, leaving a welcome freshness in its wake, some of the castle's uninvited guests declared themselves ready to depart, notably those who claimed to have urgent business to attend to – among them a couple of minor royal officials who had been sent to the neighbourhood to buy wheat for the court; a group of students late for their lectures; and several carriers who had overdue deliveries to make. Heading for their quarters in the bailey to pack their saddlebags, they remembered the courtesies.

Since Gervase had not yet returned from St Albans, they had to express their gratitude for the hospitality of Vine Regis to Dame Constance, who accepted it graciously and wished them God speed.

'Let's hope they set an example,' she murmured to Sir Guy.

'The more people who publicly see them go, the better. Perhaps we should give them a hint by stationing ourselves right at the entrance to the Hall?'

So they did, but although a few more guests chose to take the hint – another official or two, and half a dozen small traders – the guests whom Dame Constance would most have liked to see go remained immune.

After a time, John drifted over to say, 'Why are you sitting here?'

'To encourage more of our guests to say thank you and good-bye,' replied his mother mildly.

'Oh, I see.'

And then it was William. 'You're not going to get rid of the Doggetts so easily. Not until Meester Koburg goes! They're still trying to pick his brain,' he warned cheerfully.

'Thank you.'

And then came the Doggett daughter, gliding up to John's side with all her curls in place and nothing but the sweetest innocence in her smile. John twitched slightly, still torn between attraction and disapproval, as she asked, 'When does the Lord Gervase return?'

'When he feels inclined,' John told her.

Hildy, slightly unnerved, failed to respond with the winsome little flutter of her eyelashes she would have given him a few days earlier. Her pa had been saying that they should soon be setting out for home, and she had achieved nothing and had no hope of achieving anything in the time left to her. She was feeling deprived. She had abandoned any thought of enticing the horrid, frightening Meester Koburg into making her his fourth wife, and she seemed to have offended John almost beyond hope of redemption. She could probably, she reflected, bring John back to heel, but not to the extent of offering her marriage. And although she had found Lord Gervase's courtesy to her quite encouraging, she could do nothing in that much more desirable direction unless he returned to Vine Regis almost at once. She sighed heavily. She had hoped for too much at the beginning of this visit, but she was a realist at heart. She must make a different plan, that was all. If she could succeed in extracting an invitation from Dame Constance to return to Vine Regis for a longer visit, on her own, that would be a start.

As she opened her mouth to speak, she was forestalled by the lookout's horn from the tower.

'*More* strangers?' exclaimed Dame Constance, frowning slightly.

There was a bustle down in the inner courtyard, of voices speaking in a foreign language, a bustle that did not wait for the castle steward to make his formal way down but began mounting the stairs unannounced.

Hamish, on the landing, was swept aside and there surged into the Hall a huge woman crying, '*Liebling! Mein liebling!*'

Like everyone else, Dame Constance stared, then, her eyes wide, said, 'What?'

The huge woman made a bee-line for Meester Koburg, who was rising to his feet, his arms held out. '*Ach! Liebchen! Meine Frau! Woher kommst du?*'

Dame Constance said again, 'What?'

On a choke of laughter, Sir Guy, who had a skimpy but useful knowledge of several tongues, murmured, 'My little darling!' His voice broke for a moment before he went on. 'My *little* darling! My wife. Where have you been? Where have you come from?'

'. . . *der Stahlhof* . . .'

'The Steelyard . . .'

William demanded, 'What's that?'

'It's the London hall and wharf of the Hanseatic League. Hush, now I've missed something.'

William gasped, 'So when he said he had lost his wife, he meant it literally. *Not* that she'd died! Oh ho!'

Dame Constance, trying hard to smother the mirth bubbling up inside her, carefully averted her eyes from Mistress Hildegarde, who was standing with a stunned expression on her face, and trenchantly addressed William and John in turn. 'If either of you so much as smiles, I will clap you in the dungeon for a week on bread and water!'

Hamish, meanwhile, was out on the landing conferring with the two servants who had accompanied Frau Koburg upstairs. One, who spoke comprehensible English, had come with the lady all the way from Lübeck, where it seemed that the Koburgs lived; and the other Hamish recognised as one of the English attendants Meester Koburg had brought with him. He, having observed the lady's small procession on the road from the village, had hurried to join it, hoping to be helpful.

While Meester Koburg and his wife were still hugging each other – something of an achievement, considering their girth – Hamish reported to Dame Constance on what he had learned.

'It seems the lady took a fancy to visit London while her husband was there, but arrived to find the peasants' revolt in full flood and her husband gone off to Stourbridge. She took shelter in the Steelyard and when the revolt was crushed, set off to follow him. Her servants asked at various points along the route in case he had taken refuge somewhere, and that's how they landed up here. Seems Meester Koburg knew that his wife had left Lübeck – don't ask me how! – but didnae know where she'd got to.'

The reunited little darlings seemed to take up half the space in the Great Hall, even when a disapproving Sir Walter, hoping that they would at least sit down, sent a page with bread and ale to refresh the lady.

Eventually, Meester Koburg remembered his manners and brought his wife to where Dame Constance still sat by the door.

'*Gnädige Frau*,' he began, and then corrected himself. 'Lady, this is my dear wife, who has come searching for me. I haff a favour of you to ask.' He looked as if the words were choking him, the small features in the large face making him look more than ever like an inflated baby, and a bad-tempered one at that.

She smiled graciously and said, 'Yes?'

'My wife is weary after her travelling. May she stay here for a day or two before we leave, so that she may recover?'

'Of course. And I will ensure that my Clerk of the Kitchen spices her food as he does yours, as I assume you would wish?'

'*Danke!*'

A day or two, Dame Constance thought, but not a moment more. And if William were to be believed, the departure of the Koburgs would immediately be followed by the departure of the Doggetts.

Bliss.

Mistress Hildegarde unclamped her rosebud lips at last and spoke, revealing more than she knew. 'Well,' she said, 'I think it is very strange. He didn't *behave* as if he had a wife, did he?'

4

William, of course, couldn't resist going in search of Susanna to regale her with this episode, and found her in her chamber, pinning up Flora's hair.

Flora's maid was holding a hand mirror up before her and Flora was looking critical and Flora-ish. Frederick, a reluctant witness, was standing twiddling his thumbs.

Knowing his duty, William said obligingly, 'That looks nice,' then, 'Susanna, you won't believe this, but . . .'

When he had finished, Susanna exclaimed, 'How extraordinary. One doesn't expect people to mean it literally when they talk of losing their wives or loved ones. It's just a way of saying they've died, or gone to God, or . . .'

Flora interrupted. 'Was Mistress Hildegarde there?'

'Yes.'

'How did she react?'

'She was speechless!'

Flora exclaimed, 'I imagine she was. Oh, how funny! How very funny!'

She laughed. And laughed again. And couldn't stop.

William and Susanna both stared at her, until Susanna put an end to it by jabbing a pin into one of the coils over her ears and eliciting an 'Ow!' in place of the hilarity.

5

William suddenly remembered that he had another mission. 'The Lady wanted me to find you, Mistress Flora. Can you come? She is anxious to see what the painter is up to.' He added, not quite under his breath, 'And so am I.'

Susanna, anchoring the second of Flora's plaits over her ear, exclaimed, 'In a minute, in a minute!' Then, standing back to survey her handiwork, 'Yes. Definitely yes.'

Flora, staring into the mirror, was determinedly noncommittal. 'Mmmm.'

She was slightly reassured when Dame Constance greeted her appearance in the Great Hall with fractionally raised eyebrows and an approving smile. Nothing, however, was said.

In part this was because William was in full flood and not to be silenced as they moved along the passage to the Chamber. He had been in to see the painter at work two or three times in the last five days, since Lord Gervase had given permission for him to enter unaccompanied.

'Not having had anyone to translate,' he reported, 'I have had to rely more on observation than detailed information. Signor Alberti wasn't very forthcoming and his English isn't easy to follow. But you'll be astonished when you see the colours that go to make up the flesh tones. To begin with, there's a greenish earth—'

'It's called *terre verte*,' Frederick interrupted officiously, but was ignored.

'—and white, and red lake which is sort of transparent, and the defining shadows are mostly green with a bit of ochre and a touch of red. And then . . .'

As they were passing through the anteroom, Frederick interrupted again. '*I'd* like to be one of his apprentices. They grind the colours and then – see! – put them into those separate little cockle shells. Sometimes they help Signor Alberti put the right amount of each of them on his palette. I like colours. I'd like to mix the flesh tones for him. Maybe he'd let me if I was an apprentice.'

Flora said sharply, 'Frederick, you wouldn't know all that if you hadn't been sneaking into the studio again without permission. Have you?'

Cheekily, he replied, 'No, 'course not!'

It was clear to everyone that he was lying, but just then the little procession reached the Great Chamber and it became necessary to make appreciative noises, because with the flesh tones beginning to be painted in there had been an unbelievable transformation. Gods and goddesses the figures might be, but suddenly they were real and human-looking even though the faces were still blank and undefined.

Sir Guy asked, 'And does he paint the robes in next?'

'*No, non ancora!*'

Flora dutifully enquired, not yet – why not?

When everything had dried, it appeared, it was necessary to lay a thin coat of varnish over all before painting the draperies. Why?

Signor Alberti, who did not like having his concentration broken into and still more disliked having to reply to complex technical questions from a mere female, reluctantly revealed that the robes were to be in blue, and to prevent the blue from turning black – as it often did when painted on walls – it was necessary to temper it with goat's milk and a little glue water.

And there he stopped.

'A little more explanation would be welcome,' said Sir Guy hopefully, but it was not forthcoming. So, after a few moments, he had to work it out for himself.

'Yes, I see. A colour bound with water and milk would presumably not adhere well to the oil paints underneath. So the two have to be kept apart with a coat of varnish in between. Interesting!'

From the large tray of brushes lying on the table beside him, Signor Alberti selected a small, soft pointed one and, having twirled it in a mixture of ochre and red, began applying a few fine additional strokes to the godly eyebrows.

William had previously noticed the number of brushes, but not their various shapes, sizes and qualities, round and square, fine and coarse, stiff and supple. Frederick, showing off, explained, 'Those big square-cut ones are for blending edges and softening contrasts of light and shade, and the long pointed ones are for plants and flowers, and these little ones, see . . .' he demonstrated, licking his fingers first to moisten the ermine hairs, 'you twirl them round to make a really neat point for fine detail!'

'No wonder I can never find you!' exclaimed his sister. 'You must be in here most of the time, disturbing Signor Alberti. You shouldn't, you know!'

'I don't disturb him. Mostly he doesn't even notice I'm here.'

Dame Constance put an end to this exchange. 'Flora, please tell Signor Alberti how delighted I am with his work and how closely it approaches what I – and Lord Gervase, of course – had in mind. A charming and beautifully executed gallery of gods! Everyone who sees it will be impressed.'

Signor Alberti was not yet ready to be complimented. 'Wait

till finished!' he replied. But there was a faint smirk on his dark, mobile face.

6

Gervase, returning from St Albans, cast a jaundiced eye round the Great Hall and said, 'Haven't you got rid of them yet?'

'Quite a few have gone,' Dame Constance told him, 'so don't complain. And you needn't sound as if we have been sitting around doing nothing while you have been busily away.'

'I see that Hanse fellow is still here . . .'

'*And* his wife,' replied Dame Constance melodiously. 'But they are leaving tomorrow.'

'I didn't know he had a wife. And those Doggetts are still here, too.'

'They will probably go soon after.'

'Well, I hope so. I ought to get back to court fairly soon, but I'd like to see all the livestock moved into their new quarters in the bailey before I go. And we can't move the livestock in until our uninvited guests have moved out. Give 'em a strong hint.'

'What an excellent suggestion,' agreed his mother amiably, 'though the painter and two of his senior apprentices will have to remain. Do I understand you are proposing to take charge of the removal?'

'I'll supervise, of course. The baker and the brewer and the cellarer first, because with them it'll be a major upheaval. We'll shift the livestock later, as and when convenient. But Sir Walter and Master Edward can probably handle everything. Could manage perfectly well without me, if the truth be told.'

'But not – er – so briskly.'

'No.'

Sir Guy, taking pity on his wife, intervened. 'Gervase, come

213

and tell me what happened in St Albans. Did you leave our prisoners in safe hands?'

They encountered Susanna and Flora on the stairs as they made for the quiet outdoors. Gervase gave only a nod of acknowledgement to Flora, but said, 'You still here, Susanna? I should have thought Piers would have summoned you home by now.'

Susanna was slightly flustered. 'Yes, well, I have a few things to do before I go.' Trust Gervase! He hadn't even noticed Flora's improved looks. It was time to move on. Not to the embroidered surcoat – not yet – but to a long, lightweight one with a wide neck and well defined side openings, to try and improve the proportions of Flora's narrow general shape. In a pretty mid-green. Master Nicholas had a charming sarcenet that would be just right.

Susanna was doing Gervase an injustice. He had in fact noticed that Flora was looking more presentable than usual and said so to Sir Guy.

'Is she?' replied that gentleman without interest, as if he knew nothing of the great makeover, or of Susanna's undeclared purpose in pursuing it. 'I hadn't noticed. Now tell me about St Albans.'

7

As hints went, the crack-of-dawn removal from the castle into the bailey of all the bulky impedimenta of baking and brewing and wine making – the sacks of meal, the kneading troughs, the tables, the fermentation vats, the casks empty and full – had a salutary effect on most of the remaining guests. And when, with much lowing and snuffling and clucking, the cattle began to be moved into their new cowshed, the pigs into their new piggery, and the hens and geese into their new houses, it proved decisive. None of the guests in the bailey wanted wandering pigs nosing around in their bedchambers, and the general noise at sun-up promised to be unbearable. Neither Gervase nor Sir Walter felt it needful to tell them that the livestock were only in transit, on their way to the meadows for the remainder of the summer.

By the time the day ended, most of the castle's remaining guests had either precipitately departed or were preparing to do so. 'There you are!' said Gervase triumphantly to his mother. 'All it needed was application and action. Mind you,' he added, untruthfully but with kindly intent, 'I don't know how we'd have managed without these two boys.'

William, cherishing a nasty bruise on his shin after an argument with a nanny-goat which had been determined to go her own way – just to spite him, he thought – raised a sardonic eyebrow, but Frederick, who had spent much of the day chasing hens, blushed pleasedly. Dame Constance noted the colour in his cheeks and wished it were to be seen more often. Benedetta had left on the day before the battle, and William had abandoned his experiments in the kitchen, but Frederick was still sporadically sick, grey-looking and tired, not every day but too often. His hero-worship of Gervase might give him a false energy, as did his interest in Signor Alberti's painting, but he was still far from well. It continued to be a mystery, and a worrying one.

8

Blanche and Eleanor, like most children, were reluctant to go to bed at their appointed hour in high summer when the daylight had not even begun to fade. When Alice went to see that they were tucked up for the night, she was not surprised to find that, despite their nurse's best efforts, they were still running around in the nursery, playing ball.

Startled by her entrance and exclamation, Eleanor failed to catch the ball Blanche had thrown to her, and it went straight out of the window.

'I'd better go and fetch it!' exclaimed Blanche, ever the optimist.

'No, you will not,' Alice told her firmly. 'You will go to bed at once. When I see you in bed, I will go down to the court-yard and find it, though it will probably have burst, falling so far.' The nursery was high in the north-east tower, and the ball was of leather stitched round a filling of tightly-packed feathers.

'If it has, Hamish will just have to make us another one.'

'Master McLeod has better things to do than replace toys you have foolishly broken.'

'He *likes* doing things for us. He says so. Often,' objected Blanche.

'That is because he is very kind. Now, into bed with you!'

'Oh, all right.'

As she descended the stairs, Alice reflected on Master McLeod's kindness and wished very much that he would ask her to marry him instead of treating her just as someone he liked and was vaguely fond of. When she reached the inner courtyard and found him there talking to Abbot Ralph and Sir Guy, her heart – as always – fluttered at his smile. She dropped a small curtsey and went on her way.

Leaving the inner for the outer courtyard, she began walk-ing round the Great Chamber tower, past the new buildings of the bailey on her right, and towards the north-east corner of Vine Regis's island where the children's ball must have landed.

It was odd and reassuring to find the courtyard empty of

all the strangers who had filled it for so many days. Most had gone, she knew, and the others – still at supper in the Great Hall – were preparing to go. She smiled to herself, passing the bakery and the brewery and the wine cellar, all of them within easy reach of the kitchens and the Mill Tower, and thought what a transformation, what an improvement, there had been in the course of a single day. Everything was different. Everything even smelled different. And then she laughed aloud as, passing the central section of the bailey, she approached the part where the livestock were housed. *Of course* it smelled different!

She began concentratedly scanning the grass for the childen's ball, whether complete or reduced to a few scraps of leather and a scattering of feathers.

But suddenly her concentration was broken by an awareness of movement to her right and, even as she turned, a man bounded out of one of the bailey buildings and grabbed her wrist, and it was so sudden and so alarming in the renewed calm of the Vine Regis evening that she screamed. His hand tightened on her wrist and he was swinging her towards him and shouting something that she didn't understand, something that sounded like, 'Latty, latty!'

'Leave me alone!' she cried, trying to free herself.

It had no effect, so she screamed again as loudly as she could. 'Help! Help!'

He was small and black-haired and incredibly strong. She had no idea who he was except that he was dangerous, and she began fighting furiously, hoping to break her hand free from his grasp. She screamed again in increasing panic, but he only pulled her closer and shouted louder.

There was a flurry of movement behind her, and abruptly the small dark man released his grip, staggered back, and fell to the ground.

Gasping with fear and tension, Alice found another man's arm protectively round her waist. Master McLeod's. The relief was almost unbearable. Dame Constance had warned her, when she first came to Vine Regis, that she must always be careful of wandering about alone, that men naturally tried to take advantage of unaccompanied girls. But she had never before had any trouble, and had almost forgotten the risks.

The small dark man struggled up towards a sitting position, looking much offended, clutching his jaw and saying something that neither Hamish nor Alice understood.

Hamish clenched his fist again, but Alice managed to say, 'No, please don't. I'm all right. I feel safe now. But who – who is he?'

'It's yon painter fellow. Have ye no' seen him before?'

'No. The children aren't allowed in the Great Chamber, so I haven't been in there since he arrived. And there have been so many other people around that I couldn't guess who he was.'

Sir Guy's voice behind them said, 'What happened, Alice?' He sounded concerned. 'Did he attack you?'

She was anxious not to cause trouble. 'I – er – I may have misunderstood. But he startled me by grasping my wrist and shouting and pulling me towards him. I was frightened. I didn't know what he wanted.'

The two men were perfectly able to guess.

That was the point at which Abbot Ralph, at his most stately, came within hearing. 'If the man attacked Mistress Alice for – ah – nefarious reasons, then he must be sent away from Vine Regis.'

Sir Guy groaned inwardly over what Dame Constance would have to say about a half-finished Great Chamber. But Ralph was right. If the man were a danger to females, then he must go.

'Let us therefore,' the abbot continued, turning to Signor

218

Alberti, 'enquire further.' Then, in Italian, 'You were shouting,' the young woman says. *What* were you shouting?'

The stress was altogether too much for the artist's English. '... *azzurro* ... *nero* ... *voglio latte o sia di capra o d'altro non importa* ...'

A faint shadow crossed Abbot Ralph's face. 'Goat's milk? It is something to do with his painting, with blue and black. He claims he is in need of goat's milk, though that of any other animal will do! He thought, from Mistress Alice's apron and veiled hair, that she might be the dairywoman on her way to the evening milking. Since she did not appear to grasp what he was saying, he followed the common practice of saying it more often and more loudly.'

Alice, who had donned her apron earlier and forgotten to remove it, was uncharacteristically offended. 'Dairywoman? Well, really!'

'Yes, yes, yes!' exclaimed Sir Guy, striking his forehead with the heel of his palm. 'I remember. If the blue on the walls is not to turn black, it must be tempered with goat's milk and glue water. What a relief! He is, of course, a physical man, but it seems to have been a simple misunderstanding.'

'If that is indeed the case,' declared Abbot Ralph, 'then I advise that apologies should be made.'

So Hamish apologised to the painter for hitting him and the painter apologised to Alice for laying hands on her, and Alice wondered whether she should apologise to the painter for misjudging him, but decided against it.

Hamish removed his arm from round her waist.

Weakly, she said, 'I was going to see whether I could find the girls' ball. It fell out of the nursery window.'

'I'll come and help ye look.'

'Oh! Would you?'

They walked, together but apart, towards the foot of the

nursery tower and found the ball. Its leather casing had burst and there were feathers scattered around everywhere.

Absently picking some of them up, Hamish said, not looking at her, 'Alice, how would ye feel about marrying me?'

Her dark head remained bent for a moment or two, but when, her lips slightly parted, she looked up, her eyes were as bright as if with tears. 'I would like it,' she breathed. 'I would like it very much.'

With some difficulty, he said, 'I didnae know until just now how much you meant to me.' Then he did look at her and she held out her hand to him, and he took it, his chest rising and falling with the pressure of emotion but the familiar smile back in his eyes. 'My lassie. My dear wee lassie!'

'I'm not a wee lassie. I'm nineteen!'

'And I'm twice that. Does it matter?'

'No, not at all.'

9

Dame Constance exclaimed, 'Object? Why should I object? I am delighted for you. Alice is a lovely girl, and it's high time you were married. Hamish, I am *so* pleased.'

It had been necessary to ask permission of Dame Constance, whose servant he was, and he would have been surprised and hurt if she had raised any objection. But he was touched by the warmth of her response, the genuine pleasure in her face and voice.

Theirs was a strange relationship, he sometimes thought. She had been seventeen or eighteen when the late Lord Nicholas had captured him, a boy of fifteen, in the Scottish wars and brought him home to Vine Regis, where he had quickly learned to speak English and then to make himself indispensable to the life of the castle. Dame Constance and he had virtually grown up together and he knew her mind better than anyone. The difference in rank was always there, shadowing but never diminishing the depth of their friendship. He would have died for her.

She said again, 'I am *so* pleased.'

Sir Guy nodded. 'Excellent news, Hamish. Congratulations.'

Dame Constance, thinking rapidly, said, 'Vine Regis will of course make Alice a gift of her wedding gown. I will speak to Master Nicholas about it. And you may have one of the new apartments over the Great Chamber as your living quarters. Talk to Master Thomas the joiner about what furniture you want made – though, knowing you, you will want to do much of it yourself!'

He grinned. 'Aye, that's so, Lady.'

She smiled back. 'And, on the whole, perhaps we should *not* ask Signor Alberti to paint the walls for you!'

'I don't know,' he objected. 'He did me a good turn today, even if he didnae mean to.'

'Yes, Sir Guy and Abbot Ralph have *both* told me! Alice has recovered from her fright, has she?'

He nodded.

'You may consider yourself honoured, because Abbot Ralph – who is feeling benevolent, though he says he cannot approve of fisticuffs – has offered to preside over your wedding ceremony.'

'My, my!'

'Or the castle chaplain could do so, if you would prefer it. Or Father Hoby in the village, if Alice feels that would be best. Have you spoken to her father?'

'No, she's of age. And I don't want Weaver John behaving as if we're beholden to him! As for Father Hoby, well . . .'

'Yes. A terrible little man. I'm sure you know that Abbot Ralph is leaving for Stanwelle in the morning, so you should

221

speak to him before he goes, if you want to take advantage of his offer.'

'I hope he's taking his pilgrims with him?'

She laughed. 'They have already gone, on foot, of course, so he expects to reach Stanwelle before them.'

'And give them one of his warm welcomes?'

'No doubt. Now, if you are to be married – when, next month? – I will arrange . . .'

Sir Guy, who had sat silent throughout, cleared his throat and, catching his eye, she grimaced at him. 'No! I am too much in the habit of arranging things! It is your and Alice's life we are talking about, and it is for you to make the decisions. But please bring Alice to see me in the morning.'

'Yes, Lady. And thank you.'

10

Hildy was depressed. Hildy was frustrated. Hildy was desperate.

Lord Gervase had returned to Vine Regis, but she had been denied any opportunity to charm him. Indeed, she had been almost brushed out of his way as he had spent the day striding back and forth between the castle and the bailey, awarding her no more than a nod of recognition in passing.

And now her father was declaring that it was time to go – or would be when Meester Koburg and Frau Koburg had left. Tomorrow or the day after.

'But, pa, it's lovely here. Can't we stay a little longer?'

'We've already outstayed our welcome, if I'm any judge, and if you think I'm going down on my bended knee to ask, I'm not.'

Her ma said, 'You'll like to be home again, won't you, with

all your own things around you!' It wasn't a question; it was a statement.

She couldn't say, 'No,' or there would be trouble. And although she had told Dame Constance how sad she would be to go, Dame Constance had not responded with an invitation to stay, or to return.

It had all looked so promising at first, but nothing had turned out right. Meester Koburg had not only been horrible but, shockingly, had proved to have a wife already. John de Clair had been charmed by her to begin with and had then stopped being charmed, not only because he thought she was a flirt but deep down, she suspected, because she was just a merchant's daughter and therefore unworthy of him. As for Lord Gervase, he didn't know her, hadn't had time, and would probably also think that she was beneath him. Though *that* wouldn't matter if she could have made him fall in love with her, as she was sure she could have done, given time.

A voice at her side said, 'I've a message for you.'

It was Master Burnell, with whom she had barely exchanged a dozen words since she had been here.

'A message? For me?'

She was a silly, empty-headed chit from all he had seen of her, but that did not release William from his duty.

He said irritably, 'Yes, for you! It's from that pilgrim, Master Edwin.'

'But he's gone away.'

'He wouldn't have had to send you a message if he hadn't gone away!'

'Oh. No, I suppose not. What is the message?'

'He says, "Wait".'

'Wait. Is that all? What for?'

William shrugged.

'What does he mean?'

'How should *I* know? That's all he told me.'

'But how *can* I wait?'

William was exasperated. 'I don't know! I don't even know Master Edwin. He just happened to catch me when he was leaving. I was passing.'

'But the pilgrims have gone to Stanwelle. How long will it take them to get there?'

'On foot? I have no idea.' Tired of the catechism, William said, 'Now, if you'll excuse me . . .'

'Oh, yes. Thank you.'

She couldn't understand it. Why should the poor but carefree young man who looked like a marmalade cat and didn't seem to care about appearances have asked her to wait? She had liked him, but . . .

11

It seemed good to Gervase next morning, having heard about Alice's encounter with Signor Alberti, to pay a swift visit to the painter and impress on him that grabbing at girls, whatever the motive, was unacceptable at Vine Regis. It was not, he believed, a matter of words; more the conveying of a sense of authority and responsibility. His own height and air of lordship should suffice to bring the fellow to heel. He needed no translator.

'Morning,' he said.

Signor Alberti tossed his head.

Carefully slow, Gervase went on, 'Here at Vine Regis our women are accustomed to going about their business in safety.'

Signor Alberti tossed his head again. 'Was a meestake. A mees- a meesunderstanding. Ees all.'

'It must not happen again.'

Signor Alberti snorted. 'Will not,' and continued with his varnishing.

Patronisingly, Gervase said, 'Your painting is coming along well,' then, turning to leave, almost tripped over Frederick, who had been listening carefully to how the Lord Gervase imposed his will on others.

Gervase looked at him, 'Why are you following me around?'

'I'm interested.'

There seemed to be no answer to that. Gervase looked at the boy more closely. There was a smear of white at the corner of his mouth. 'Wipe that milk away,' he said.

Frederick drew his thumb and forefinger across the corners of his mouth and then licked his fingers.

'That's better,' Gervase told him. 'Cleanliness is very important.'

Then, with Frederick following close behind, he left the Chamber to join Dame Constance at breakfast in the Great Hall.

'I've made it clear to the Italian fellow that we won't stand for him frightening our women,' he told her.

'Have you? How helpful,' she said.

He laughed suddenly. 'That's a nasty bruise Hamish gave him. He's a good painter, mind you. I like what he's done so far. Did goddesses wear jewellery, do you know? He's drawn some in.'

'I have no idea.'

'No. Well, I'll have a look in another day or two when the varnish is dry. I want to see what blue he's using for the robes. We don't want it too bright, do we?'

'No. It might keep you awake at nights.'

Gervase usually knew when his mother was teasing him, so he smiled dutifully and said, 'Ha, ha!'

Master Edwin returned from Stanwelle not on foot but on horse-back. He rode well, Gervase noted, and looked better-dressed and cleaner than when he had left.

'You back?' Gervase said, as the young man dismounted.

This statement of the obvious produced a slightly worried grin. Then, 'Yes, I was wondering whether Master and Mistress Doggett were still here?'

Controlling his revulsion, Gervase said, 'I believe so.'

'And – er – young Mistress Hildegarde?'

'Her, too. There's talk of them leaving after dinner today.'

'Oh.'

Helpfully, Gervase added, 'If it's Mistress Hildegarde you want, I think I saw her going into the orchard.'

Master Edwin's grin lit up the courtyard. 'Thank you.'

And off he went, leaving Gervase with eyebrows raised and speculations chasing through his mind. But it was none of his business, so he went off to talk to Sir Guy about a small legal matter to do with a lease on one of the Vine Regis manors.

Master Edwin found Mistress Hildegarde at the far end of the orchard, absently tearing petals from a daisy and looking downcast. Her maid was nowhere in sight.

He said in a thrilling tone, 'You waited!'

Looking up at him, she refrained from replying that the choice had not been up to her. Instead, she smiled waveringly. 'Why did you want me to wait?'

He went down on his knees. 'I have something to ask you.'

'Oh, have you?'

'Yes, I . . .'

He was looking lover-like, she thought, wide-eyed and breath-less, which was strange since they were barely acquainted. She liked him very much, but that meant nothing. He was poor, and not at all the kind of man she would be prepared to marry. Or be allowed to marry.

Seeing the blankness of her gaze, he rose to his feet and turned away. Speaking with his back to her, he said, 'We scarcely know each other, but I loved you the moment I saw you!'

'Oh.'

'Could you love me, do you think?'

Her heart was pounding away under the silken gown. 'I – er – I might.' And then more strongly, 'But it wouldn't do. I'm awfully expensive.'

He swung round. '*Why* wouldn't it do? Somewhere under your well-drilled exterior, there is a real, mischievous human being. I saw it one day when we were talking to Dame Constance – just a glimpse, no more. But if you no longer needed to behave with propriety, if you could learn to be yourself . . .'

Down on his knees again, he took her hands. 'Say you will. Please say you will!'

'I can't. I can't change myself.'

'I don't ask you to change yourself. Just to *be* yourself.'

'But you haven't any money,' she wailed. Even as she said it, she knew how crude and vulgar it sounded.

He looked at her, his expression serious. 'If I had, would it make a difference?'

If there was one thing she was sure of, that was it. 'Yes,' she said.

He hesitated, but he knew enough of the world and of women to accept that security was of primary importance. A woman's only security lay in the coffers of the man on whom she depended.

'I am not poor,' he said after a moment.

'But . . .'

'I may look it,' he admitted, 'but pilgrims have to, unless they wish to risk being attacked and robbed.'

She was not convinced. In any case, not being poor was a very different thing from being rich.

'Don't worry,' he said. 'I am rich.'

'*Rich?*' It came out as a squeak, and he laughed.

'Not quite yet. But my grandmother promised to bequeath all her worldly goods to me if I would make the pilgrimage on her behalf. And I have made the pilgrimage, and she was dying when I set out. In a few weeks, and when all the formalities have been completed, I will be rich.'

'Ooooh.'

'*Now*, will you marry me?'

'Rich? Really, truly rich?'

'Yes. Really, truly rich.'

It made all the difference in the world. She had never expected to be offered marriage by someone who was not only rich but likeable – lovable!

Her hand at her throat, she gasped. 'Do you mean it?'

'I mean it. Will you marry me?'

'Yes.'

'May I kiss you?'

'Yes.'

He kissed her, and she liked it, the warm feel of his lips on hers. She nestled comfortably into his arms. He smelled much nicer than horrible Meester Koburg; of horses rather than ginger and garlic.

After a while, a difficulty occurred to her. 'Oh dear, what will pa say?'

'Won't he like it? Won't he think me a suitable husband for his lovely little daughter?"

'No. He'll think you're not respectable. He has a suspicious nature, you see. Even if you give him proof of your

228

grandmother's legacy, he'll think it's fraudulent. He'll be furious. He'll cut me off without a penny.'

'Does it matter?'

'Not at all. Not if you're rich. Oh, how different life will be, how much, *much* better!'

She jumped to her feet, took his hands, and they danced laughingly together round the orchard bench as if it were a maypole.

At last, breathlessly, he said, 'Do you want to stay and face him and tell him? Or will you come with me now, today, and be free of it all?'

She stared at him for a frozen moment, then on a sudden wave of happiness exclaimed, 'Let's go now!' and they ran hand in hand back through the orchard and into the courtyard, and Master Edwin mounted the horse he had borrowed from Stanwelle and, with Mistress Hildegarde perched behind, rode off over the drawbridge with no more farewell than a merry wave of the hand to Hamish, who happened to be passing and interestedly watched them disappear into the distance.

13

There was a grand fuss when the Doggett daughter did not turn up for dinner. The unfortunate maid was sacked on the spot for having failed to keep an eye on her mistress. That her mistress had instructed her to stay indoors and see to the packing was ignored.

Lord Gervase remarked casually that the pilgrim fellow had come looking for the young woman and had found her in the orchard, he thought. More than that he did not know.

'Oh dear,' murmured Dame Constance, 'I hope she remembered to take her comb and her curling iron with her.'

Loftily, Gervase remarked that if the Doggetts had time to waste, they were at liberty to search the castle.

The Doggetts' enquiries at first failed to elicit any useful answers, although every soul in the castle except for themselves knew by then that Mistress Hildegarde had gone riding off with *a man*. It might have been different if the Doggetts had not been so dislikeable. Only when they questioned a lad in the stables who was not acquainted with them did they discover that a young man and a young lady had ridden off together going Woldesb'ry way. 'Wur on a gelding come fr'm Staaanwelle. I knowd 'im.'

Master and Mistress Doggett argued loudly and at length over whether they should pursue the fugitives to Stanwelle or to Woldesbury. It was not to be until several weeks later, by which time they were at home and had reached the 'She's no daughter of mine!' stage, that they received a message from Hildy, announcing her marriage and revealing that she had gone in quite another direction, to her newly wealthy husband's home at Etchingham. *Wherever that might be!* snarled her pa.

Meanwhile, Flora, in a very Christian spirit, said that she wished Mistress Hildegarde well, remarking only that, with parents like hers, it was not surprising that the girl should have developed into a scheming little minx.

14

With the departure of the dreadful Doggetts just after that of the equally dreadful Koburgs, Vine Regis began to feel like itself again.

Plumping herself down on a stool beside Gervase in the Great Hall, Susanna said brightly, 'All this romance in the air! Don't you feel you are missing something?'

'No.'

'Well, you are.'

He glanced up from the notes and calculations in which he was engrossed. 'Are what?'

'*Missing something!*'

'Oh. You women and your obsession with romance! I'll never understand it.'

'Well, you might at least try.'

'Why?'

Breathing heavily through her neat little nose, she retorted, 'Because it's high time you remarried, and you have to make *some* concessions to women's weaknesses.'

'Nonsense.' It was said kindly rather than critically. 'You know perfectly well that romance has nothing to do with marriage.'

She herself had been betrothed to Gervase after his first wife's death and could have – should have – married him three years ago, but then Piers had come into her life and she had learned that romance had *everything* to do with marriage.

Not everyone was so fortunate, and she knew it. She sighed. 'I know marriage is a business arrangement, but on a personal level it's a partnership. Two parts of a whole. I mean, look at your mother and Sir Guy.'

'Ah, but they're very special people!'

'We're *all* very special people. Everyone in the world is special in one way or another.'

He laughed. 'I wouldn't choose to argue that in a court of law!'

'Perhaps not. What I am trying to say is that, romantic passion may not be in *your* nature . . .'

'It isn't,' he assured her.

'. . . but if you love, or even just like your partner, the world becomes a much more warming and welcoming place.'

She couldn't very well remind him that she understood his first wife, Felicia, to have been a young woman of such paralysing refinement that she had drained the vitality from everyone around her, even from the air they breathed, which would have been enough to put any man off love and marriage.

Disconsolately, she added, 'And you feel lost when you are separated.'

'I can see that. Why have you not gone rushing back to Lanson, now that all's safe?'

'Because Piers is away in the south looking at a barbary mare he's thinking of buying for the stud, and he wants me to stay here until he gets back.'

'Poor Susanna!' Gervase rose to his feet and stretched. 'Well, if you have finished giving me the benefit of your advice, I am off to see how the painter is getting on with varnishing the Great Chamber. And then on Friday I have to set out for court.'

'So we won't see you again for another three months?' It might almost have been deliberate, Susanna thought with exasperation, although she was aware that the official routine was three months at court and three months at home.

'It depends,' Gervase replied. 'The revolt has thrown everyone's timetable out, so I may be back sooner – or later.'

'Very helpful!' Susanna said tartly.

15

Signor Alberti was perched on a ladder close by the fireplace in the Chamber, hard at work.

'Is the varnish dry already?' Gervase planted a hand on the wall by the door and found himself adhering to it. 'No, it isn't.'

Detaching his hand, he left a neat palm print on the fleshy posterior of a very small satyr.

'Ees not dry *there*!' snapped the painter. 'Ees dry *here*! Here I try effect.'

Gervase tilted his head to study the effect of the high-waisted, low-necked blue gown on the figure of a reclining Venus – or Ariadne, or whoever she was – and decided that he liked it. Or was the blue perhaps a little too strong? If the figures round the room were all clad in that same blue, it was going to be overpowering.

He said hopefully, 'Different blues, paler blues, for the other figures, and white edges to the robes?'

'No. Gold.' The painter fluttered his fingers commandingly in the direction of the apprentice who was scooping yellow paint from one of the cockle shells onto the rectangular wooden palette. '*Oropiumento, si. E pennello fine.*'

Gold wasn't going to quieten the blue down. Gervase scanned the walls, trying to visualise the overall result. He needed Mistress Flora to make his views clear to the painter.

Turning back to Signor Alberti who, eyes still on his Venus (or Ariadne), was blindly holding out a hand for palette and brush, he saw that his own faithful shadow, Frederick, was 'helping' by twirling a small brush in the yellow paint intended for the gold edging. But the paint seemed to be too thick for the brush to be shaped into the delicate point required so, while Gervase watched frowningly, the boy used his fingers to improve it. He handed the brush up to Signor Alberti with a sigh of satisfaction, and then began licking the surplus paint off his fingers.

Gervase, offended, said, 'No. Wipe your fingers with this!' and held out the linen handkerchief that men at court had begun to adopt, following the young king's example. But before the boy, still licking, could make use of it, Signor Alberti glanced down at him, stared at him for a surprised moment, and then

233

let out a loud squawk of, 'No, *no, raggazzo cattivo!* Ees bad. Ees *oropiumento*. Ees *velenoso!*'

Gervase said, 'Speak English, please!' but Signor Alberti only waved his hands about in seeming horror.

'I was just helping!' wailed Frederick. 'Why is he shouting at me?'

Striding over, Gervase forcibly wiped the boy's hands and mouth and said, 'Come with me!'

Then he marched him off in search of Mistress Flora.

16

They found her immersed in astrological charts, looking puzzled. Frederick's destiny was seemingly much improved, which was a relief, but she had just cast her father's horoscope – which she had fallen into the habit of doing occasionally – and could make no sense of it at all. He was alive, certainly, but all around him was confusion.

She was startled when, dragging a reluctant Frederick by the hand, Lord Gervase arrived beside her and declared, his formal courtesy in temporary abeyance, 'This brat of a brother of yours!'

'Ye-e-es?'

'Just now, in the Great Chamber, he was licking some yellow paint off his fingers. Signor Alberti got very excitable about it. Horrified. Jabbered away in Italian. I didn't understand a word he said, but his reaction was extreme. Almost fearful. It occurred to me to wonder whether the paint might be what has been making Frederick sick and causing everyone so much worry.'

Frederick said, 'But that's the first time – ever – that I've licked the *yellow* paint!'

Gervase looked at him piercingly. 'And what about other

234

colours? What about that white the other day? I thought it was milk, but it wasn't, was it?'

Sulkily, 'No.'

Gervase said, 'I suggest, Mistress Flora, that you take Frederick to discuss all this with Signor Alberti. Perhaps you should ask Master Henry the apothecary to go with you. If any of the paints are toxic, it must be well known – to painters at least – and the apothecary might be able to match Frederick's symptoms to the known dangers.'

Thoughtfully, Flora said, 'He only spoke of poisoning in general when I first consulted him. But I suppose . . .' Turning to her brother, she said sadly, 'Oh, Frederick! How *could* you?'

'It was me that was sick,' he pointed out defensively.

'But didn't you even *think*? You're old enough to put two and two together.'

'No, I didn't think. You all kept talking about eating this and drinking that, and I wasn't eating or drinking the paint. I was only licking the tiniest drop of it, and it tasted pretty nasty, I can tell you.'

She turned back to Gervase. 'I cannot say how grateful I am to you.'

He was embarrassed. More than that, he was touched – an unfamiliar sensation. 'I don't deserve your gratitude. If the paints prove to be the source of Frederick's sickness, I take no credit for discovering it. I simply happened to be there when the possibility presented itself.'

'You are much too modest.'

'Not at all.' He had stiffened up again, but she recognised now that there was quite a kind and considerate person under all the starch. He said, 'Forgive me, I must leave you now. I have matters to attend to. But you will let me know the result of your talk with Signor Alberti?'

'Of course.'

17

'*Oropiumento?*' Flora echoed doubtfully. 'The word doesn't mean anything to me.'

'In English it is "orpiment",' the apothecary told her grimly. 'Which is to say yellow arsenic.'

'*Arsenic!*'

'Yes. And the *biacha* of which Signor Alberti speaks is not just white paint but white lead.'

Faintly, she said, 'And the green *verderame* must be verdigris?'

'Yes. In other words, copper rust. Shall we go on?'

'No! Arsenical poisoning and lead poisoning are quite enough. Is verdigris as dangerous?'

'Probably only in the longer term. But now you will understand why I was originally unable to make a satisfactory diagnosis of your brother's illness. There has been a confusion of symptoms because of the different poisons, and he has of course been consuming only the smallest quantity of each and at different times. The first attack was the worst simply by the fact of its being the first. Since then his system has to some extent become accustomed.' He paused before concluding, 'Very satisfactory.'

Flora stared at him for a moment. *Satisfactory?* But then she realised that he was rejoicing at having found justification for his earlier failures of diagnosis.

She turned to Signor Alberti and tried to discover politely why he had not stopped Frederick from poisoning himself. Her politeness was wasted.

Signor Alberti embarked on an impassioned tirade of which the essence was that Frederick was *uno raggazzo cattivo* who was always hanging around in the Great Chamber watching the artist at work or in the studio watching the apprentices.

Today was the first occasion on which the signor had observed the boy licking paint from his fingers, and he had hastened to make it clear to the lord that the paint was poisonous. But perhaps such a *raggazzo cattivo* would be the better for being poisoned!

When the tirade ended, Flora told Frederick that Signor Alberti said he was a bad boy, with which judgement she heartily agreed. 'But I need to know why no one has seen you licking paint from the brushes or from your fingers before, because you must have done it often. The truth, now, Frederick!'

She had to drag it out of him. 'I want to be a painter,' he whined, 'you *know* I've always wanted to be a painter . . .'

'Only since we've come here!'

'No, always. And I need to practise. But I don't have any brushes . . .'

'So?'

'So when I was in the studio I got a piece of parchment and when the apprentices weren't looking, I dipped my finger in the paint and used that to draw with. I'm getting quite good at it.'

Finger painting.

It was all so simple.

She sighed. 'Perhaps when we get back to Coteley I can find someone to give you lessons.'

'Oh, good. And then I can have some brushes of my own.'

18

This last made Gervase laugh aloud when Flora reported it to him.

'Children are resilient, aren't they?' he remarked to his mother later.

'More so than their elders,' she replied. 'Poor Flora has had a very trying time with him. She will probably find it hard to stop worrying.'

'Mmmm.' After a reflective moment, he went on, 'She's a nice girl, isn't she? As well as being clever, I mean. And she's better-looking than I thought when she first came here. I don't know why. Perhaps it's because she's tidied herself up a bit – living up to your and Susanna's example.'

'It's possible,' agreed Dame Constance with a private chuckle. Susanna's ingenious matchmaking seemed to be working well in one direction at least. Whether it would work with Flora was another matter entirely.

Chapter 8

1

B Y THE time three weeks had passed, Frederick was quite restored to health, and everyone felt the better for it. Even Flora stopped looking as if all the cares of the world were upon her shoulders. Her newly elegant shoulders. The weather having turned cooler, over the leaf-green kirtle she now wore a mid-green sideless surcoat shaped in to the waist, with a low wide neckline, open armholes stretching from shoulder to hips, and a front panel decorated down the centre of its length with a full row of gilt buttons. It flattered her figure, as a satisfied Susanna had known it would. And since the plaits coiled over her ears were not only uncomfortable but interfered with the wearing of her spectacles, she had had her hair cut to chin length and curved boyishly under. Flora herself was so much cheered by Frederick's recovery that she even admitted to liking her new look.

During the course of those weeks, Dame Constance, relieved

of the burden of the castle's unwanted guests, had been indulging in some constructive thought about finishing touches in the decoration of the Great Chamber.

To Flora, she said, 'I have one or two ideas that I would like to discuss with Signor Alberti, who is in the very last stages of his work. Will you come with me? It may become a little complicated, so I will need your help. Your most tactful help!'

'I will do my best.' Flora smiled mischievously and Dame Constance twinkled back in response.

'You know, when you first came here,' she said, 'I found myself wondering if you *could* smile. What an improvement.'

Flora blushed faintly. 'I know. I was depressed and I must have been incredibly depressing for everybody else. But despite my worries about Frederick, I have been much, much happier here than at Coteley, and I thank you for it.'

They had reached the entrance to the Great Chamber, and Dame Constance said, 'It has been a pleasure. Now, tact at the ready, if you please.'

Signor Alberti was delicately intent on the face of Bacchus, touching in the fine and final details of eyebrows, lashes, and nostrils in ochre and lightening them with pure white.

One or two of the other faces were still blank and featureless. 'What we need to know first,' Dame Constance murmured to Flora, 'is whether Signor Alberti is good at catching a likeness.'

Flora gave a little choke of laughter. 'I should be very surprised indeed if he said he wasn't.'

'So should I.'

'I will start, I think, by telling him how impressed the Lady is by the vitality of his portraiture . . .'

Signor Alberti listened, unmoved, while he signed off the second Bacchic eyebrow with a flourish and then, turning to his visitors, embarked with enthusiasm on the subjects of portrait-ure in general and drawing from the life in particular.

It took more than frequent interventions of, '*Si, si, grazie!*' from Flora to stem the flow, but in the end he talked himself out.

Turning to Dame Constance, Flora said, 'As we guessed, he is a genius, no less, at catching a likeness. To put it briefly, it is a matter of painting the soul, the passions, the strength, the weakness, the character – all through the hint of a smile, a twist of the lips, the raising of a brow, a sparkle in the eyes. Shall I go on?'

'No, thank you. Does he need the living presence before him?'

'That depends.'

'Hmmm. Well, perhaps he would set about representing the soul, the passions, and all the rest of it, of my son Gervase.'

Flora's eyebrows rose. 'I can't think the Lord Gervase would approve of having his soul painted on the walls.' She giggled.

'No, and that is why I am not going to tell him. It simply occurred to me that, just as the images in church windows often immortalise those who have contributed to their cost, so the head of the family should be immortalised in paint. Signor Alberti has seen Gervase often enough. Could he incorporate his features from memory? I think that Mars, god of war – the figure with the helmet on the left – would be an appropriate identity for him.'

Signor Alberti had no difficulty with that. His visual memory was faultless and the lord's features were strong and angular.

'I think also,' Dame Constance remarked, 'that it would make Blanche and Eleanor very happy to be painted. As those two cherubs, perhaps.' She waved a hand at the two small figures floating in the sky above Venus and Mars, scattering what appeared to be rose petals over them. 'The girls can come and sit for Signor Alberti to draw them, since their childish faces are unformed and he can hardly be expected to memorise them.'

That also was agreeable to the signor, and Dame Constance knew that Blanche would be ecstatic.

'Shouldn't you be represented, too, Lady?' Flora asked.

'As whom? I am not of an age for Venus or Ariadne . . .'

'You should be the mother of the gods! I can't remember her name.'

'No, but she was undoubtedly as fat as she was fertile. Furthermore, if memory serves, she had some very reprehensible habits. I would prefer not to be associated with her.'

Flora's eyes had been straying and suddenly she laughed aloud. 'I've just seen – look, there, by the window! – an attendant nymph, or *half* an attendant nymph peering out from among the foliage. Oooh, wouldn't Mistress Hildegarde be cross if she knew she had been reduced to near-invisibility!'

'I wondered when you were going to notice,' Dame Constance responded dryly. 'Now, only one thing remains, and I doubt if Signor Alberti will like it. But is there some very small and unobtrusive corner of this very large painting where Frederick might be permitted to make his mark?'

Flora gasped. 'After all the trouble he's caused everyone? No, no. You musn't reward him!'

'It's not a reward. I just think it would make him so happy to wield a real brush loaded with real paint. If he could point to, say, Jupiter's toenail and say, "*I* painted that".'

'It would make him the happiest boy on earth!'

Signor Alberti was not enamoured of the idea of letting the *raggazzo* loose on the godly toenail – which carried its own weight of soul, passion, and character – but ultimately conceded that it might not ruin his great work if the boy were permitted to paint a final layer of shadow, no more than an inch or two, on the hem of one of the robes. In the darkest corner of the room, naturally.

'Finally,' said Dame Constance, a picture of innocence, 'would you ask him when he expects to be finished?'

'I don't think I dare! Oh, well . . .'

2

'At least we've escaped alive,' Flora said cheerfully as they left. 'He seemed to think we were criticising him for being slow – though he's been quite quick, really, hasn't he?'

'Amazingly so.'

'Is there some reason, other than a natural desire to be rid of him, for wanting to know when he will finish?'

'Yes, of course. We are proposing to give an extravagant reception for Hamish and Alice when they marry, and it seems to me that the Great Chamber would be the perfect place for it.'

'What a lovely idea! And so – er – symbolic.'

Dame Constance raised an enquiring eyebrow.

'Symbolic of newness and freshness and beginnings and . . .'

'Yes, I see. I hadn't thought of it that way. Anyway, not only does the painting have to be finished, but the carpentry, too. The benches and shelves, in particular.'

'Have they decided where the actual ceremony is to be held?'

Dame Constance smiled. 'They both feel that Abbot Ralph's offer to perform it at Stanwelle would be altogether too grand for them. And though Alice says she *ought* to be married in the village church, she quite understandably draws the line at having her wedding presided over by dreadful little Father Hoby. So our own chaplain, Father Sebastian, will marry them quietly in the chapel here. It is the best solution, I think.'

'I'm sure it is.' Then, 'Oh dear, I've just thought – when the painter finishes, you won't need me any more, will you? I will have no more excuse for staying.'

'My dear, you must stay for as long as you wish! I enjoy having you here. And you must certainly stay for the wedding at least.'

Flora's lips quivered. 'Thank you. You are so kind to me.'

Dame Constance thought, but did not say, *Little do you know!* Sir Guy had heard nothing about Flora's father from his associate in France and assured Dame Constance that it was too soon to expect a reply. 'I don't want to pursue it with Gervase,' he had said, 'since I didn't tell him the content of my message, and you know what he's like about sticking to the rules – utilising official privilege for private purposes, tut, tut! In any case, all France is smouldering on the edge of revolt. We cannot be sure that our heralds have even succeeded in reaching Paris or Vincennes or Meaux, or wherever the court may happen to be. So, have patience.'

Which made it all the more surprising that, when the lookout's horn announced 'Strangers approaching' four days later, the strangers should turn out to be Flora's father with his retinue.

3

Flora, who had no great interest in the wonders of Nature, was standing by the roadside hedge with Susanna, dutifully laughing at the antics of a blackbird which was all too clearly exasperated by the ever-open yellow beaks of its hungry infants.

'They look just like buttercups opening and closing,' said Susanna.

'Buttercups don't make so much noise.'

'Oh, look! She's found a lovely big fat worm for them.'

Susanna turned towards Flora to ensure that she had noticed, but Flora had gone.

Gasping, 'Father? It's my father!' she had picked up her skirts and was running in a most unladylike way towards the group of half a dozen horsemen approaching from the east, crying, 'Father! Father!' as she went.

The tall, middle-aged, weary-looking man leading the group hauled on his reins and slipped from the saddle, holding out his arms to his daughter, who ran straight into their embrace.

They walked the short remaining distance to the castle, and Susanna could hear Flora's questions tumbling out.

'When did you leave Paris? Why did we hear nothing from you? Are you well? How did you know I was here?'

'One thing at a time, my child. I have come from Coteley Valence. Where is the boy? Where is Frederick? He has been ill, I am told.'

'I don't know where he is at this moment, but he has fully recovered. Oh, Susanna, this is my father, Maître Chandos. And father, this is the Lady Susanna Whiteford of Lanson, which you must have passed on your way here.'

'I believe so.'

And then he had to be formally greeted in the courtyard by Sir Walter, and relieved of his helmet and sword, and led up to the Great Hall where, almost at once, Dame Constance and Sir Guy came to welcome him. Both wore an expression that it would have been hard for anyone other than themselves to disentangle into its component parts, being equally compounded of pleasure, embarrassment and guilt. Flora saw only the pleasure.

Dame Constance said, 'You must be tired, Maître Chandos, and no doubt hungry. We ourselves have just finished supper, but I will have you taken up to one of our guest chambers and have food brought to you. I am sure you and Flora have much to talk about. And afterwards, when you have rested, perhaps you would give us the benefit of your company?'

'I will be happy to do so.'

In the handsomely appointed bedchamber in the west-facing range of the castle, Maître Chandos ate his way appreciatively through a bowl of fish pottage, a spit-roasted spring chicken, and a dish of blamanger, while his daughter talked without cease until, at last, she said shamefacedly, 'Why have you not stopped me? You must be exhausted.'

'I am tired,' he admitted. 'Too many days on horseback. I shall lie down and rest for a little, I think.'

He went straight off to sleep and slept all through the evening and throughout the night. Flora had to restrain Frederick physically from rushing in and bouncing on his bed, crying, 'Papa! Papa!'

4

In the morning, with Flora and Frederick, Maître Chandos attended High Mass in the castle chapel and then waited, in conversation with Sir Guy, while Dame Constance had her routine pre-breakfast conferences with her household officers.

'From what we hear,' Sir Guy said, 'the French king's death last September must have sent all the seigneurs, councillors and prelates into an extreme state of political – er – perturbation, as royal deaths are wont to do.'

Maître Chandos's lips twisted sardonically. 'You might so describe it. And since, at the gates of heaven, even kings are conscious of the impression they will leave on earth, it is not unusual for them to bequeath to their heirs duties it is impossible to fulfil.'

'In this case, the abolition of the hearth tax?'

'Yes. The basic property tax on which the whole function-ing of the state depends. Quite impractical to abolish it, of course. It deprives his successor – in the present case, the Regent, since the new king himself is only twelve years old – of the means of governing. The promise naturally caused wild excitement among the people, and even more excite-ment when they realised that the hearth tax would have to be replaced by other, newer taxes ... Ah, well. It has all been very difficult, and the scramble for power around the throne has kept me much occupied, even on the margins as I have been.'

'I can imagine,' said Sir Guy sympathetically, reflecting that Maître Chandos did seem to have *some* excuse for neglecting his family in England. Two pages now appearing from the kitchens, bearing jugs of small ale, bread and cheese, he said, 'Ah, breakfast. Will you join us?'

Some little time later, quietly entertained by Flora's suppressed impatience at the ever-lengthening analysis of French affairs, Dame Constance said helpfully, 'I hope, Maître Chandos, that you will be our guest at Vine Regis for as long as is conveni-ent to you. Now, on such a lovely morning, may I suggest that Flora takes you for a stroll in our orchard?'

Flora flashed her a look of gratitude but Maître Chandos said, 'First, I must thank Sir Guy, as I should already have done, for arranging for me to receive the message which has brought me back to England.' He rose to his feet, a very tall, very thin, grey-haired man with an air of distinction about him, and bowed formally to Sir Guy. 'I thank you, sir.'

His daughter blinked in astonishment. 'The message?'

Dame Constance said, 'We did not tell you about it, in case it brought no result, in which case you would have been disap-pointed.'

'I deduced from the message,' Flora's father explained, 'that something I believed had been done has not been done.'

'Something? What something?' Flora asked. 'No, it's all right, father. You don't have to be careful what you say. Dame Constance and Sir Guy know all about my situation.'

He frowned slightly. 'Very well. When I sent you and the boys back to England, I instructed my man of business to arrange for you, Flora, to draw an income from your late mother's estate. Unfortunately, not until several months after the event did I discover that my man of business had been killed in a riot in the Languedoc – and what he was doing there remains a mystery! Since he was in general an efficient fellow, however, I assumed he had made the income arrangement immediately after I instructed him to do so, and long before he met his untimely end. I gather now that he did not, and I am sorry for it.'

And so you should be, thought Dame Constance. But it was reassuring to know that Maître Chandos had after all employed a man of business instead of, as had originally appeared, simply leaving everything in the air.

Flora exclaimed, 'Does that mean everything will be all right now? What a relief! Are you going to arrange an income for me? Because I cannot – I really *cannot* – go on sharing Coteley with Stephen and Benedetta!'

'I perfectly understand that,' her father replied fastidiously. 'Benedetta strikes me as a sluttish young woman. Not the kind of wife I would have chosen for my son.'

'But what now, father? What next?'

'I suggest we do as the Lady has suggested, and go for a stroll, when we can talk more.'

Or talk more freely, Dame Constance thought. He was a very contained and careful man.

Arm in arm, they crossed the small bridge to the orchard, leaving Frederick behind. 'Find my body servant,' his father told the boy. 'Somewhere in my baggage is a gift I have brought you from France. He will look it out for you.'

'Oh, what is it?' Frederick's face fell. 'Not a book? I don't like books.'

Maître Chandos eyed him coolly. 'You must learn to like them. As it happens, I have brought you, not a book but a chessboard and pieces. I will teach you to play.'

'Thank you, papa!'

'It will be good exercise for his mind,' Maître Chandos remarked to Flora as the boy ran off.

'I have been exercising *my* mind according to your teaching,' Flora said with a happy smile.

He smiled back, his hard face softening. 'You look well on it. In fact, you look as well in body as in mind. You are learning to dress and groom yourself just as you ought.'

She blushed. 'The Lady Susanna deserves the credit for that. She says that being comfortable is all very well, but being stylish is better.'

'Hmmm.'

She squeezed his arm. 'Oh, papa. I am so happy to see you!'

'To see me alive and moderately well, you mean?' He grimaced. 'There have been times when I would not have expected to hear myself utter those words.'

'But you are here now. Are you going to stay, or must you go back to France?'

'We will talk about that later. Now, it is clear to me that you have told Dame Constance and her husband a great deal about your private affairs . . .'

'They have been *so* kind to me.'

'Yes, I understand that. And you may of course tell them whatever you wish to tell them of what I am about to say to you. It is for you to decide. It seems to me that they may have become like substitute parents to you . . .'

She could only laugh. Impossible to think of Dame Constance as a mother or Sir Guy as a father. They were friends, friends, *friends*, with no age barriers.

'But that is by the way. Where your late mother's estate is concerned, it naturally belonged to me, as her husband, both before and after her death. However, I have always intended to make it over to you, not just the income but the estate itself. It is called Lesselney and it is in Somerset, about half a day's ride from here. There is a pleasant stone manor house and a small acreage of land which should, if properly managed, provide you with an adequate income. I will help in the early days, if need be . . .'

She stopped dead. 'Do you mean it? Oh, papa, *do you mean it?*'

'Of course I mean it,' he replied crisply.

'An estate of my own, where I can be my own mistress? I can hardly believe it! It is all I have ever wanted.'

'Well, if that is the sum of your ambitions, I am disappointed in you.'

She stared at him for a moment, her eyes unfocused, then, breaking away, began to dance, whirling round and round until she was giddy. 'It is so – so – *so* wonderful, I can't believe it.'

His mouth twitched. 'Try!' he said.

Laughing and crying at the same time, happiness welling up inside her, she gasped, 'Yes. Oh, yes! I will, I *do* believe it!'

It took some little time for her to come down to earth, for it to occur to her to ask, 'And what do you mean to do, yourself? Must you go back to France?'

'I should, but I have had enough of affairs of state. I think

I will acquire a place for myself here in England and settle down.' He raised a calming hand. 'No, your mother's estate in Somerset is yours and yours alone. I do not suggest sharing it with you.'

'But . . .'

'There are reasons.'

His face was in shadow, and she peered at him. Was he blushing? No, impossible. Guiltily conscious of relief, she repeated, 'Reasons?'

He sighed heavily. 'Very well. You must know soon enough. It is my intention to marry again. There is a lady in France to whom I have become attached.'

Flora couldn't think why she was so astonished. Men who had lost their wives invariably married again as soon as possible and why should her father be different? Perhaps it was so unexpected because he had taken so long about it.

She gathered herself together. 'Oh, I am *so* pleased!'

'Are you?'

'Yes, of course. How lovely!' Almost as tall as he, she leaned up and kissed his cheek. 'Will your lady be content to live in England?'

'Let us hope so. But she, like you, will wish to be mistress of her own household, and I have no desire to find myself acting as a buffer between my wife and my daughter. What I want is peace, in a home of my own.'

Flora laughed. 'You deserve it. Tell me about your lady.'

'She is French, but fluent in English. Thirty years old. Not clever but intelligent and quickwitted. Blonde and handsome, if perhaps a little fair of flesh. She has been twice married to husbands of the minor nobility and twice widowed. She has three sons, and will be prepared to accept Frederick into our household – if he wishes to come.'

That, too, was a relief. 'Will I like her?'

251

'My child, how can I tell! But I can think of no reason why not.'

They continued walking and talking for more than an hour, with Flora trying to conceal her fizzing excitement, her desire to rush off and tell Dame Constance and Susanna how her world was about to change.

6

Dame Constance was clearly pleased. But when Flora boasted to Susanna, 'My own household! Now we can forget all about the "need" to find me a husband!' she had the oddest sensation that Susanna was far from pleased. 'Are you not happy for me?' she asked a little doubtfully.

'Yes, of course I am,' Susanna said crossly. 'But I still think you need a husband.'

Flora laughed. 'Oh, is that all?'

It was not, of course, all.

The trouble Susanna had gone to, the time and thought she had expended, the planning designed to bring about a match between Flora and Gervase – everything looked as if it were to be wasted. Gervase was away at court and now Flora was about to set up her own household in Somerset; only half a day's ride away, perhaps, but it might as well have been a year's. All the useful intimacy of having the two of them meeting in the everyday context of life at Vine Regis would be lost.

'My father,' Flora said, 'is very grateful to you for helping me to improve my appearance . . .'

'Oh, is he? How nice.'

It was almost too much for Dame Constance. Her voice quavering slightly, she murmured, 'Susanna's taste, as we all know, is impeccable. I had been intending to comment on the

252

success of your new look, Flora, and it is good to know that your father approves.'

Sir Guy cleared his throat and said, 'Yes, indeed.'

Susanna, who thought he was the most wonderful man in the world – after Piers, of course – glared at him.

7

After breakfast next day, Flora rode off with her father to inspect her new estate at Lesselney. They took servants and pack horses with them, laden with sheets and fresh bed straw, in case it proved desirable to stay for a night or two. Maître Chandos had warned Flora that the place was probably in need of repair and refurbishment, but that cheered rather than discouraged her. She loved being occupied.

The ride was pleasant, the weather warm but not oppressively so, and the larks were warbling in the heavens. The wild flowers of high summer were in bloom everywhere – rose-purple mallows by the roadside, pink willowherb in the damp of the ditches, yellow St John's wort in dry places. Flora had been learning all the names from Susanna – though with increasing reluctance because, whenever she congratulated herself on having mastered the name of everything within sight, some anonymous little green shoot would without warning expand hugely in size and burst into a riot of violent colour which usually clashed nastily with that of its neighbours.

Maître Chandos sighed contentedly. 'One forgets, you know. I have not been in this part of the world for many years, but it brings my whole boyhood back to me. I was reared partly at Coteley and partly at Morelney, not far from here. Well, now, let us see what state the place is in. The grounds look well enough with those few sheep keeping the grass cropped. At least the house has not fallen down, though the steward, however dignified his title, is in fact no more than a caretaker. He must be a very old man by now.'

The house was square and plain, though the stone mullioned windows were graced with trefoil arches at the top. There was one central chimney which led Flora to sigh at the prospect of an old-fashioned fireplace in the centre of the floor. However, when they entered through the ancient oak door, sagging on its hinges, she discovered that the central chimney was simply left over from times past, and that there were wall fireplaces, unseen from the direction of their approach, built on to the outside of the house at the back, together with a kitchen block.

Years of dust lay thick over everything – floor, table, stools – and Maître Chandos remarked, 'I suppose old Edward and his wife must live in the kitchen.' Then he raised his voice and shouted, 'Ned! Ned!'

It was several minutes before a door opened at the far end of the hall and an ancient retainer appeared, mumbling, 'Here be Oi. Oo waaants me?'

Maître Chandos and his daughter exchanged glances as they mentally translated his dialect into an English they could recognise, and then both began to laugh.

8

Back at Vine Regis, Dame Constance was saying to Susanna, 'We must talk.'

Susanna tossed her head pettishly. 'No longer any *need* for a husband! After all my efforts!'

'Yes, but there is a limit to what you can achieve. You can't organise other people's lives for them.'

'Why not? *You* do.'

Sir Guy gave a choke of laughter, and his wife glared at him. His eyes alight with amusement, he said, 'Please don't think I dislike being glared at, but I should prefer it not to become a general habit. I must go and do some work, so I will leave you two in peace – if that is the word.'

Dame Constance watched him go, a smile in her eyes, then turned back to Susanna. 'What I was trying to say was that there is only so much you can do. As I think you know, I have become quite fond of Flora and I feel that she and Gervase would suit each other well. From what Gervase said to me before he left for court, he is already half convinced.'

'Oh, *is he*?'

'But don't be too optimistic. Flora is the difficulty, especially now that she has the prospect of Lesselney to care for. Can she be persuaded that she wants a husband as well as a household of her own? Can she be persuaded that she wants Gervase as a husband? Neither of them is exactly hot-blooded . . .'

'I know. Isn't it depressing!'

'Not necessarily. I have an idea of how a marriage between them might be arranged – unconventional, perhaps, but practical.'

'What is it?'

'I can't tell you that! The whole virtue of unexpressed ideas is that, if they don't work out, no one is any the wiser, whereas if they do work out one can take all the credit. And more!'

'That sounds shockingly cynical to me.'

'Possibly, but what you – and I – must remember is that we have both, in the past, talked to Flora altogether too much about the desirability of her having a husband, which is likely to invalidate anything we say in the future. So we must guard our tongues. Maître Chandos might possibly be our most import-ant ally, though we don't yet know his views.'

Susanna giggled. 'You think we need allies? You don't feel that the – er – the impassioned style of Gervase's proposal alone would suffice to sweep Flora off her feet?'

If Dame Constance's cast of feature had allowed for dimples, the dimples would have shown. 'Quite so,' she said. 'But I also think we need more reliable help than that of Maître Chandos. We need an outsider. I had thought of Master William.'

Susanna was taken aback. 'But he and Flora don't get on!'

'I know. Which, as I see it, could be an advantage.'

She broke off suddenly at the sound of the lookout's horn. 'Well, well. "Friends approaching" – and who should those friends be, unless my eyes deceive me, but Gervase and his retinue. What excellent timing.'

9

'I am home because I have the king's leave to attend Hamish's wedding. Old family retainer, and so on,' Gervase announced. 'Hallo, Susanna, you still here?'

'As you see,' she snapped.

He regarded her percipiently. 'Have I said something to offend you?'

'No, no.'

'Good. Well, I would like a private word with my mother, if you will excuse us.'

'Of course.' Susanna stalked off.

Resignedly – for it seemed that Gervase would never learn tact – Dame Constance suggested, 'Let us go into my garden in the courtyard.'

When Dame Constance was seated, with Gervase standing as he preferred, he launched straight in to what he wanted to say. 'As you know, since Felicia died I have always intended to marry again. Looking back, I am glad that the match you arranged for me with Susanna fell through. She has too sharp a tongue, and we would not have suited. But I have been thinking hard about marriage in these last few months and my mind is made up.'

A little uneasily, but with an appearance of calm, she said, 'I have been living in expectation of your bringing a potential bride home from court.'

'Hmmm. I might have done but, you know, pretty though they all are – or most of them – they don't have anything else to commend them. Not a brain amongst the lot.'

This was a new come-out. She surveyed him pensively. 'I cannot believe that you want a clever wife!'

He frowned. 'Not *too* clever. But, thanks to you and Isabelle, I have learned that beauty without brains is not enough.'

'Thank you,' she murmured.

'On the other hand, any woman who has brains but no beauty would have a hard time of it at court. So, as I say, I have been thinking about it and I have decided that Mistress Flora would suit me well . . .'

Dame Constance heaved an inward sigh of relief.

'She is undoubtedly clever – I am sure you will agree – and she is much better looking than I thought when we first met. I don't quite know why. Something to do with her clothes, perhaps?'

'Perhaps.' Looking down on her from above, Gervase failed to see the twinkle in his mother's eye. Helpfully, Dame Constance went on, 'She is not beautiful in the orthodox sense, but she has style.'

'Yes!' He was surprised, and pleasantly so. 'That is just what I was thinking. So you would approve, would you, if I took Mistress Flora to wife?'

'Very much so. I like her, and I think you would indeed suit very well.'

'Splendid!'

'Gervase, do please stand back a little. You are looming over me. If you would sit down it would be even better.'

He obligingly stood back, though he had a knack of seeming to fill small spaces. 'Well, that is one problem resolved. However, I need your advice about something else. Whose permission should I ask before I address myself to her? As I understand it, her father is in France, no one knows where. Should I go to her brother, do you think?'

She smiled. 'No need for that! Maître Chandos arrived here two days ago. He has gone off with her to Lesselney, to inspect a small estate which he means to make over to her. And she is of age, of course, so his permission is not strictly speaking required.'

'That's true, I suppose, but I like to do things properly. How convenient that he should suddenly have turned up, after all this time!'

'Yes, isn't it! Gervase, will you *sit down*! And stop fidgeting.' He sat.

She said, 'There is something you should know. Flora is not one of those young women whose only ambition is to find a husband. Indeed, she has quite strong views about female independence and considers it unreasonable that society always expects women to marry. In principle, she would much prefer to be her own mistress.'

'I didn't know that.' Understandably, he did not see it as good news.

'No, don't let it raise concerns in your mind. She is a perfectly sensible girl and I believe her opinions have much to do with her upbringing. My impression is that her father has always encouraged her in the belief that his clever daughter should have the freedom to be clever, rather than to be dependent on . . .'

'Yes, yes. On a husband! I see.'

Dame Constance took a deep breath. 'But if you can convince her that, with a little flexibility, you and she would deal well together – as I believe you would – there should be no difficulty.'

He sat doubtfully for a moment, his lower lip trapped between his teeth. Then, 'Should I ride over to – Lesselney, did you say? – and speak to them both together? Or speak to Mistress Flora first? Or to her father first? Or would you do it for . . . ?'

'No, I would not!'

If only Gervase had delayed his return for another day or two, Dame Constance would have had a better idea of whether her plan to persuade Flora to take a more favourable view of matrimony was likely to succeed. She most certainly did not want Gervase charging in before the ground had been prepared.

She said, 'I don't think it would be wise to ride over to Lesselney. If the place is as neglected as I think it must be and if they are in the midst of discussing what to do about it, your presence might be intrusive.'

Her son looked offended.

'I mean that only in the sense that, in an atmosphere of dust and disuse, talk of marriage might seem out of place.'

'Rather the opposite, I should have thought,' Gervase retorted with infuriating alacrity. 'It emphasises the choice and provides the answer.'

'You may be right. But the contrast will be greater,' said his mother, rapidly retrieving the initiative, 'when she returns to Vine Regis from decrepit Lesselney. She should be back in a day or two, and I would recommend that, before you speak, you give her time to recover from what will have been a tiring expedition.'

'I suppose so. But the sooner everything is settled, the better.'

'Don't be too hasty.'

'No.' He leapt to his feet. 'I must go and have a word with Hamish. Are the wedding preparations going well?'

'Yes.'

10

Susanna was not alone in feeling frustration over all her seemingly wasted effort on Flora's behalf. William, too, contemplating the trouble he had gone to in his endeavours to identify the source of Flora's little brother's illness, was inclined to brood over the injustice of Lord Gervase simply sauntering in and discovering the answer by accident. Indeed, if it would not have appeared impolite to miss The Wedding, William would already have left Vine Regis for home.

He was thus very much surprised to receive a request from Dame Constance that he should come and see her in her private chamber as soon as convenient – which he took to mean, 'At once.' Hastily changing his everyday doublet for the new one with the pouter-pigeon padding and the long funnel-shaped sleeves, he replaced his hood with his best hat, high-crowned and with a peacock-feather plume, and hastened off to obey the Lady's summons.

Dame Constance welcomed him kindly and asked him to sit down. Was he well? Good. It was some little time since they had last talked.

Then, 'I need your help,' she said.

'Yes,' he said. 'Of course,' he said. 'Delighted,' he said.

She laughed. 'No need to look so worried.'

'I'm not. Worried, I mean. Far from it.' His spirits had perked up amazingly at the prospect of being helpful, although they sagged again a moment later when the Lady said, 'It is to do with Lord Gervase and Mistress Flora.'

'Oh, is it?'

'To put it plainly, Gervase wishes to marry Mistress Flora . . .'

William blinked. 'Really?'

'Yes, really. However, as I am sure you know, Mistress Flora has – er – "no opinion of men", and would much prefer to have a household of her own, uncluttered by husbands.'

Austerely, William said, 'She has made no secret of it.'

'And now her father is making the estate of Lesselney over to her, so it has ceased to be an either/or situation.'

William was profoundly uninterested in the futures of Lord Gervase and Mistress Flora but, since he had to say something, he made do with, 'So Lord Gervase is going to have to look elsewhere for a wife?'

'Not necessarily. I believe Flora might be persuaded to change her view if the right arguments were put to her by someone with – so to speak – no axe to grind.'

'Do you mean me?'

'Yes.'

There was a moment's vibrating silence, then William sighed. 'I am happy to do anything you ask of me, Lady.'

'Thank you. Now, Hamish and Alice's wedding takes place in three days' time, and I anticipate that Flora and Maître Chandos will return here from Lesselney tomorrow. Gervase intends to speak to Maître Chandos tomorrow, but I have told him he must give Flora at least another day to recover from her exertions at Lesselney before he puts his proposal directly to *her*.'

William gave a spurt of laughter. 'You feel that the shock might be too much for her?'

Dame Constance ignored his ill-judged frivolity. 'Before then, you will have to contrive to have a private conversation with her – the forthcoming bridals should be a convenient starting point – and I believe she will then need some little time to think over what you have said to her.'

'Which will be?'

'Which will be . . .'

11

The absentees returned to Vine Regis just before supper next day, Flora full of excitement, Maître Chandos his usual controlled self.

Introductions having been made, Gervase told Maître Chandos that he would be grateful for the favour of a private word with him after supper.

'Of course,' replied a slightly surprised Maître Chandos.

Gervase was nothing if not thorough when it came to explanations. There was never any real problem about *what* he was explaining, though there were times when he omitted to mention *why* he was explaining it. This was one of those times.

By the time he had taken Maître Chandos all the way through the size and location of his various estates, the history of his past life, his present employment at court, and how his future seemed likely to develop, Maître Chandos was having a struggle to stay awake.

'I am telling you all this,' Gervase said at last, 'because I believe your daughter and I would suit well and I would like your permission to ask for her hand in marriage.'

'*Dieu de dieu* . . .' muttered Maître Chandos. Then, 'I apologise. That is not very polite.'

'Well, I wouldn't know about that. I am not fluent in French.'

'I was merely expressing surprise. My daughter has said nothing to me about your proposal.'

'She wouldn't. She doesn't know about it yet.'

Maître Chandos drew a calming hand across his forehead. 'Ah,' he said. 'And you think that if I give my permission, all will be settled?'

'No, but it would help.'

'Well, you have my permission to address her, certainly, but it is entirely up to her whether she agrees to wed you or not. I firmly believe that women have rights . . .'

'Oh, so do I!' Gervase interpolated virtuously.

'. . . and those rights include taking a hand in their own destiny. To the best of my knowledge, my daughter does not wish to be wed. She is a clever young woman and feels she would be diminished by marriage – would necessarily be forced to rely on her husband rather than on herself.'

'That would depend on the husband, would it not?' Gervase, who had failed to take to Maître Chandos, was beginning to feel slightly irritable. 'However, now that I have your consent, I will speak to your daughter tomorrow.'

12

'Is it *you* he wants to marry? Or *me*?' Flora enquired tartly.

'Flora!' exclaimed her father, unaccustomed to his formerly quiet daughter being so outspoken, and wondering what had brought about the change. 'The Lord Gervase is perhaps a little old-fashioned. But he is being perfectly correct, asking my permission before he addresses himself to you.'

She sniffed. 'Well, it's the first I've heard of it. If he had come straight to me he would have saved us all a good deal of trouble. Anyway, I don't understand why he should want to marry me; he's never given any hint of it. And I don't want a husband.'

'Are you sure?'

'Yes.'

She paused.

'No.'

She paused again.

'I don't know.'

Her father said nothing.

'All I want,' she resumed more firmly, 'is to run a household of my own with no interference from anyone else. People keep telling me I need a husband. Well, I don't. Though if I have to have one,' she added fairmindedly, 'Lord Gervase would do as well as any. He appreciates that I am not just some empty-headed female, and underneath that starchy exterior he is quite a good and kindhearted man. But *really*! It is all too exasper-ating, having to choose. Marriage or independence? What is your view, papa?'

Maître Chandos shook his head. 'No, I cannot give you advice. I don't wish to influence you. It is *your* future that is at issue, and you have to make up your own mind.'

13

She didn't want advice. She didn't need advice. What she wanted and needed was to have a rational, intelligent discussion of her situation with someone who could be open-minded about it. Which ruled out the husband-obsessed Susanna.

Who could she talk to? She would have had no hesitation about approaching Dame Constance except that it was Dame Constance's son who was the problem. But there was no one else so, taking a deep breath, Flora knocked on the door of Dame Constance's chamber and was relieved to find her there and alone.

After the usual exchange of courtesies, Flora said, 'I imagine that you may know that the Lord Gervase has spoken to my father about the possibility of my becoming his wife?'

Dame Constance smiled with her eyes only. 'Yes.'

'He has not yet spoken to *me* on the subject . . .'

Oh, Gervase, Gervase! that young man's mother thought. *You should have warned Maître Chandos to say nothing to Flora before you spoke to her yourself.*

Aloud, she said, 'Oh, dear. Gervase does like to do things according to the rules.'

'Yes, I understand that. But there are one or two questions that occur to me and I hoped you might be able to answer them.'

'Of course, if I can.'

'You know, I think – for I have said so, often enough – that I have no desire for a husband. That I would prefer to have a household of my own?'

'I remember your exact words the first time we talked. "I have no opinion of men". Susanna was dreadfully shocked!'

Flora gave a small smile. 'I had every justification at the time. I felt badly let down by my father, my brother . . .' She stopped abruptly. 'Looking back, I wonder why I condemned the entire male sex on the basis of only two sinners. Silly of me, I suppose. But it did clarify my mind and emphasise my desire for an independent existence. I would still prefer to have a household of my own – and I wanted to ask you, if I agreed to marry Gervase would I have to come and live at Vine Regis?'

With invisible care, Dame Constance replied, 'It would be customary.'

'Would you mind, having me here?'

'Not at all. I would like it.'

'But I would not have a household of my own, and I would be bound to tread on your toes.'

Dame Constance laughed aloud. 'I remember that, when

Susanna was betrothed to Gervase, her entire ambition was to replace me as Lady of the Castle.'

'Oh, I would never think of such a thing!'

'Some day you would have to. I cannot live for ever.'

Flora shuddered violently. And then, almost on a wail, 'I don't know what to do. To marry Gervase or devote myself to Lesselney.'

Sympathetically, Dame Constance said, 'Much depends on how you feel about Gervase. Could you live comfortably with him?'

'I don't know. I like him. At least, I *think* I like him. Is that enough?'

'Liking often grows into love. But if you are asking my advice, I can't help you. I don't mind giving an opinion, but advice – never. I'm afraid, my dear, that you must make up your own mind.'

Just then, there came a knock on the door and it was Susanna, glancing from one to the other a little suspiciously. But her errand was to ask Dame Constance if she would like to come and see Alice in her bridal gown. Master Nicholas was just taking in the last few tucks in the final fitting.

Everyone was used to seeing Alice in the dull blues of her everyday dress and to recognise that, despite the unflattering garb, she was a pretty girl. But now she was more than that. She was a very pretty girl indeed, the creamy tissue of the low-necked gown with its latticework of finest gold threads making a perfect setting for her soft dark curls and lovely complexion. She was wearing a charming gold necklace with a baroque pearl hanging from it, a gift from her future husband.

'*Yes!*' exclaimed Dame Constance. 'Perfect, quite perfect!'

Alice's shy smile lit up her face, and Flora thought, *How happy she looks.*

14

For almost the first time in her life, Flora found herself dither-
ing. There was one point at which her brain and her tongue
were so disconnected that, if Gervase had approached her, 'yes'
might have emerged as 'no', and 'no' as 'yes'.

But Gervase, following his mother's instructions, did not
approach her, and Flora could not guess, as he went striding
purposefully about on estate business, that he was deliberately
giving her time to think.

It added an element of mild irritation to her indecision, so
that when William 'accidentally' encountered her in the orchard
he had every excuse for asking why she was looking so
distracted.

At any other time, she would have regarded his question as
intrusive, but he had chosen his moment well.

'If you really want to know,' she said petulantly, 'I have
always, and publicly, maintained that given a choice between
two options I would have no hesitation in deciding. I didn't
think the choice would ever arise.'

'And now it has?'

'Yes.'

'And the decision is not so clear cut?'

'No.'

'And your pride is at stake if you go for the option you have
always – um – derided?'

'I suppose so.' It was said rather gloomily.

'Pride is a form of vanity, you know.'

'It isn't,' she flared.

'Yes, it is.'

Flouncing on along the grassy walk, she flung back at him,
'I don't see why I should have to choose. I can't choose. I see
no good reason why I shouldn't have both.'

William, who knew perfectly well what she was complaining about, said, 'Well, I can't offer you an opinion unless I know what the question is.'

'I don't want your opinion.'

'That's all right, then.'

'Oh, fiddle! I have always said, and believed, that I don't want a husband, that I want a household of my own.'

'And now you can have one at Lesselney . . .'

'*But* Lord Gervase has decided he wants me to be his wife.'

'God's bones, does he indeed?' William responded – very convincingly, he thought.

'Yes.'

'So what's the difficulty? Don't you like him?'

'Yes, I do. If I have to marry someone, I had rather it was him than anyone else. But I also want my independence, to be my own mistress. I want both, but I have to choose between them. *Why* should I have to choose? I don't *want* to choose. I *can't* choose.'

'I don't see why you're making such a fuss about it,' William said dampingly. 'There's no reason why you can't have both. Use your common sense.'

'What does my common sense have to do with it?'

William ticked his points off on his fingers. 'One – you could behave conventionally; you could say, "Yes, please, Lord Gervase, I would like to marry you and devote my life henceforth to your wellbeing". Two – you could say, "No, thank you, Lord Gervase, I'd rather be independent and devote myself to the wellbeing of Lesselney". Which would not only be unconventional, but pretty insulting to Lord Gervase . . .'

'Oh dear, yes it would, wouldn't it?'

'Three – you could agree a compromise that suits everyone.'

'*Every*one? Who's everyone?'

'Where have your wits gone a-begging? You, Lord Gervase, and Dame Constance, of course.'

'There's no need to be so impolite about it! Anyway, I still don't understand.'

William sighed heavily. 'It's simple. You could agree to be married to Lord Gervase, but not all of the time. When he's at court, which he usually is for three months at a stretch, you wouldn't need to stay at Vine Regis and get in Dame Constance's way, you could stay at Lesselney and run it as you wish. If Lord Gervase wants you to be at court for some particular event, that wouldn't be too much of a torment, would it?'

'What you're suggesting is that I should be a part-time wife!'

'Why not, if it suits everybody concerned?'

After a seemingly interminable moment, she said thoughtfully, 'But it would look so odd to other people.'

'Does that matter? Everyone knows you're clever, so people *expect* you to be odd.'

It was hardly a sensible answer but, to William's relief, she said, 'I'll think about it.' And then, as an afterthought, 'Thank you. You've been – er – quite helpful.'

15

Vine Regis might be very large and very grand, but it was just like any other household when there was a wedding in the offing.

With Dame Constance in charge, there was of course no sense of panic, just a general air of purposeful bustle. The happy couple, having paid separate visits to the castle chaplain, might go about their duties as they always did, but everyone else was very busy indeed and the young pages who were sent scurrying about the castle with messages and instructions were beginning to show signs of wear and tear.

Flora, whose offer to help in any way she could had been gently turned down by Dame Constance, decided to soothe her whirling brain by a study of her almanac. Having failed to find any other quiet corner where the light was adequate, she made her way to the Lady's alcove table in the Great Hall, and began setting out her papers and writing implements.

She was just uncorking her little ink bottle when a voice behind her said, 'Ummm', and caused her almost to jump out of her skin. Her hand jerked and a splash of ink landed on the table top.

'Oh dear!' she gasped distractedly. At least it hadn't landed on her parchments, but it would soak into the table top unless someone could produce a cloth quickly. She tried to attract the attention of one of the pages but, before she could do so, the voice behind her exclaimed, 'My fault entirely. Allow me to help.'

It was Gervase, who produced one of his handkerchiefs and mopped the ink up with it. 'Useful things, these,' he said. 'The king has introduced a fashion for them at court.'

'Oh, really?' she said, staring up at him, still startled and a trifle nervous.

Deceived by the magnifying effect of her spectacles, Gervase thought, *She's frightened! Why should she be frightened?* So he smiled at her reassuringly.

Susanna could have told her that Gervase's smile, which was very rare – it not being thought proper for lords to go about smiling at people – had the effect of transforming him into a different person, softening his hard good looks, straightening his saturnine brows, and easing his air of formality. Susanna would have added that his smile could not of course match the brilliance of Piers' smile or that of his father, Sir Guy, but it was unusually attractive just the same.

Flora had not yet met Piers nor felt the full blaze of his father's charm, so her standards of comparison were not so high. She thought simply, *Oh-h-h-h!*

Gervase said, 'Shall we go outdoors and find a few moments' privacy? I imagine you know what we must talk about?'

Flora waved a limp hand at her papers, but he said, 'Leave them. They will come to no harm.'

She gave a small laugh as she removed her spectacles and ostentatiously tucked them away. 'As long as we are sure that Blanche is safely up in the schoolroom.'

'Yes, she's a bright little thing, isn't she? I'm proud of her. She takes after her grandmother.'

Daringly, she asked, 'Not after her mother?'

'No.' He thought for a moment. 'I hope *our* children will take after you.'

This was rushing things, to put it mildly, and enabled her to respond rather coolly when, having reached Dame Constance's private garden, he said, 'Your father will have told you that I wish to have you for my wife, and that he has no objection. We have spoken in general about marriage settlements and the like. May I now ask *you* whether you are prepared to take me for your husband?'

'I am not sure that I want a husband,' she replied. 'And I wouldn't want one – er – all the time.'

A lesser man than Gervase would have gaped at her. He said merely, 'And what do you mean by that?'

Hastily, she gathered her thoughts together and tried to phrase them lucidly and not too insultingly. 'I mean that I would prefer not to find myself forever dancing attendance at court, though I would attend, if required, on occasion. When you are at Vine Regis, I would be prepared to be here, too. The rest of my time I would hope to spend at Lesselney, running my own estate there.'

'Hmmm. So you *are* prepared to marry me, but only under conditions?'

'Er – yes – I think so. I know it sounds strange, and of course it's usually the gentleman who lays down conditions, but . . .'

'But you don't really want a husband. You want to have complete control over your own life.'

With a trace of embarrassment, she looked away. 'I have always said so.'

'So I have been told.'

Firing up in her own defence, she exclaimed, 'Well, how would *you* feel about it? Would *you* be prepared to give up everything you treasured, all your beliefs and principles, for the sake of having a wife? If we marry, the law says that I become your possession. How would you feel if the law said you would become *my* possession?'

Gervase, a fair-minded and honest man, frowned. 'I don't know. It's a difficult question. I would probably hesitate to give up *everything*. Though I suppose it would depend on the wife.'

They stared at each other uncertainly.

Gervase broke the silence. 'So we both have to choose. You whether to devote yourself wholly to me, or wholly to Lesselney, or to divide your devotion between us. And I whether or not I am prepared to marry you under the conditions you have set. Have you a particular preference?'

She hesitated. 'I believe I should stand by my often stated principles, but I – I haven't really made up my mind.'

He still thought she was frightened. Of what? Not of him, surely? With a blinding flash of inspiration, he decided – quite wrongly, as it happened – that she was frightened of the physical side of marriage.

He smiled at her again, intending to be reassuring, but she thought, *Oh dear, have I gone too far?* Insensibly, she had come round to wanting to marry him.

He said, 'Perhaps you could make your mind up by tomorrow evening? And so will I. We will talk again after the wedding, not before. If we agree to marry, we must not announce it or let it be obvious immediately. We wouldn't want to overshadow Alice and Hamish's great day, would we?'

'Oh no!'

'Fine!' said Gervase in his usual brisk tones. 'Well, I think we can go back indoors now.'

'Yes,' Flora agreed weakly, hoping her knees would stop shaking for long enough to carry her there.

Consulting Dame Constance an hour or two later, Gervase was pleased to discover that she regarded the conditions as an excellent solution to Flora's doubts and Gervase's desires. 'How interesting,' she said. 'If I were you, I should agree, without hesitation. Flexibility is much to be preferred to rigidity, especially when such flexibility is designed to keep the two of you happy and contented.'

For the first time in years, he said, 'Yes, mother, I am sure you are right.'

Fortunately, Sir Guy was not present, otherwise she would have been quite unable to keep a straight face.

16

Alice and Hamish had been quite decisive about the arrangements for their wedding. Indeed, Weaver John was still sulking over his second daughter's refusal to be married from 'home' in the village. She remembered all too well the excitement that had attended the wedding in the village church of the Lady Susanna to Master Piers; all those people coming from miles around to gape at them and then to scramble for the coins tossed among them by the groom. Alice wanted a quiet wedding and, as far as Hamish was concerned, what Alice wanted Alice must have.

So they were wed in the private chapel of Vine Regis by Father Sebastian, with only a handful of witnesses – Maître Chandos, Dame Constance and Sir Guy, Gervase, Susanna and Piers, a few of the senior household officials, Flora, William, a selfconscious Weaver John and all six of Alice's sisters as attendants.

They made a handsome couple, Alice radiant in her cream-and-gold tissue gown and the fine golden veil over her dark curls, and Hamish tall and stalwart in a sandy-coloured doublet and hose very different from his usual grey liveries. There was something unusually touching about the way they looked at each other, about Alice's adoration and Hamish's determination to protect his beloved wee lassie from all the pains and sorrows of the world.

After prayers and Mass, the couple knelt under a canopy for a blessing on their marriage and the anointing with holy water of the ring that represented the plighting of their troth.

The bride, still shy after three years' residence in the castle, had also declared herself terrified at the prospect of presiding over a grand banquet for a vast number of guests. So there was to be no sitting down, no ceremonial serving of gilded swans or peacocks in their plumage, no speeches. All was to be informal, and the kitchens had excelled themselves in producing a wonderful array of foods that could be eaten with the fingers, while all the guests chatted happily, strolling around or perching on the carpenter's handsome new cushioned stools and benches.

There were small omelettes rolled up with fine slices of salted sturgeon inside and a trace of green sauce, pigeons roasted on the spit, individual venison pasties and others filled with lightly spiced chicken. There were cheese pastries made with fine white flour and filled with apples and honey, small custard tarts delicately flavoured with ginger, and crispy wafers, their batter as light as air. There were bowls of tasty sauces for dipping, as well as comfits and sugared almonds and candied aniseed to finish off, and wine, ale and hippocras to drink.

Dame Constance found it interesting – for want of a better word – that although most of the guests saw each other every day, they still found plenty to talk about. It was something worth bearing in mind for future occasions.

The decoration of the Great Chamber had much to offer in the way of things to talk about, and Dame Constance – as so often in these last weeks – had difficulty in stifling her laughter, because Signor Alberti had deigned to stay for the wedding reception in the certainty of seeing his work widely admired. In general, she supposed, he received compliments only at second hand, passed on by the nobles who had commissioned him. But today he was able to be present at his own grand opening, however lowly and ignorant the critics.

The said critics, fortunately, were without exception awestruck and admiring, and indeed the impact of his work was spectacular in the quietest and most elegant way. All the strong colours had been calmed by a combination of his painterly talent and the techniques that seemed to Dame Constance to have been haunting everyone for weeks.

The finished effect was wonderfully pleasing, the pale oak dado surmounted by an airy haze of sky and landscape, full, but not too full, of figures – figures lying, standing, sitting – all of them real, almost human but strangely ethereal. The goddesses were willowy yet voluptuous, the gods muscular yet graceful. They made a select company to be in; they were a presence, but not oppressive. In Dame Constance's view, they were just right.

Gervase said, 'I like it. I don't know how much we're paying

Signor What's-his-name? – Alberti – but he's worth it. In fact, he has produced a Great Chamber that is truly worthy of Vine Regis. Don't you think so, mother?' He stopped suddenly, his eyes fixed on the image of the god Mars. It was the first time he had looked at all the figures in detail. He exclaimed, 'Who's that? Is it John, or is it meant to be me? Do I look like that?'

'Most of the time,' Dame Constance told him sweetly.

'One might call it a speaking likeness, in fact,' Sir Guy confirmed.

'I look rather bad-tempered,' Gervase complained.

'No, just warlike.'

The children, too, were taking a personal interest. Blanche, prancing around, was telling anyone who would listen, 'Look, that's me up there in the sky. And that's Eleanor. We're cherubs, that's what we are!'

'Cherubs, pooh!' said Frederick and, not to be outdone, pointed out, 'You just sat there so Signor Alberti could draw you, while *I actually painted* that bit there, down at the hem . . .'

John, surrounded by all six of Alice's sisters, was in his element. None of the girls was as pretty as Alice, but none was as shy. They were all teasing John and he was loving it. But he was in no danger, his mother thought.

Sir Guy, divining, as so often, what was in her mind, said firmly, 'No. Leave the boy to find his own way.'

'But it has taken seven years, from start to finish, to find Gervase a second wife . . .'

'That's because he doesn't fall in and out of love every five minutes.'

'And John does! That's why . . .'

'That's why you feel you need to take a hand.' Sir Guy smiled at her understandingly. 'Don't. He *needs* to fall in love, and that's something you can't arrange. He will know when he meets someone he can live with for the rest of his life, and that someone is unlikely to be a suitable match found for him by his mother.'

'I suppose not.'

The moment soon came when Hamish and Alice took their formal farewell of their guests, and left to mount the stairs to the bridal chamber.

Dame Constance chuckled. 'Oh dear, poor Alice. She has spent half the day reminding herself that, for this afternoon at least, she is not in charge of Blanche and Eleanor and doesn't have to tell them to behave. It occurred to me that I might send them off with their nurse to spend a few days with Susanna and Piers, but Susanna was horrified at the thought. She said it would be better for the girls to stay here and become better acquainted with their new stepmother – *if* Flora and Gervase agree to make a match of it.'

'We'll know soon enough. I am, of course, no judge,' Sir Guy went on mendaciously, 'but it seems to me that Flora has gone to some trouble to look her best today. Perhaps that means something?'

'Perhaps,' his wife smiled back at him, mischief in her eyes. Flora was indeed looking as stylish as Dame Constance had once hoped she might, in a gown of a lovely clear red, a coronet-like chaplet of matching taffeta twined with pearls on her perfectly coifed head, and a quite extraordinary quantity of jewellery – everything from amber paternoster beads to gem-studded girdle and a ring on every finger. The spectacular golden brooch set at the centre of her low oval neckline took the form of a twelve-pointed star and was set with pearls, amethysts and rubies.

Apologetically, she had told Dame Constance, 'My father brought all my mother's jewels from France for me, and he expects me to wear them. They're a bit old-fashioned, and *so* heavy when I wear them all at once, but I don't really have any choice. Do I?'

Dame Constance had said, 'No, you don't. But just think how bright and cheerful they will make you look and feel!'

That had been a little optimistic. In fact, Flora looked as if she would have liked a corner to hide in, except that there were no corners in the big, circular Great Chamber. So she had retreated to one of the window embrasures where, glancing at her occasionally, Dame Constance had seen her hazel eyes – no spectacles today! – gazing a little wistfully at the idyllic Hamish and Alice, and at a Susanna ecstatically reunited with her adored Piers. Dame Constance thought she had probably been watching herself and Sir Guy, too, when they were unaware of it. All of them excellent advertisements for the married state.

William, beside her, said in an undertone, 'Well, come on, Lord Gervase! Stop strolling around gossiping with people and do something useful.'

What an irrepressible boy he was! Dame Constance tried to look as if she had not heard.

At last the moment came when Gervase, a trifle selfconscious – though no one but his mother would have known it – made his way across the room to where Flora was standing by the window.

'You look – ah – very splendid,' he said, and she blushed faintly.

He, too, was looking splendid in the gold-embroidered crimson doublet and hose he had worn – although she did not know it – to the king's coronation three years before.

She murmured, 'Thank you.'

He took a deep breath. 'I have to say that I agree, without qualification, to your conditions. So, now, I ask you again, will you marry me?'

Seeing that she was as nervous as he, he smiled at her blindingly.

She gasped and then, a slight quiver at the corners of her

mouth, smiled back and said without hesitation, 'Yes. With all the pleasure in the world.'

At which point he laughed with delight and she laughed, too. And he took her hands in his and swung her out into the room, and they laughed together, and danced together, and their steps matched perfectly.

Dame Constance gave a silent but heartfelt sigh of satisfaction.